Author's Note

I started writing this book before the decision to overturn
Roe v. Wade was made.

It's not lost on me that this book addresses abortion and is set in Texas.

I hope Kai and Olivia's story can be a safe place for women everywhere
to sit in their feelings and know we are not alone.

Women are the most powerful creatures on the planet,
which is why someone is always trying to take our control
away. But just remember, ladies…

…this our pussy we can do what we want.

Playlist

As Fast As You Can —The Foreign Exchange, Carmen Rodgers
It Will Rain—Bruno Mars
Stitches—Shawn Mendes
Fool For You—CeeLo Green and Melanie Fiona
Right My Wrongs—Bryson Tiller
Halfcrazy—Musiq Soulchild
Happy Without Me—Chloe x Halle & Joey Bada$$
Adorn—Miguel
The Sweetest Thing—The Refugees and Lauryn Hill
The Boy is Mine—Brandy & Monica
Sure Thing—Miguel
Cinderella's Dead—EMELINE
Shea Butter Baby—Ari Lennox & J. Cole
Watch n' Learn—Rihanna
Leave the Door Open—Silk Sonic
Oh My God—Adele
Boss Bitch—Doja Cat
Dusk Till Dawn—ZAYN & Sia
Through the Fire—Chaka Khan
Confidently Lost—Sabrina Claudio
Ordinary People—John Legend
Comfortable—H.E.R.
Rocket—Beyoncé
Hrs & Hrs—Muni Long

WHERE WE FOUND OUR
Passion

Prologue

Kai

"HELLO?"

"Hi, Kai." That voice. It's cold and distant, a tone I've never heard directed toward me, but fuck if it doesn't still light a fire inside of me.

I've been waiting by the phone for hours to see if she'd call me or if she'd once again push me to the side.

I can help her.

She just needs to let me.

"Are you okay? I saw." There's no point in pretending that I didn't witness her tear her ACL on national television tonight.

She sighs. "No." Good. I'm glad we're not starting this conversation off with a lie.

"How can I help?"

She laughs but there's no humor in it. She's barely holding it together.

I don't, really. My schedule shouldn't allow for another client right now, but I know I'll make it work. I'd rather cut off my own arm than reject her. A part of me always knew it, but this moment just confirmed that I would still, to this day, do absolutely anything for this woman.

Part One

CHAPTER
One

Olivia
Twelve Years Old

"**S**TUPID AUSTIN," I MUMBLE TO MYSELF AS I KICK THE SOCCER BALL I'm practicing with in our front yard. It bounces off the white brick of the house wildly before I stop it from going into the street. Why did we have to move here?

"Stupid Mom," I grumble as I line the ball up with the exact brick I want to hit.

"Stupid Dad." My next shot is sloppy, and I cringe as the ball doesn't hit anywhere near my mark. I trap the ball beneath my cleat upon its return.

I can't focus. There's too much rage and annoyance flowing through my body. I do a few toe taps and then line up one final shot. I close my eyes and take a deep breath, then I let go. It crashes against the brick and then whips past my face.

"Ow." My body spins around at the voice I just heard. A tall boy stands across the street rubbing the back of his head. My soccer ball sits at his feet.

He turns around to face me and I'm taken aback. He's sort of...beautiful. His brown skin is highlighted by the sun setting behind him, and I've never seen a more glorious mess of curls on a boy before. He tilts his head as if he doesn't know what to make of me, probably because I'm just standing here like an idiot instead of apologizing and going to get my ball. He bends to pick it up, and I think he's going to throw it back to me, but instead he looks both ways and crosses the street over to my yard. "This yours?" he asks, holding the ball out to me.

"Umm, yes. I'm sorry. I shouldn't have kicked it that hard." I wince as I grab it out of his hands. So lame.

He chuckles and it's a cute sound. I decide at that moment I'd like to hear what his full laugh sounds like. He's tall and his deep-brown eyes are a little harsh, but his cheeks have a roundness to them that don't match the rest of his body, so I can't tell if he's my age, younger, or older. "That's okay. You must've been really mad about something."

"Something like that."

He considers me for a moment but doesn't ask about what made me mad. I'm grateful. "You've got some power in that foot of yours."

"Thanks. I'm practicing for team tryouts."

"With that kick, I'm sure you'll make the team." I don't know why but his compliment makes my neck feel hot.

"You like soccer?"

"I like all sports, yeah. But I think soccer might just be my favorite now."

"All sports, huh?"

"Yep. You don't believe me?"

I shrug. "I mean all sports is a bold statement. Do you know how many sports there are?"

Another chuckle. I'll get that full belly laugh soon enough. "Okay, try me."

I drop the ball to the ground, crack my knuckles, and narrow my eyes at him. "Okay, well I guess I can assume you like the obvious ones—soccer, basketball, football, baseball."

"Yep, yep, yep, and yep."

"Hockey?"

"Yep."

"Swimming?"

"I mostly pay attention to it during the Olympics but yeah."

"Archery?"

"Archery is badass." He lifts his eyebrow, testing to see if I'll challenge him. I won't. I have no way to verify if he's telling the truth right now, but I just want to keep him talking a little longer.

"Tennis?"

"Serena Williams is my favorite player."

"Serena Williams is everyone's favorite player." I rest my hands on my hips.

"Yeah but she's really mine. I saw her play for the first time when I was seven with my dad. We watch her play together all the time now."

"Golf?"

His eyes crinkle in the corners, and he flattens his lips into a thin line before he responds, "Yep."

I point my index finger in his face. "Liar!"

And right there, I get the belly laugh I've been craving. "You got me. The one sport I don't like."

"Mm-hmm, I'm sure there are others, but it's okay; my point's been proven."

His curls bounce as he shakes his head in disbelief, eyes still shining with laughter. "You just move in?" He glances behind me to my house.

"Yeah, last week. From Houston."

"Makes sense. We stayed at my Po Po's house last week so I missed you."

"Your Po Po?"

"My grandmom." My eyes light up at his response. He calls his grandmom Po Po. That's so cute.

"Ahh. That's a cute nickname."

"It's Chinese."

My brows furrow. "Are you Chinese?"

"Half. I'm half Black, half Chinese."

"Cool." He seems to like my response.

"Well, welcome to the neighborhood. I'm Kai." He holds his hand out, and I internally laugh at the manners on this kid before grabbing his hand and shaking it.

"I'm Olivia."

The smile he rewards me with after I share my name blinds me. Wow, his teeth are unbelievably white.

"So what made you guys move?"

I roll my eyes then rub them to cover it up so he doesn't think my irritation is aimed at him. "If you ask my dad, he'll tell you it's because there's a coach at the high school in this area he wants me to work with. But since high school is two years away for me, I say it's because he was tired of living in the house where my mom abandoned us."

That might be too much information too soon, but I'm just too tired to care.

"Your mom left you?" His eyes widen after he asks and he starts waving his hands in apology, but I stop him.

"It's okay. Yeah, she did. Last year. She gave up her Broadway dance dreams to follow my dad to Houston for his NBA career. But then he fractured his pelvis and that ended that. That was a year before I was born, and I guess my mom stuck around because she thought eventually I could carry out her legacy for her." Too bad I can't find a beat to save my soul, but I can drive a soccer ball down a field with precision.

I knew my mom and dad fought constantly about her lost dreams because they never bothered to keep their voices down, but I never thought she'd leave us. Or maybe I did, but I thought maybe she'd take me with her, or at least say goodbye. She left like a thief in the night, and I haven't heard from her since. When she left, Dad started putting the pressure on me to practice harder. I think he thinks that if I become a soccer star my mom wouldn't feel like she wasted her time birthing me and she'd come back. Wishful thinking on both of our parts.

"Sorry," I blurt out. "That got too heavy. You just met me and I'm telling you my life story. I swear I'm not a weirdo or anything."

His chestnut-brown eyes bore into me with such intensity that my step falters. I've never had a boy look at me like this before, but I don't think I want him to stop.

"Nah. I don't think it's weird at all. I think your mom's missing out."

"On what?"

"On you."

I wipe sweat from my brow that wasn't there a moment ago.

We continue standing in my front yard just talking. I learn that he's my age and we'll be going to the same school this year. He's got a younger sister, and they live with his mom and dad but visit his grandmom a lot. It feels like a long time goes by in his company and yet not enough.

My eyes start darting from Kai to the street, searching for my dad's car. He should be home from the store soon, and he'll lose it if he sees me socializing instead of practicing.

I try to think of a nice way to get Kai to leave, but before I get a chance, a cute little girl with bone-straight hair bounces out of his house and waves her hands at us.

"Kai! Mom said it's time to come eat!" She darts across the street, and I hear him softly scold her for not looking both ways before crossing. She ignores him and grabs his hand but stops to look at me. "Who are you?"

"I'm your new neighbor, Olivia."

"Hi Olivia, I'm Kylie. I hope you'll be my new friend. I'm tired of hanging out with my brother."

Kai's eyes bulge, and he wraps his arm around her neck to give her a noogie while she squirms and laughs to get away. I can't help but laugh at the scene in front of me.

"I'd love to be your friend, Kylie. And you know what? My friends call me Liv or Livvy so you can too." She flashes a wide gap-toothed smile at me before grabbing Kai's hand again and dragging him toward their house.

"Okay. Bye, Livvy!" she shouts excitedly.

Kai turns to me, stopping her progress. "See you around, Olivia. Next time, try not to aim your ball for my head though."

"No promises, but didn't you hear me when I said my friends call me

Liv or Livvy? You don't have to keep calling me Olivia." I mean, I hope he wants to be friends or I might just die from embarrassment.

His lips turn up in a sly grin, like he's the only one in on the joke. I just better not be the punchline. "I heard you. We're friends now." He leans in a little so only I can hear him. "But I don't wanna be like everyone else." I'm left standing there, mouth wide open before he throws a "Bye Olivia" over his shoulder and heads into his house.

I think I might like this city after all.

CHAPTER
Two

Kai
Twelve Years Old

"THIS IS CRAZY. I CAN'T HAVE YOU BEATING ME LIKE THIS IN MY OWN house." I lightly push her and she falls over on the side of the couch, laughing.

Since that day in her front yard, Olivia and I have spent every day together. When I'm not with her while she's practicing, she's over at my house hanging out.

She's the best friend I've ever had.

"Get on my level and maybe you'd win once in a while," she teases. We've been playing *Super Smash Bros Melee* for the last hour, and she's beat me almost every time.

"Nah, let's turn on items. I'm done playing with you."

She shrieks, "No! We're not turning on items. That's so dumb."

There goes that eye roll she's always throwing my way. "No, you're the one who's scared since you wanna turn on items."

"Pick up the sticks, Olivia."

She blows out a harsh breath and picks up the GameCube controller. I asked my mom to get me a purple one just for her to use since it's her favorite color.

I make my character selection and wait for her to pick Samus like she always does. "Jigglypuff? Since when do you play with Jigglypuff?" I've been playing with Link this whole time, but I'm tired of her talking crap so I'm ready for her.

"Don't worry about me, just pick your player."

She mumbles something under her breath about me being a fool before she makes her selection and the game starts.

As soon as the fight starts, she throws her best attacks at me. I knew she would. She's so competitive, which is why Samus is the perfect character for her, but I'm just laughing because she's about to be so mad.

Jigglypuff falls asleep, and she makes the mistake of stepping into my area. That's all it takes. I blast her into the air and win the round.

She turns to me stunned. "Did you…did you just rest smash me?"

I can't help it. I burst out laughing. I don't have to look at her to know she's seething with rage, but I can't stop cracking up. There's nothing more embarrassing for someone who takes the game seriously to lose by Jigglypuff falling asleep and then knocking you into space.

"I did."

"I'm gonna kill you."

"Don't talk about it, be about it. Let's go."

Turns out, Samus is no match for Jigglypuff. Not when she just keeps walking into my traps. And yes, I have items on but that's because the game is a lot more fun with them. There's no shame in my game.

"I hate you."

"You could never."

"Whatever. I gotta pee. Be ready to lose when I come back."

I'm not sure what happened in the bathroom, but the Olivia that comes

out is not the same one that went in. She's fidgety and refuses to sit back down on the couch.

I try to get her to go back to playing with me but she refuses. "No, you go ahead. I'm gonna take a break."

"Are you sure?"

She hugs herself tight without looking at me. "Yeah, I'm good."

I can't help but feel like I did something wrong here. Is she that upset about the Jigglypuff thing?

Should I apologize? I don't know what to do. She bites her bottom lip and turns toward my front door and that's when I catch it. The small red splotch on her pants. I turn to where she was sitting on the couch and there's no red there, but I'm sure she's still freaking out.

"I'll be right back." I jump off the couch and run to my parents' room. They're lying in bed watching a movie. "Mom, can I talk to you for a minute?"

She and Dad share a look, but Mom gets right out of bed and comes to my side. "Sure, sweetie. What's up?"

"Could you come help Olivia? I think she just got her first period." We learned about periods in health class, and Mom told me it was important to pay attention to that stuff because I have a younger sister who might need my help one day. Olivia doesn't have her mom around to help with these things. That's fine; she can share mine.

"Oh goodness, that poor girl. I'm on it."

I put my hand out to stop her from going out to the living room. "Just… don't tell her I told you." I don't want her to be embarrassed.

She gives me one of those "you did good" smiles and kisses my cheek. "You got it."

I wait a minute before following her back out. When I get there I see Olivia hunched over, but she straightens the moment she sees my mom walk out. I hear my mom ask her to come help her with something, and Olivia looks nervous but she just nods before her eyes fly to me. "I'll be back."

"Cool, I'm just gonna play till you get back."

I turn the game on classic mode and try to keep from listening in on whatever is going on back there. Another fifteen minutes goes by before I

hear the washing machine shut, and Olivia and my mom's laughter echoes down the hallway. I jump up and run to the kitchen and back just as Olivia reappears.

"Hey." She shuffles over to the couch nervously. She's wearing different pants. I recognize them as a pair of my mom's sweatpants. She probably thinks I'm going to mention it but I'm not. I just hand over the carton of cookies-and-cream ice cream I grabbed out of the freezer for her. I don't know if it's going to make her feel better, but whenever my mom has her period she always eats a whole carton in one sitting. "Oh, thank you."

"No problem. Ready to lose again?"

Her mouth splits into a wide grin, and she takes a huge bite of her ice cream then sets it on the coffee table. "Ready."

A few hours later, my mom and I stand by the window watching Olivia to make sure she gets inside her house okay. As she gets to her door she turns and waves to us before going inside. My mom walks over to the couch to grab the sweats she borrowed.

"She's such a nice girl. I like her a lot. It's so sad that her mom isn't there for her."

"Yeah."

"You did good, Kai. Anything she needs, you just let me know. Okay?"

"Yes, ma'am." She ruffles my hair and goes to her room. I start to go to my room to get ready for bed when I hear a thud outside. I go back to the window and find Olivia outside with her dad. She's changed from her jeans to sweats and a hoodie, and she's doing dribble warm-ups. What is going on? When she left my house, she was tired and her stomach was hurting her, so why would she be outside practicing right now?

Her dad has his back to me while she's facing me, and as if she knows she's being watched, she looks up and locks eyes with me. It's written all over her face that she doesn't want to be out there, and I feel bad. Her dad

is probably making her run drills because he thinks she spent too long over here "goofing off."

I'd do anything to put a smile on her face right now. I grab my sneakers and open the door as quietly as I can. I sit on my front step and nod my head at her to let her know I'm with her. If she has to be outside, I'll be out here too.

She puts her hands on her hips with a heavy exhale, careful not to look directly at me and call her dad's attention, but I see the smile I wanted grace her face.

My dad moves the curtain aside and looks at me questioningly, but then he sees Olivia in her yard and he must know what I'm doing, so he just nods and closes the curtain. As the hour goes on, it gets chillier outside, but I don't go in until she does. Her dad runs inside but she lingers for just a moment to mouth a silent "thank you" to me. She doesn't have to thank me.

That's what best friends are for.

CHAPTER
Three

Olivia
Thirteen years old

TODAY IS GOING TO BE A GREAT DAY.

The weather is absolutely perfect. The sun is shining brightly enough that I can feel its rays kissing my skin with a delicate grace as I stand on my front lawn, but it's not so hot that I'm sweating through my shirt.

My dad actually decided to leave me alone for a day and let me just be a teenager.

I get to go to the fair today, which I've never been to before, and the best part? I get to spend the day with my favorite boy.

Ugh, I've got to play it cool.

Kai has been my best friend for a year now, but in the last three months, I don't know what happened. One minute, I was whooping his butt in *Super Smash Bros* and making fun of him with Kylie and the next I was wanting to run my hands through his curls and make him my first kiss.

My first real crush. I mean, yes, David Beckham makes an appearance

in my dreams every night. Have you seen that smile and that curved free kick? Unreal. But this is a real boy we're talking about! A boy I can touch, who I do touch. Often.

Did that sound weird? I just mean we hug a lot, and play fight, and bump fists. You know, all the actions of best friends. Which is all we are so I need to lock this crush down because I can't lose him.

All I've ever wanted to do is play soccer.

And then I met Kai.

Don't get me wrong; it's still the only thing I want to do. Soccer is the blood in my veins, but Kai is the air in my lungs. I can't live without either one.

"Are you ready to go or do you want to pray to the sun god some more?"

Oh crap. Of course, he caught me facing the sun with my eyes closed and hands out to my sides like a weirdo.

I spin around and there he is—the beautiful boy with the beautiful smile. He looks good in his *Space Jam* T-shirt, basketball shorts, and Air Force Ones. His lips look soft and welcoming. *Stop looking at his lips.*

"And what's wrong with praying to the sun god?" I place my hands on my hips as I ask.

He snickers beneath his hand. "Nothing. Send a prayer up for me too." He looks from my hair all the way down to my shoes before speaking again. "You look nice."

My hair is freshly done so *that* I can understand, but looking down at my denim shorts, old T-shirt, and shells, I'm not sure how I look different from any other day. The shirt is tight and doesn't completely cover my stomach because I've had it since I was seven, but since I'm still waiting for the day when I'll need more than a sports bra to support me, there's not much to look at.

"It's about time you noticed." His megawatt smile smacks me in the face, and I swear I hear him mumble, "I always notice," which makes the butterflies in my stomach flutter. But then the flutter turns to panic when he steps in closer and reaches his hand out to touch my hair. I step out of the way of his hand just in time. "Are you crazy, Kai? I didn't spend hours with Ms. Patrice and her hot comb yesterday just so you could mess my hair up

before we even get to the carnival." Ms. Patrice is Kai's aunt, and she always offers to do my hair for me since my dad has no idea what he's doing and doesn't care to learn. She's been teaching me how to do different styles for myself too. I told her next time I want to do a roller set.

"Yeah, my bad. Say your last prayer and let's go already."

I roll my eyes and he grabs my hand to pull me across the street to his parents' SUV where Kylie and her best friend, Tylah, sit giggling about something in the second row. A chorus of "hi Livvy" hits my ears, and I manage to take my eyes off the spot where Kai's hand touched mine to say hi back and climb into the third row.

Mr. Morris, who was standing by the open front door of their house when I walked over, walks down the driveway and jumps in the driver's seat. "Hi, Liv. How's it going?"

"Good, Mr. Morris. Thanks for letting me join you today."

"Oh no problem, sweetie. I'm just glad your dad said yes."

You and me both.

Mrs. Morris runs out to the car moments later and then we're off.

The carnival is packed when we get there. Once we have our wristbands, Mr. and Mrs. Morris give Kai and me permission to run off on our own so long as we meet them in front of the carousel in four hours. We take off, ignoring the cries of Kylie and Tylah, who were told to stay close to Kai's parents.

The first thing we do is the rides. Kai demands to get on the roller coaster first while I demand to hit the Tilt-A-Whirl first since I have no food on my stomach. We rock, paper, scissors to decide who wins, and of course I come out on top so we head toward the Tilt-A-Whirl.

"Ugh, whose idea was it to get on that?" I bend over and dry heave once we get out of the way of foot traffic. On the plus side, I haven't thrown up since there's nothing for me to throw up. On the down side, dry heaving hurts like hell. Kai just looks at me with mock disappointment.

"Yours."

"And why did you let me decide that?"

"Since when do I let you do anything?" I glare at him and he throws his hands up in surrender. "Don't blame me, blame rock, paper, scissors."

I groan loudly right as a group of kids walk by. "That ride should be abolished!"

Kai's eyes widen before he howls with laughter, bending over to match my position. I should kick him in his kneecap.

"Are you done?" I ask, standing at full attention.

He continues howling like a big dummy for another minute before standing up and wiping a tear from his eye. A genuine tear. It was not that funny.

"Yep, I'm done. Come on, badass. I'll take it easy on you before we hit the roller coaster." He wraps his arm around my shoulder, and all that anger melts away with his touch.

We stuff our faces with cotton candy, funnel cakes, and pizza while playing Whac-A-Mole, ring toss, and challenging each other to a water gun shoot-out. Kai wins me a stuffed animal at the hoop shot game, and we track down his parents so they can hold the gigantic bear while we go cause more trouble. He proves to be slightly stronger than me at the high striker game, but I refuse to acknowledge that. I finally get my revenge once we get on the roller coaster when Kai screams like a baby as we hit a sharp slope. He refuses to let me buy the picture of him midscream from the photo stand, but I sneak back and buy it anyway while he's off getting us churros.

We've got another hour to kill before we have to meet back up with his parents so we decide to ride the Ferris wheel. As we move through the line, Kai seems distracted and nervous. I'm not sure what happened or how to pull him out of it.

Once we get to a seat and are strapped in, I hope the awkwardness will dissipate but instead it multiplies. We have no choice but to sit close to each other, but it feels like we're miles apart. What happened?

I replay our entire day in my head, and I can't think of a single moment that could've ruined his mood or made him uncomfortable. It's not like him to hold anything in—we tell each other everything. So, I do the only thing I can think of. I talk.

I ramble on about school and how we'll be starting high school soon

enough, my love of the movie *Bend it Like Beckham,* and everything I can think of while Kai just sits there quietly.

I don't want to have to do this but I'm about to start my rant on why New Edition's "If It Isn't Love" is a better song than "Can You Stand the Rain" when he cuts me off and turns my world upside down. "Can I kiss you?"

Those butterflies in my belly have turned into a stampede of elephants. Did he just say what I think he said? "W-w-what?" I stutter.

He turns to face me, his eyes shining with an intensity I've never seen there before. "I would very much like to kiss you, but if I do that means you'd be mine so I need to know if you'd be into that."

My mouth is dry and my arms are sweaty, but my brain still isn't fully registering what this means for us. While my heart is trying to process my emotions, my head is trying to process his choice of words. "Yours? What does that even mean? Do you even know?"

"Exactly what I said. You'd be mine."

"What movie did you steal that from?"

"Why do you think I stole it?"

"Because you're thirteen. You didn't come up with that on your own."

"Why are you being difficult?"

"When have I ever not been?" I pause and raise my eyebrows, causing him to give me that grin I love so much. "Yours, huh? And would you be mine?"

"Of course. You'd be mine and I'd be yours. Equal."

Equal.

This is really happening.

"What if you're a bad kisser? Then I've locked myself into a 'yours and mine' thing without an escape."

"How would you even know if I am? You've never kissed a boy before."

Damn him for knowing that. "And you have?"

"I've never kissed a boy, no."

I smack his arm. "You know what I mean!" I know everything there is to know about Kai Morris, and if he hid a first kiss from me there will be hell to pay.

His chuckle soothes the elephants back into butterflies. "Our first kiss is gonna be great. You know how I know?"

"How?"

"Because it's us. And there have never been two people who fit more perfectly than us."

Well, if I wasn't on board before there's no way I wouldn't be now. "I...I could be into that."

"Sooo...yes?"

I nod my head with so much enthusiasm I think it's going to fall off. "Yes."

I don't even get a second to be nervous because the moment I say yes his lips are touching mine. It's awkward at first because neither one of us can decide which way to tilt our head, but it doesn't take away from the magic. His lips are pillowy soft and perfect. They feel like clouds, the kind that you could spend an entire day watching and wishing they'd carry you away.

Too soon, the kiss is over but instead of backing away he rests his forehead against mine. I've never seen his eyes this close before but now that I'm staring at them, I see the smallest hint of gold there. It's my new favorite view in the whole world.

I have no idea what to do with my hands so I slide them over his shoulders and coil one of his curls around my finger. "As far as first kisses go, that was not bad," I tease, ignoring the stammering heartbeat in my chest.

He chuckles, and the scent of cinnamon wafts on his breath. "Not bad at all, Olivia. Wanna go for good?"

This time it's me who kisses him, our unsure head tilts settling into a comfortable rhythm. A perfect fit, just like he said.

By the time we meet up with his parents an hour later, I've had my third kiss. And my fourth. And my tenth. Who knew kissing could be this fun?

"Liv, you need to focus."

I sigh and sink down to the slightly damp ground with my head in my hands. Dad has had me up since the crack of dawn running drills. I play on

21

a rec soccer team during the summer to keep myself in good shape, and I messed up during a game yesterday so Dad has been riding me hard.

"We don't have time for a break," he admonishes.

There's never time for a break. There's never time for anything but soccer. That used to make me happy, but now it feels suffocating.

"Dad, please."

"No, Liv. You brought this on yourself. You've been spending too much time with that boy. You're losing focus on what's important." If only he knew that in the past few weeks, Kai and I have graduated from just playing video games to playing video games while sneaking in both make-out sessions and gentle kisses. He'd lose it. I don't care; he can call Kai a distraction all he wants. I'm never giving him up.

I get back to my feet and stretch my neck before signaling him to continue passing me the ball so I can work on my drop kick.

Once he's worked me until my legs feel like jelly and I've done my cooldown jog, I start my stretches in the hopes that he'll just leave me alone for the rest of the day.

"You know, I'm doing what I can to help you."

No such luck.

"Yep. I know, Dad."

"I don't think you do. You didn't want to dance. You wanted soccer so badly that I fought for you and then your mom left. Now I'm trying to help you accomplish the goals you said you wanted, and you're too distracted to care."

And there it is.

The not-so-subtle dig that I'm the reason Mom left. The reminder that he fought for my love of soccer and that means I somehow owe him all my blood, sweat, and tears. I didn't know having my parent stand up for me meant I signed away my freedom on the dotted line. I think about Kai's parents and how they encourage him and Kylie to do what makes them happy. When Kylie decided piano wasn't for her and wanted to pick up art instead, they didn't even bat an eye.

I don't have that kind of freedom.

"I do care, Dad."

"Prove it, then."

Hours later, when my dad is fast asleep and the rest of the world seems to be as well, I find myself back at the field by our house. I should be sleeping too. God knows I need it since I started my day before any human should, but I can't get my brain to shut off.

My head is clouded with the misgivings of Jason Harding.

Soccer, that's what I want. But soccer isn't going to bring her back, which is all my dad seems to care about now. I don't even understand why he wants her back. She left us. We weren't good enough for her.

I wasn't good enough.

What if I never am?

"Hey."

I spin around and am almost knocked off my feet before Kai pulls me into his waiting arms.

"What are you doing here? You can't scare a girl like that."

"I saw you sneaking out of your house and wanted to see what you were up to. I should've known. Do you ever take a break from practicing?" He plants a soft kiss against my lips, chasing away all my demons.

"According to Dad, I take too many." He frowns at that, and I bring my finger up to smooth the puckered skin between his eyebrows back down. "It's fine, I just need to get another hour in and I'll be satisfied."

He sighs and bends down to pick up the ball by my feet. "Okay then, let's get started."

"You're staying?"

He tilts his head to the side as he considers me. "Did you think I would leave you out here alone?"

We spend the next hour running through drills and laughing the entire time. I remember why I love this sport so much, all thanks to my favorite boy.

Kai quiets the noise.

CHAPTER
Four

Kai
Fourteen years old

"You were amazing out there," I say as I wrap my arms around Olivia and plant a kiss against her soft lips.

She squirms, trying to pull away from me, but I don't know why she wastes her time. After every practice, she tries to get away from me saying she's too sweaty and gross for me to kiss her, and every time, I ignore her and hug her and kiss her anyway because there is no better feeling than connecting my lips with hers.

I didn't think we'd get this far when I asked if I could kiss her last year. The thought had crossed my mind so many times, but for some reason that day I couldn't keep it to myself anymore. If she had said no I would've been crushed but she still would've been stuck with me as a friend. I could never give her up. I'm just glad she said yes, and now I get to kiss her whenever I want, so if she thinks her being hot and sticky is going to keep me away

Finally, she gives in and hugs me back, leaning her head into my chest. "Ugh, I was okay. I missed two goals though. Didn't you see?"

Now that's what drives me crazy. I grab her arms and hold her out so I can see her face. A sheen of sweat coats her brows and hairline, though her edges remain perfectly laid. Her lips are twisted up in confusion, but it's her eyes that I really want to see or rather I want them to see me when I say what I have to say.

"I said you were amazing out there and I meant that." I hate when she doesn't see herself clearly. I take a step back from her so that I can hold my hand out in front of her face. "You see this?"

Her brows furrow. "Uh, your hand? Yeah, I see it."

"Pretend this is your mirror."

"I'm lost."

"Pretend I'm holding a mirror up to you so you can see yourself. The real you. Not the version your dad wants you to see." Her dad comes to all of her games and he never has a positive word to say afterward, only ways to improve. I hate it. Why can't he see the raw talent his daughter possesses? "So what do you see?" I ask.

She blows out a harsh breath and studies my hand as if the lines in my palm can give her the answers she wants.

"I see…a sweaty girl who's exhausted after practice."

"Okay. Fine. What else?"

She looks around to see if her teammates are watching her literally talking to my hand, but no one is paying us any attention. Most of them are packing up and heading out.

"Kai, can we do this later? At your place?"

"Nope. We can't leave this spot until you tell me what you see."

"Well, it's not actually a mirror so I can't see anything."

"Ohhh, my bad. I thought I was dating Olivia, the girl with a wicked imagination."

She slaps me in the chest, rolling her eyes. "Alright, fine." She straightens her back and levels her eyes back on my palm. "I see a girl who

loves this sport so much. A girl who's really freaking good at it too. A girl who needs to stop being so hard on herself."

"Good. That's good. What else?"

"You want more?" Her eyes double in size.

"I want you to keep talking until you actually believe the words coming out of your mouth."

She stomps her right foot and starts to say something but I cut her off. "Don't tell me. Tell the mirror."

She closes her eyes for a brief moment and then locks her eyes onto my hand. "I see a girl who is gonna be a pro soccer player one day. I see a girl who's gonna win a World Cup one day. I see a girl who loves soccer. I see a girl who loves...herself!"

"Say that again."

"I...I love myself," she stutters.

"Again."

"I love myself."

"Louder."

"Kai..."

"Louder, Olivia."

"I love myself!"

"One more time."

"I love myself!" I catch the look her coach gives us when Olivia shouts that, but I can't be too focused on her. Not when Olivia's bright smile demands my attention.

"How'd that feel?" I ask.

She giggles. "Actually? Really good. I'm kind of a boss."

I step into her and brush another kiss against her forehead. "Nothing kind of about it, Olivia."

She steps out of my hold and looks up at me, wiggling her eyebrows. "And that right there? Is why you get to kiss me in all my sweaty glory."

I make the most out of that prize before I wrap my arm around her shoulders and walk her home.

"You know I don't need a babysitter, right?"

As much as I love my Friday night tradition of making dumplings with Po Po, I want my parents to know they aren't slick. It's no coincidence that Po Po started this tradition on my parents' weekly date night.

Mom looks at my reflection from the mirror in her and Dad's room while she applies another coat of lipstick.

"Babysitter? Po Po isn't coming over to babysit. Why would you say that?"

"Because she's not coming over until you leave and she's staying until you get back. That's babysitting."

"Are you too cool for your grandmom now?" she asks.

"No, but I'm fourteen and I don't need a babysitter."

Her brows rise and her eyes lower as she inspects me. "Mm-hmm."

"What she's trying to say,"—my dad's loud voice echoes through the hallway as he comes around the corner—"is that we know you don't need a babysitter, but number one, Kylie does, and number two, you can't have both. Either your grandmom comes over or Livvy doesn't. Because we're too young to be grandparents."

It takes everything in me not to suck my teeth at that. You get caught making out with your girlfriend in your room one time and suddenly your dad acts like you're an after-school special.

Olivia and I have been exploring our bodies together but we haven't had sex nor have we talked about it yet, so they don't need to worry about that.

But I won't lie, I've thought about it. More than a few times.

"Kai, are you listening?" my mom asks, grabbing her sweater off her and Dad's bed.

"Yep, got it. No Po Po means no Olivia."

She cups her hand against my cheek and smiles. "You'll understand when you're a parent one day."

They hug and kiss Kylie and me goodbye before walking out to greet Po Po as she pulls into the driveway, then get in their car to leave.

"Po Po!" Kylie screams as she runs and jumps into her arms. She catches her with ease, hugs her tight, and whispers something in her ear before

lowering her to the ground and holding her hand the whole way back up to the house. Her salt-and-pepper hair is braided down her back and swings as she walks. Her kind eyes light up when they see me, and her hand is already rising to touch my cheek before she even reaches me.

"And how is my little wolf?"

"I'm good, Po Po. You have anything you want me to get from the car?"

"Oh yes, baby, if you could get the shopping bags from the car that would be great." I nod my agreement as I walk past her to the car while Kylie trails behind Po Po, talking a mile a minute.

As I watch Po Po pull out the sesame oil, soy sauce, pork, and other ingredients out of her bags, my eyes keep drifting to the window in the living room.

"Why don't you just go get her?"

"What?" I ask, confused because Po Po has her back to me.

"You keep looking out the window for Olivia. Why don't you just go get her?"

She always knows what I'm up to, I don't know how she does it. I shake my head in disbelief and mush Kylie's face when she sticks her tongue out at me.

As I'm opening my front door, Olivia opens hers. She closes her door behind her quietly and locks it, her face turned down in concentration, but when she turns around and catches my eye, her grin splits wide open. She throws her arm up in a wave to me, causing her shirt to rise above her belly button. I lick my lips at the sight.

Before I know it, she's across the street and in my arms. "Hey babe. Guess what?"

"What?"

"I'm down for doggie time tomorrow. The warden is giving me a rare morning off."

Auntie owns a dog salon where she offers full and mini grooming services. During the summer, I normally help her out every other weekend by coming to clean. Olivia has been wanting to come with me to help out with

some of the grooming, but her dad never lets her take the weekend off from practice. I wonder why he had a change of heart this time around.

"That's great. You know she'll be happy; she stays in my face about bringing you." Auntie loves Olivia. The two of them are thick as thieves.

"I know she is gonna work me hard. I'm ready though. We have a lot to catch up on."

"Oh yeah, like what?"

"Like this smelly guy I'm dating."

"Oh wow, so this is how you tell me you're dating somebody else?"

Her eyes bulge out of her head. "What?"

"You said you're dating a smelly guy and I don't smell, so you must be talking about somebody else."

She slaps my arm. "Shut up, always acting a fool."

I chuckle and wrap my arm around her shoulders, leading her into the house.

She leaves my arms the minute she hears the water running in the kitchen and runs toward the sound. "Hey G!"

Po Po smiles brightly at her. "Hi, my little tulip. Wolf can finally stop pacing the floor now that you're here."

"Okay, okay, you don't need to hype it up."

"Yeah, he kept watching the window like a sad puppy. He looked pathetic," Kylie teases.

"Spell pathetic," I command.

Her lips curl up and she places her hands on her sides. "I can spell better than you, fool."

"Okay, prove it."

Her back goes straight and her eyes narrow until they're nearly closed. I know she can spell the word, but I also know she's torn between proving she can spell it or refusing just because I challenged her, which will only lead to me teasing her more.

She clears her throat. "Pathetic. K—A—I. Pathetic." Olivia bursts out laughing while Po Po lifts her hands to her face to cover her smile. I buck at Kylie and she takes off running but pauses behind Po Po to say, "Should

I use it in a sentence?" And that's a wrap. I take off chasing her around the house, finally catching her near the couch and tackling her there.

"Alright you two. If you don't help, you don't eat. Let's go."

I release Kylie from her headlock but push her back into the couch cushions before making my way back to the kitchen.

"Those look great, Tulip," Po Po praises Olivia as she pinches the ends of her dumpling dough. The four of us have been sitting around our kitchen table making dumplings for the last hour. We have about fifty ready to cook. It might seem that fifty is too many dumplings for four people—well, six since we'll leave some behind for my parents—but that would be wrong. Olivia can never get enough of Po Po's dumplings, and Kylie may only be ten but she eats like a grown man.

"Thanks, G. I've come a long way since I started making these with you guys."

"Yeah, yours used to look like balls of poop," Kylie states matter-of-factly. Her tongue sticks out of the side of her mouth as she focuses intensely on pinching the disk of dough in her hands.

"Ya Tou, that's not nice," Po Po admonishes but Olivia just laughs.

"Nah, she's right, they did. But now mine look even better than Kai's."

Kylie gives her a look as if to say *now you're taking it too far.* I think it's the repetitive motion that soothes me but I've always loved making dumplings, and I've become really good at it. Each one comes out looking exactly the same with the perfect dough-to-meat ratio.

Po Po even gives Olivia a look that says she's trippin' but Olivia just smiles and keeps pinching. Her long dark hair is pulled up into a bun but a few strands are loose around her face. She looks so beautiful; I want to wrap one curl around my finger and kiss her, but I don't want to hear Kylie's mouth about being gross at the table so I don't.

We continue assembling in comfortable silence for a while before Po

Po asks, "So, summer is coming to an end and high school is right around the corner. Are you two ready?"

Olivia drops her head slightly and lets out a small sigh. "Yeah, I guess."

"That didn't sound convincing. What's wrong?"

"I'm just nervous is all." She shrugs.

"About starting at a new school?" Po Po asks.

"No, it's not that. It's just my dad is putting all this pressure on me for soccer tryouts when the school year starts. He wants me to make varsity. I just feel like my chances of that are low. I'm just a freshman."

I reach under the table and grab her knee. She puts her hand on top of mine and squeezes but never takes her eyes off Po Po.

"Hmm. And do you want to make varsity?" she asks.

Olivia's brows furrow and she shifts uncomfortably in her seat before she bites down on her bottom lip the way she does when she's deep in thought. She's been pushing herself and her body to the limit to keep up with her dad's demands, but I don't think she's ever stopped to consider what it is she wants.

"I...I think I do." She pauses to reconsider. "Yeah, I do. It would be so cool to make varsity, and I think it would help me get noticed by college scouts. But still, the chances of making it—"

I cut her off, saying, "Hey."

Her eyes fly to mine, shocked at my interruption and my tone. I give her knee another squeeze to reassure her. "Do we need the mirror again?" I start to hold up my hand but she grabs it and holds it in her lap with a laugh. "If making varsity is what you want then you'll do that because you're just that good. One of these days you're gonna have to accept how ridiculously talented you are. And if you change your mind and you don't want it then that's fine too. Do what makes you happy and forget everyone else."

"Even you?"

"I'm always gonna root for the thing that makes you happy so we'll never be at odds, but if we ever are then I stand by what I said, yes."

She doesn't say anything but she doesn't have to. The look on her face tells me how much she needed my words, how much she appreciates them and me. Nothing I said is new. I've told her before how talented she is and

how hard I ride for her, but she needs reminders and I get that. When the two people who are supposed to be your first source of unconditional love and support deprive you of that, it's easy to forget your worth. So I'll remind her as much as I need to until my love outweighs their neglect.

Kylie blows out a raspberry with her lips. "Ugh, eew. They're about to do that nasty kissy stuff."

Po Po snickers and winks at me before taking Kylie to the kitchen to start cooking, and Olivia and I do the nasty kissy stuff for a minute before we join them.

A couple hours later, dumplings have been consumed and Olivia and I have made our way to the front steps to sit and talk. I sit on the steps while she excitedly paces back and forth.

"What do you think high school will be like?"

"Like Kylie. Loud and obnoxious."

She slaps my arm in jest. "I'm serious!"

I grab her arm and pull until she falls into my lap. "I'm serious too. I don't really care what high school will be like. You'll be there, so I'm cool."

She looks up at me as though I'm the answer to every question she's ever had, and I mentally vow to always be that for her.

"You have a point."

I kiss her forehead, nose, and lips then take my hand and pat my stomach. "I could go for a pb&j sandwich."

You would think I said I wanted to eat human toes the way she looks up at me in horror.

"You're serious? You just ate your weight in dumplings."

I shrug. I can always make room for peanut butter and jelly. It's my comfort food. I tell her this and her eyes soften as she stands and takes my hand, leading me inside to make sandwiches for everyone.

Turns out, high school is different from middle school but also the same. Olivia and I have two classes together—biology and English, and we have

the same lunch period—but for the rest of the day we're separated. Within the first week, we both settle into our friend groups. Me, with a few of the guys I play basketball with in the neighborhood and Olivia with a few of the girls from her gym class.

There are a few girls who I always see giving Olivia shit but she assures me it's nothing to worry about. I don't know if I believe her. I don't hit girls. I think guys who do are the scum of the earth. However, I will call Auntie so she can call her best friend's daughters, who I call my play cousins, to come handle things. I don't want anyone messing with my girl.

Today after school, Olivia has soccer tryouts and I can tell she's nervous. At lunch, everyone chats about their weekends but Olivia just offers one-word responses. She doesn't even react when I take her butter crunch cookies and switch them with my Famous Amos cookies.

I turn my body so that both of my knees are touching her, and I lean down to whisper in her ear. "You're overthinking. You're gonna kill it today."

Her vacant eyes come to life as she turns her head to smile at me. "You know what I love about you?"

My heart stutters for a moment at her use of the word love. I always thought I'd be an adult before I experienced love like my parents, but then I met Olivia. "What?"

"You always think the best of me. Meanwhile, I was over here distracted by my thoughts of throwing tryouts to spite my dad."

This catches me off guard. I know she hates the pressure her dad puts on her but never once has she mentioned doing anything to derail her goals.

"Tell me what's up."

She reaches her hand up to smooth the wrinkle between my eyebrows. "I'm not gonna do it. I'm gonna kill it, like you said. But for a minute there, I thought about how satisfying it would be to see my dad's face if all his hard work went up in smoke."

"It's not his hard work. It's yours. He can't take it from you."

She lets out a whimsical sigh before leaning in to kiss me, then jumping into the conversation with our friends.

After school, I make my way to the bleachers so I can be front and center for my girl. Her friends have their own practices to attend so they can't be here, but my boys are here with me to support. I look across the bleachers and scowl when I see her dad watching the field with his arms crossed. Parents don't normally come to tryouts but of course he's made the time to come watch and criticize his daughter. I consider going over to him to tell him he needs to leave but then Olivia and a bunch of other girls run out to the field and she smiles brightly at me.

She sees her dad but barely spares him a glance before she starts her warm-ups, so I know I don't have to worry about her.

Olivia is murdering tryouts. She's a beast on the field, lightning fast and creating space between defenders where there shouldn't be one, but she's also methodical in her movements. Opponents try to use her momentum against her, but she's prepared for that, pivoting and transferring the ball before they even realize she's moved.

She's magnificent to watch but she also understands the importance of teamwork. I've seen a lot of players only rely on their team when they can't get out of a bind, but Olivia brings her team into the fold without pressure. She anticipates not only her opponents' next moves but her teammates' as well, passing the ball flawlessly to where it needs to go, giving them the opportunity to demonstrate their skill and strong offense.

It's clear the team respects her judgment, looking to her for silent guidance as they fly down the field. She's somehow able to be both an encouraging teammate and ruthless opponent in the same breath.

Her teammate comes out and swings the ball over to Olivia who has all the time and space in the world because her opponents have failed to mark up, and she launches the ball into the far corner and scores.

Olivia celebrates by pretending to strum a guitar and then her teammates lift her up in congratulatory hugs before the game resumes.

That varsity seat is hers for the taking.

CHAPTER
Five

Olivia
Fifteen years old

I'M IN THE BATHROOM AT SCHOOL, FIXING MY HAIR, WHEN ALTHEA AND her minions, Kara and Amina, walk in. These girls have been on my neck since freshman year. All because they're thirsty and want Kai for themselves.

Sometimes I look at him and wonder if he's really all that cute for these girls to be trying so hard to steal him from me, but then I laugh at myself because I know he really is that cute, plus he's perfect. So I get it, but they are trying my patience.

"Oh look, it's O," Althea teases. Her minions laugh though I don't recall hearing a joke.

"Hi, ladies. Having a good day?" I ask, trying to kill them with kindness. Althea looks me up and down, a scowl forming on her lips. I guess she doesn't like what she sees.

"I don't understand what Papi Kai sees in you. You're flat as a board

on both sides and you talk like a white girl. You can't even dance. I saw you trying with your friends the other day. Boring."

Kara puts her finger in her mouth, pretending to gag. Jesus, are we sure we're in high school?

"You keep calling him Papi Kai but you know he's not Hispanic, right?" I ask, ignoring her comments about my shape. They don't faze me.

She looks flustered, not used to not getting the reaction she wants out of people.

"Ugh, who cares? He's still a papi."

I roll my eyes.

"How'd you get him to date you anyway, O?" I hate this nickname. Who gave them the right to give me one? "Did you pay him?" Amina asks. Kara laughs but Althea just watches me closely.

"Sorry, how to get a boyfriend classes are full. Maybe try again next year."

I head for the door, but of course Althea blocks my path. "You think you're better than us?"

"I never said that."

"But you thought it," she insists.

"You don't know what I think. You don't know me. You thought that because I'm the quiet girl who minds her business that I was an easy target, but understand this—I eat bullies like you for breakfast. You ain't saying nothing I haven't heard before. I'm an Oreo because I can't dance and I play soccer. I'm so skinny, why does Kai even want me? I'm a loser. When you come up with something original, I'll be impressed. But right now, you bore me." The girls look baffled that I blew up at them, but I stand my ground. The biggest bully I know calls me his daughter so I'm not afraid of these girls. I've grown tired of being nice.

I walk past Althea and out the door. Kai is standing a few feet away, talking to his friends. As if he senses my presence, he looks up and locks eyes with me, his smile wide. Until he sees Althea, Kara, and Amina walk out behind me and his eyes narrow.

I chuckle under my breath and give him a subtle shake of my head so

that he doesn't call his play cousins down here. He's been chomping at the bit to handle Althea and the Pips but I can handle them myself.

"Fuck!" I yell. There's no reason for the expletive to leave my mouth. It just feels good. I've discovered that I like cursing, a lot.

Kai, who is watching me pace back and forth across this patch of grass, smiles at my outburst. He convinced me to skip last period today because he could tell my nerves were shot. So, now we're sitting in the park close to school. Well, he's sitting; I'm pacing like a maniac. Today is an important game. The most important game I'll probably ever play in high school.

When I made varsity last year and then became captain this year, I gained a lot of attention. Some good and some bad. The best comes in the shape of Coach Shannon Naughton from Rice University. I want to play at Rice just to play under her. She's the best of the best. Coach Turner, my current high school coach, is great. I see why my dad was excited for me to work with him. He pushes me and I've grown under his guidance. But Coach Naughton is a badass and she's also one of the few Black female coaches in Division 1 soccer, and I want to soak up all her wisdom. She somehow noticed me and told me she'd be at today's game. I know I still have two years to prove myself but this game today will set the tone. If I don't blow her away I can kiss an opportunity to get her to come back goodbye, but if I kill it then this will open so many doors.

Tired of watching me pace, Kai stands from the bench he was perched on and grabs my shoulders. "What do you need from me right now?"

And this is why he's perfect. This is why Althea and her girls are obsessed. Ugh, Althea. I was fine after their bullshit in the bathroom earlier but then they proceeded to test me. Kai, Althea, and I are all in the same English class this year. We've been working on a group project for the last week, with me being assigned to a different group than them. All through class, I had to sit and watch her drag her nails down his arm and across his

back and listen to her laugh a little too loud at everything he said. Every time her hand touched him I wanted to snatch it right off her wrist. Kai is mine.

That sparks an idea in my mind. I grip his hands and smile up at the eyes that constantly make me dizzy.

"You can sit back, relax, and enjoy the show."

"The show?"

"Yep." I don't allow him to ask any more questions. I just push him back onto the bench, grab my phone, and pull on my favorite hoodie.

I scroll through my music library until I find the song I want and then I channel my inner artist.

Monica and Brandy's "The Boy is Mine" plays through my phone speakers, and I immediately join in about how girls seem to be confused. I don't want to say Monica and Brandy should step aside for me but I'm killing this performance. Kai's smile tells me he agrees. Another reason he's perfect; he feeds into my delusions.

Once I finish my stellar show, Kai gives me a round of applause so I reward him with a kiss.

"You feel better now?" he asks.

"So much." He grabs my hand and leads me back to the school.

My team and I are on fire today. This is by far the best game I've played in my life. I've officially entered my Brandy and Monica era because you can't tell me that little performance earlier isn't the reason behind this hall of fame worthy game. My superstitions won't hear it.

I drive the ball down the field, drawing the attention of a couple defenders, but as they've done this entire game, they leave too much space for me to slip through. I know they're probably thinking I'll run it down myself, but I know my teammate Raynelle is waiting on the outskirts. All I have to do is open the channel for her.

Boom! The moment the ball hits her foot she sails it beautifully past the goalie. Raynelle slides across the grass in celebration and we all join her, hitting a push-up at the same time.

Raynelle's goal plus my two brings our score up to three. The Westlake Redfish have let us into their heads and we're not letting up. Their striker

fights for possession with two of my teammates and though she comes out on top, she's frazzled and her shot is no good. It strikes the woodwork and goes outside the post.

The game is coming to an end and my team is still on fire. Raynelle wins possession of the ball and flies down the field. She has the wherewithal to know her defender is right behind her, but she's already curled the ball my way and I hit a header straight into the pocket.

A fucking hat trick. I just hit a fucking hat trick.

My teammates launch themselves at me, bringing my focus back, and I watch as Raynelle drops to her knees and flings her palms backward. Our other teammate Billie slides to her butt, pushing her legs up by Raynelle's sides with her feet flexed. Natalie, another teammate, bends so her torso is directly above Billie's head and her hands rest against Raynelle's shoulders. My turn. In a swift move, I jump onto Natalie's back, grab Raynelle's outstretched palms, and rest my feet in Billie's hands. We move our limbs to resemble a bicycle while the rest of our team laughs and salutes us.

Game over.

"Hi, Olivia?" Holy shit, Coach Naughton is really standing in front of me right now.

"Y-yes."

She holds her hand out for me to shake, and I try not to squeeze too tight from excitement. "I'm Coach Naughton from Rice." I nod my head enthusiastically. It's all I can do to keep from screaming in her face. She laughs as if she can see the energy pouring out of me. "That was an amazing game."

"Thank you."

"You've got raw talent and good instincts. I like how you led the team out there."

You better say something better than thank you. "Thank you, Coach." *Oh my gosh, something else!* "Our team works well together." *Okay, that's something.*

"Getting seniors to follow you as a sophomore is pretty damn impressive. Is your plan to join the league?"

"Absolutely."

She nods her head. "You'll definitely get there. Hell, you're almost ready for it now. You just need more experience leading and to work on your dribbling a little bit. I've gotta run but I'll be keeping tabs on you, Olivia."

"I appreciate that."

She waves goodbye, and I hold my breath until she's out of my line of vision.

I barely turn back toward the field when I'm tackled by my friends, Janelle and Imani. Kai follows closely behind them but gives them their space to shower me with love. He shoves his hands in his pockets and winks at me.

"Bitch, you did that!" Janelle shrieks.

"Yeah, that was your best game yet," Imani cosigns.

I give a fake curtsy and dust my shoulders off. "Thank you, ladies."

We spend another three minutes gushing over the highlights of tonight's game and my brief conversation with Coach Naughton. From the corner of my eye, I see none other than my dad moving toward me. I thought he'd be tied up talking to Coach Turner a little longer but no such luck. The girls see him heading our way and they send me a determined look before they run to cut him off. He won't entertain a conversation with them for long, but it will be long enough for me to have a moment with Kai before he ruins my night.

"That was incredible, baby," he says as he kisses my lips softly. "Brandy and Monica did the trick, huh?"

I shrug. "Apparently. So, I hope you know that's my new pregame ritual now."

"Cool, as long as I get front row seats to every show."

"Of course. I can't perform without my number one fan."

"That's right. I want merch." He looks over my head and his face falls so I have to assume my dad shook off my friends. "Can I see you tonight?"

"Yeah. He should be in bed by ten. Come over then." Sneaking Kai into my room at night is easy because Jason Harding may be a hard ass, but he's an even harder sleeper. Nothing wakes him up once he's out.

Kai nods his approval and kisses my forehead, nose, and lips before walking off.

"That was a decent game, Liv." I turn at the sound of his stiff voice. His eyes are following Kai off the field.

"Thanks, Dad. Coach Naughton was impressed." His nostrils flare with the mention of Coach Naughton, and I cough to hide my laugh. Coach Naughton may be the best of the best but there's one thing she's not—a man. And in my dad's eyes, the lack of an appendage between her legs is always going to hold her back from measuring up. It eats him up that I want to work with her so badly.

"I saw you speaking to her. Did she mention your dribbling in that first play?" Of course, he wants to know if she spoke about my shortcomings, not my strengths.

"Yes, she said it needs some work." His tongue touches the inside of his cheek at this. He doesn't want to admit it, but he's pleased. I won't waste my time explaining that she didn't dwell on my shortcomings or make me feel like it outshined my talent. That I didn't want to hang up my cleats after speaking with her. No, it's best that he thinks his self-appointed coaching rival agrees with him on where I fall short.

CHAPTER
Six

Olivia
Sixteen Years Old

"OH MY GOD, GET OVER!" AUNTIE YELPS, GRIPPING THE CEILING handles in the car for dear life. I swerve lanes and then slam my foot against the brake, and Kai makes a dramatic show of banging his shoulder against the back of my seat.

I turn and glare at him when he breaks into a full belly laugh. "It's not funny."

A horn honks behind us. "Pull the hell over, girl! Worried about Kai's ass when you bout to kill us all!"

"Yes, ma'am." I pull over to the side of the quiet street and wait for Auntie to catch her breath.

To be fair, for a newbie I'm a pretty decent driver. That turn just got away from me. I tried to fix it but ended up in oncoming traffic, but I got us back in the right lane before that truck got too close. She should be proud of me.

Auntie finishes what was an awfully long silent prayer and then levels

me with a look that tells me today's driving lesson is over. "Get out of the car, Liv. I will drive us home."

"I can drive us home, Auntie."

She holds her finger up to him with her eyes closed. "Boy, my nerves have been played with enough for the day."

She gets out of the car and Kai laughs again. "Ima start calling you Tokyo Drift."

"You better not! Stupid-ass movie." Kai still hasn't stopped laughing about how much I hated that movie when I loved the first two so much. As far as I'm concerned the series ended with *2 Fast 2 Furious*.

He starts to tease me some more but he's interrupted by Auntie banging on the hood, telling me to get my ass to the passenger side.

When we get settled back in the car, I turn to Ms. Patrice with pleading eyes. "Auntie, did I ever tell you how much I appreciate you giving me driving lessons since my dad always acts like he's too busy?"

She rolls her eyes. "You don't have to butter me up. I'm still gonna teach you. I'm gonna have to invest in hair dye since you 'bout to make me go gray, but it's fine. You did alright, last incident aside."

"Ahh!" I reach over and hug her tight. "Thank you, Auntie!"

"Yeah, yeah, you're welcome. Now, unhand me. I've worked up an appetite now fooling with you two and I want some barbeque."

"You sure you don't want me to drive, Auntie?" Kai leans forward in his seat so he can look at her face.

"I'm positive. You do your driving with your daddy. My nerves can't take both of you."

I stick my tongue out at him and he pinches my side before leaning back in his seat.

Once we get to Ms. Patrice's favorite barbeque spot, it doesn't take long to place our order and find a table to sit down.

"Alright, so what are your plans for the rest of the day?"

"Practice, practice, practice." My father's stipulations for allowing driving lessons today was that I'd go out and practice with him later. Practices

with him never end well. I always walk away wanting to take every jersey and pair of cleats I own and burn them.

Kai nudges my elbow, a subtle gesture to let me know he's here. He offered to come with me but it's better to face it alone. One of us should get to keep our good day intact.

I give him a small smile which triggers his own before he turns to his aunt. "I'm helping Po Po later. One of her friends from the community center isn't able to make their Mahjong game so I said I'd step in so they didn't have to cancel. I'm gonna try to get her friends to play Uno after."

"You got Ms. Maggie playing Uno?"

"Yeah, she's getting good at it."

"A little too good," I cut in.

Kai laughs. "Oh yeah, you know the last time we played she actually said 'Uno, motherfuckers' when she put her card down. Excuse my language."

Auntie falls into a fit of laughter, choking on her strawberry soda. Our order number gets called and Kai quickly grabs everything for us.

"So, don't you guys have a dance coming up? I feel like Xay told me you did."

My shoulders slump and I avoid making eye contact with Kai. "Yeah, we have the Homecoming dance coming up but I can't go."

"Oh, why not?"

"My dad conveniently scheduled a visit to the University of Maryland for us for that weekend. He's claiming it's a bonding trip for us and a chance for me to see the campus and meet the Terps coach." A waste of time if you ask me since I've made it clear I don't want to play for anyone but Coach Naughton. He's doing this on purpose because he hates how much time I spend with Kai.

Auntie looks at both of us with soft eyes. "I could talk to him," she offers.

"No, it's okay. We both know that won't do anything." The last time she tried telling him to ease up on me a little bit he politely told her to fuck off which led to her impolitely telling him to watch his mouth because she's not the one. She might end up in jail for assault if she tries talking some sense into him again.

Auntie whispers something under her breath but I do manage to catch the words "go upside his head" before she pastes a smile on her face and asks another question.

Kai stays quiet while Auntie and I talk. He says it doesn't bother him that we can't go to the dance but it's eating away at me. Sometimes I feel like I'm holding him back. Would he be happier with someone whose family is less...complicated?

"So, are you gonna tell me what's wrong or do you need more time?" My eyes zone in on a patch of green paint on the wall just past Kai's head, but he grabs my chin and moves my face so I'm forced to look in his eyes. "You can talk to me."

Kai should be at home sleeping right now, but instead he's in my room, courtesy of my window, rubbing my feet after a grueling practice with my dad. Sometimes I wonder what I did to deserve him but then I think that he might just be some kind of reward from the universe for dealing with the parents I was given.

"I know, sorry. I'm just in my head."

"Okay. About what?"

"Well," I move my legs out of his lap and plant my feet on my plush carpet. "It's just...are you sure you're okay with not going to Homecoming?"

His jaw drops. "That's what's upsetting you? You think I care about missing some dance?"

"It's just that my dad keeps getting in the way. He's always finding some way to keep us from spending time together, and it drives me crazy so I can't imagine how you feel. I don't want you to look back on your high school years and wish things were different."

He rolls his eyes and then in the blink of an eye he's on his knees in between my legs. "Do I wish your dad would stop riding you so hard so you could enjoy life more? Yes. But there's not a single thing I would change

about you or us. It's just one homecoming, Olivia. There will be others. If I wanted to go, I could go with friends but I just don't care to go. Okay?"

"But…"

"But, nothing. You're acting like we're missing our senior prom or something." He sees the panic in my eyes and cuts me off once again. "And even if we do end up missing that too, who cares? When I look back on high school I'm not gonna be thinking about some dumb dances or your dad. I'm gonna be thinking about that time we skipped school to sneak into a showing of *Batman Begins.* Or the time you got sick from eating so many dumplings. Or the time you laughed so hard soda came out of your nose after I slipped on a wet spot on the cafeteria floor. I'm gonna think about how lucky I was to have met you and how lucky I am to keep knowing you. I'm gonna think about how much I love you."

"You love me?" I ask the question but I don't know why. Kai has been proving his love every day since that kiss on the Ferris wheel.

He chuckles and leans forward, wrapping his arms around my waist. "Don't ask questions you already know the answer to."

I grab both sides of his face. "I love you too, Kai."

"I know."

"Whatever." I laugh. "And I, um, I think I'm ready."

At that his eyes widen and he licks his lips. "Ready? For…"

"Yeah. For that."

I wasn't planning on telling him that tonight. It's been on my mind for a while, but I wanted to wait until this weekend since both of our parents will be working.

"Are you sure?" He tilts his head.

"Yes. I've thought about it a lot. Why? Oh God, are you not? That's okay, we can…"

He brings his hand around to lay on top of mine. "Don't freak out. I'm ready too."

"You are? Since when?"

"Mmm, like a year ago."

A year?! I've been confident that I'm ready for sex for a few weeks. He's been ready for a year! "Why didn't you say anything?"

"I don't know. I just figured when you were ready you'd say something. I didn't want you to feel pressured."

I lean down and kiss him softly. "Okay. Okay, good. Let's do this."

I reach down to pull his shirt up, but he grabs my hands. "Woah, woah. Slow down. We're not about to have our first time when your dad is downstairs sleeping. We have time. I want it to be perfect for you."

"I want it to be perfect for you too."

"It's already perfect for me because it's with you."

"You know, I'm waiting for the day when I find out that you're not actually real. That you're a rom-com movie clone or a science experiment for the perfect man come to life." He laughs and nuzzles his head against my stomach. "I'm so serious. How do you always know exactly what to say?"

He shrugs. "I don't. I just say what feels right. I watch how my dad treats my mom and how happy she is and it just...comes to me."

Like I said, some kind of reward from the universe.

"Don't ever change, Kai."

"Wasn't planning on it." He kisses me deeply and I moan into his mouth. He pushes up off his knees and pins me against the bed, climbing on top of me.

I wrap my arms around his neck and my legs around his waist and give in to the feeling. I can feel him growing hard between us, even through his sweatpants, and I reach down to run my palm against him.

He bucks under my touch and breaks free of our kiss. "Shit." He jumps off my bed and I sit up to watch him. "I'm gonna go before I change my mind about waiting."

"What if I want you to change your mind?" I bat my eyelashes. He leans forward and kisses my forehead, nose, and lips.

"Soon, Olivia. Very soon. Come close the window behind me." And with that, he's gone. I fall asleep with a smile on my face.

CHAPTER
Seven

Olivia
Seventeen Years Old

"Livvy, can I ask you a question?" Kylie taps on the middle console in my car.

Driving lessons with Auntie paid off because I passed my driver's test on the first try. My dad agreed that if I passed he would help me get a car so that I could take myself to practices and games over the summer. Now, I'm the proud owner of a deep crystal-blue 2002 Nissan Altima. The top of the passenger window has duct tape on it to remind me not to put it down because it won't come back up and my blinkers no longer turn off automatically but I love my little hoopty. I call her Freeda, short for Freedom.

Today, I cut out of practice early to pick Kylie up and take her to Whataburger. She hasn't been herself lately. Yesterday, she didn't even make fun of the way my dumplings looked when we were finished. I wasn't at my best because Kai kept teasing me under the table. She didn't even act grossed out or remotely interested when Kai kissed me at the table either. We both

agreed that something is up with her so while Kai is helping Ms. Patrice at her shop today, I'm taking Kylie for a girls' day.

"Yeah, of course. What's up?"

"How did you know you wanted to play soccer for the rest of your life?"

"Hmm, well when I was little my mom really wanted me to dance. She kept signing me up for every dance class imaginable but I just didn't have the gift of rhythm. I hated it and I hated seeing my mom's disappointed face after every class. And then one day, I think I was around seven, my dad brought home a shit ton of balls. Basketballs, footballs, soccer balls, golf balls. The list goes on. He gave me a rundown on what to do with them and then he literally made me try every single one."

"Like a field day?"

"Yeah, kind of." At the time, I thought he was actually trying to help me figure out what I liked so I could stop suffering in dance classes, but now I'm not so sure what he was trying to do. "So I tried everything and I was good at a few things, but when I held that soccer ball I just knew. I picked up on the basics quickly. It was as easy as breathing and it felt incredible. I've been hooked ever since."

She seems to consider my words and then looks out of the window. "Hey, what's going on?" I ask.

She lets out a sigh that's deeper than any thirteen-year-old should have in her body. "I don't want to paint anymore."

"Oh really? I thought you loved it."

"I used to, but it's just not fun for me now."

"Well that's okay. You don't have to do it anymore."

Another heavy sigh. "I already feel bad that I stopped playing piano and now this."

"Well, you do know you're only thirteen, right? You don't have to know what you want to do for the rest of your life today."

"Says the girl who has known she wanted to play soccer since she was six."

"Seven."

"Whatever. And Kai knows he wants to do something with sports

medicine. And Tylah knows she wants to be a singer. And I just don't know; things seem fun at first and then I lose interest."

"So you haven't found your thing yet. That's okay. You have soooo much time. My friend Imani plays volleyball, and she's really good at it but she says it's just for fun. She doesn't plan to do it forever. She might not even do it past high school."

Her breath hitches and her eyes flutter. "Really?"

"Yeah and she's not even sure what she wants to study in college, if she goes at all."

"That's good to know." She starts picking her nails in her lap just as I pull into the Whataburger parking lot.

I shut off the car and turn to face her. "Don't put so much pressure on yourself. Do you know how often I think about quitting soccer?"

She blinks for an extremely long time and shakes her head in confusion. "What? Why would you do that? You love soccer."

"I do, but my dad is a lot. He sucks all the joy out of it, and there are days where I just dread stepping on that field."

"Wow. I didn't know that. I'm sorry. What helps you not quit?"

"Honestly?" She nods her head. "Your brother. He makes me remember why I love what I do."

She wrinkles her nose. "Ugh. I guess that explains why you willingly put your mouth on him."

I smack her arm. "Smartass. That's part of it, yeah."

She pretends to gag. "Well don't tell me the rest. Gross."

"Oh stop it. When you start putting your mouth on somebody, I'm gonna tease you relentlessly."

She hides her mouth beneath the collar of her shirt and my jaw drops. "Oh my God, are you putting your mouth on people?!"

"Eeew, stop saying it like that."

"You said it first."

"Yeah, but it's weird when you do it."

"Stop evading the question."

"I'm not kissing anybody! But there's this boy in my class that doesn't completely suck."

"Ooooooh, a crush."

"I didn't say all that."

"You didn't have to." I poke her cheek. "That smile you're trying to hide says it all."

She closes her eyes and dodges my finger. "Ugh, fine. I'll tell you about it. But burgers first."

"Deal." She grabs the handle of her car door, but I grab her hand before she can step out. "Are you feeling any better about the art stuff?"

Her smile is wide and bright. "Yeah, much better. I'm gonna tell Mom and Dad I don't wanna do it anymore and let my next hobby come to me."

"I'm proud of you."

"Thanks, Livvy." She leans across the console to give me a hug and then jumps out of the car and slams my door shut.

"Hey, what I tell you about slamming my doors? Freeda is sensitive."

"God, I love you," Kai grumbles as he kisses a path from the sensitive spot behind my ear down to the curve of my neck.

It's not exactly comfortable straddling his lap in the front seat of his car, but we have to steal our moments when we can. Since our first time last year, we cannot get enough of each other. He's perfect in every way, and after the day I had I want to soak up all his perfection. My dad found Kylie's Whataburger cup in my car because I stupidly forgot to check behind her yesterday, and he went off on me about taking my training seriously. It turned into an all-out drag-out fight about boundaries and ended with me in tears. He always knows how to reduce me down to nothing.

When Kai asked me to sneak out and take a drive with him, I couldn't say yes fast enough.

"Mmm, I love you," I whisper back. I hum in contentment when he pulls my shirt over my head, leaving me in my bra.

"How was your day?" he asks as he bites my neck.

"It was, ahh, it was fine." My words falter when he sucks on my earlobe.

"Just fine?" He kisses my collarbone.

"Mm-hmm, just fine." I trace the planes of his chest under his shirt before I push it up and over his head.

"What'd you do?"

I giggle as he licks the shell of my ear. "Fought with my dad. Same shit, different day."

He stops kissing me and sits up to make eye contact with me. "Are you okay?"

"Yessss, I'm fine and I don't wanna talk about him. I wanna do more of this." I grab him and kiss him, licking his bottom lip until he grants me entrance so our tongues can meet.

"One day, you won't have to deal with him anymore."

"Oh yeah? Where's he gonna go?" Because I can't imagine a day where he won't be up my ass.

"Well, you'll be in the pros and I'll be a world-renowned physical therapist and we'll be too busy jet-setting to listen to him. He'll be lucky if he hears from you on birthdays and holidays."

"Jet-setting, huh? I like that. What else will we be doing?"

"Whatever you wanna do, baby."

"Hmmm. I want a beach house somewhere."

He sucks his teeth. "Easy."

"I wanna get married in your parents' backyard."

"Oh yeah? They'd love that."

"And at least three kids."

"I'll give you all the kids."

"I wanna make you happy."

He kisses my shoulder blade and pushes my bra strap down my arm. "You already do that."

"I promise I'll never stop loving you, Kai."

"That,"—he gives me a short but heated kiss—"is all I ask for."

CHAPTER
Eight

Kai
Eighteen Years Old

"H APPY GRADUATION DAY!" My parents, Auntie, and Po Po shout at the top of their lungs.

It's the morning of graduation and my dad and Auntie teamed up to make a huge breakfast for Olivia and me. Meanwhile, Olivia's dad is at work but he claims he'll be at the ceremony later.

"Thank you, everyone," Olivia and I say in unison.

"I'm so proud of you both." Tears well up in my mom's eyes as she speaks, so I pull her into a hug and Olivia joins in.

"Don't you start with the waterworks, Lisa, because then I'll get started." Auntie starts patting under her eyes with a tissue and my dad rolls his eyes.

"Will you both calm down? This is an exciting time!"

Auntie slaps him in the chest and he laughs. "We know what time it is, fool. I just can't believe they're headed off to college soon. Who told y'all

"That's a great question," Po Po chimes in.

"Wait for me!" Kylie yells from somewhere behind us.

She comes running out to the kitchen wearing the Rice University hoodie my mom bought for me the moment Olivia and I received our acceptance letters.

"Why do you have my hoodie on?"

"It looks better on me."

"Says who? You look like a T. rex with your big head and little arms." The hoodie practically swallows her whole, with the arms going well past her hands so you can't see them and the hem stopping at her knees.

She sucks her teeth. "I came down here to be nice and bring you a graduation gift but now only Livvy gets one." I pull her into my arms for a big bear hug and she squirms in my hold. "Don't try to get on my good side now."

"Love you too, sis," I say as I kiss her on the top of her head.

"Love me enough to let me keep your hoodie?"

Like she doesn't already know she'll get whatever she wants from me. "Yeah, yeah. Bleed me dry."

She finally hugs me back. "Thanks, big brother. Love you too."

She steps out of my hold and pulls out two small packages from the pocket of my, I mean her, hoodie. She hands one to each of us and prompts us to open them.

Carefully wrapped in bright pink tissue paper are homemade friendship bracelets. Mine has beads in different shades of blue, and Olivia's has green beads and soccer ball charms. In the middle of both of ours is Kylie's name spelled out in letter beads.

She then pulls the arms of her hoodie back to reveal two bracelets on her arm. Each one matches our bracelets but one says 'Livvy' and the other says 'Kai' in the middle.

"So you don't forget me when you're off at school." She shrugs.

Olivia shrieks and wraps Kylie up in a warm embrace that Kylie happily accepts. They talk excitedly, and I tune out when their voices reach an octave too high to comprehend, but I do slide my bracelet onto my wrist and wipe my eyes before I dig into my breakfast.

"Can you believe high school is over?" Olivia's voice is whimsical as she stares up at the sky in my parents' backyard.

The graduation ceremony is over and my parents put together a dinner for me, Olivia, our friends, and their families. Olivia's dad made it to the ceremony but I am surprised that he came to the dinner as well. He's been very quiet all night, but I won't complain about that.

I step up behind her and wrap my arms around her waist. The smell of vanilla and strawberries wafts off her and wraps itself around me, putting me in a trance. Every part of her calls to my very essence. It's impossible to even see past her. "It feels like just yesterday you were freaking out about freshman tryouts."

She turns in my arms and drapes her arms over my shoulders. The moonlight reflecting off the rich brown of her skin makes her look like a goddess.

"Hmm and now I get to do it all over again."

"And you love every minute of it." I start swaying us from side to side, dancing to the music I can only hear when I'm around her.

"You're right, I do." She beams. "Thank you."

"For what?"

"For being you. I think I honestly would've lost my shit without you."

"You would've had it under control."

"You know what? You're right; I probably would've eventually. But it wouldn't have been the same. Because everything is better with you."

She kisses me and then wipes the remnants of her lip gloss off my lips. I kiss her again because there's no part of me that minds the taste of her lip gloss.

"I'm gonna go in and find Kylie to make sure she doesn't try to get out of our run tomorrow." Kylie decided to try cheerleading this year so she and Olivia have been going on runs together every Saturday morning. "You coming?"

"Nah, I'm gonna stay out here for a minute."

"Okay, take your time, babe."

The moment Olivia leaves, there's a shift in the air. I immediately feel irritated when I hear a familiar voice behind me, but I don't let it show.

"Congratulations, Kai." Olivia's dad steps out from the patio door and I wonder if he's been there long.

"Thank you, Mr. Harding. Are you proud of your daughter?"

"For doing what she's supposed to do and get her education? I suppose." I don't know why I bothered asking.

"Right."

"So I understand you'll be attending Rice as well, correct?"

He knows damn well that's correct. Olivia and I have been planning to attend school together since starting high school. I didn't care what school we went to so long as it had a kinesiology program, so when Olivia decided she wanted to go to Rice to train under Coach Naughton, I was on board. "That's right."

"Is that where you wanted to go or you're just following my daughter's dreams?"

My eyes narrow at the accusatory tone in his voice. "Olivia and I came up with a plan together."

"That's great. It's sweet to see such young love." He takes a step forward so that he's face to face with me. The slight scowl on his face tells me he expected me to move aside but I don't. I square my shoulders and meet his gaze head-on. "Have you thought about what comes after college? My daughter plans to go pro. She could end up anywhere."

"Her career is what's left to question. Once we graduate and she gets selected for a team, that's where I'll make my home base. I can do physical therapy anywhere."

"How noble of you."

"It's not noble. Being together makes us happy, so we'll do what we have to do to stay together."

"And how long do you think that'll last?"

"How long what'll last?"

"Being happy."

"With all due respect, sir, that's none of your business. Olivia and I are good."

He lets out a dry laugh. "None of my business. Funny. You misunderstand, son. I'm trying to help you because at the end of the day, Liv is my daughter so I know her better than you think. At some point, she will realize that sacrifices have to be made to have the career she wants. I'm just trying to get you to see the inevitable."

He doesn't know Olivia at all. Both he and his ex-wife have tried molding Olivia into carbon copies of themselves and they've both failed. It drives her dad crazy that she isn't some robot he can control, and I can't do anything but laugh at his pitiful show of power. I pat him on the shoulder and step around him. "Have a good night, Mr. Harding. I'm gonna go find Olivia."

CHAPTER
Nine

Kai
Nineteen Years Old

SHE'S PREGNANT. HOLY SHIT, OLIVIA IS PREGNANT. I'm not surprised since we were lax with protection but I'm…in awe. A baby, with the love of my life. It's early—way earlier than we planned—but I'm beyond happy.

We're holding off on telling the family for now until we see them for Thanksgiving, but I'm already in planning mode. I've asked my boss at H-E-B if I can work more hours, and I'm going to look for a second job for the summer. The baby is due in June so I'll have to be mindful of that, but I'm grateful that we'll get to at least finish out sophomore year and have the summer to get acquainted with parenthood before having to balance classes.

I'm going to have to ask my parents to help us with a deposit on a place in Houston so that Olivia can come back to school once the baby is born. I doubt she'd want to make a two-hour plus commute every day so that we could move in with my parents back in Austin.

I'm distracted from my thoughts by Olivia's phone call. "Hey," I answer.

"Hey, Baby Daddy," she giggles.

"What are you up to?"

"I just got out of my internship so I'm about to run my ass back to campus and take a nap."

"Are you literally running because you sound out of breath?"

"Oh shut up, I do not."

"Yeah you do. It sounds like you after you sing both parts in 'The Boy is Mine.'"

She cackles and the sound fills my body with pride. "And see, this is why I never defend you when Kylie starts roasting you. I hope our baby takes after her."

"Damn, turning my own child against me?"

"You damn right. Anywho, I just called to tell you I plan to be knocked out until it's time to go to practice so don't call me."

"I got you. You need anything?"

"Nope, all good. But I will see you tonight, right?"

"Yep. I'll come meet you after practice and walk you back."

"Such a gentleman."

"I'll show you a gentleman tonight."

"Aht aht, that's how we ended up in this position."

"I see no problem with that."

"We're supposed to be working on our papers, not fooling around."

"Okay, I'll fool around and you focus on your paper."

"Goodbye, Kai."

I chuckle. "Bye, love."

⚕

Something is wrong.

I haven't seen Olivia in three days. I keep texting her and calling her, trying to make plans, but she keeps blowing me off. She says she's not on campus but I don't know where she would be. She didn't mention any plans

with Kylie or her teammates, and I've seen her roommate on campus a couple times.

Why is she avoiding me? It would be one thing if she just took a few days off to go somewhere to get away, but she's acting cagey. Her messages are short and dismissive and she won't even hold a conversation with me over the phone. When I ask her what's wrong she says nothing.

Today, she has class, so I know she has to be somewhere on these grounds and I'm going to find her.

I called out of work tonight because Olivia finally started texting me back, but she sounds weird. Honestly, she sounds drunk but I know she wouldn't be with the baby.

Now, I'm making my way to someone's dorm room because that's where she said she is.

"Yoooo, you lookin for Liv?" some guy slurs as he steps out of the dorm room Olivia sent me to.

"Yeah, she in there?"

"Yeah, I saw her earlier. She's fine as hell, bro. Good looks locking her down."

I don't even have the energy to deal with that so I step around him in search of Olivia. When I find her, she smiles at me which makes my shoulders sag in relief. That is until I get close to her and smell the alcohol coming off her. What the fuck?

When I ask her what the fuck she's thinking she blurts out, "I'm not pregnant anymore."

It feels like the ground falls away beneath my feet. Is this why she's been avoiding me? She's been dealing with this loss by herself? Fuck, I feel like a piece of shit.

"I didn't lose it. I went to the clinic and...you know," she explains.

I'm...confused. From the moment we found out about this baby, we've been nervous as hell but excited. At least I thought we were, but maybe it was

just me. We've been talking nonstop about our plans so that when we tell our parents we'll already have answers to all the questions they're going to ask.

If she changed her mind, that's fine. I can't tell her what to do with her body so I would've accepted it no matter what, but why didn't she tell me first? She went through all of that by herself and for what? That's not who we are. She knows damn well I would've wanted to be there to help her through it.

She starts ranting about leaving school to join the draft, and I feel like I'm back in my backyard the night of graduation talking to her dad. She doesn't want me to come with her. As if the idea of me transferring schools to wherever she gets drafted is the most ridiculous idea she's ever heard. She's not making sense. It's as if Jason Harding wrote this shit and she's just reading off a teleprompter.

What the fuck did he say to her? Because I don't even know who's standing in front of me right now.

When she tells me I'm holding her back, I can't hold back anymore. "The fuck you say?"

"I said, you're holding me back. I have an opportunity to get the very thing I've been working my whole life for, and I realized it would be silly for me to pass that up just for a piece of paper."

I can't even listen to the bullshit she's spewing anymore. I don't even know how I get through the rest of our conversation before she storms off.

She may have thoroughly pissed me off tonight, but I still need to make sure she's safe so I text her to check in. She's at least graceful enough to let me know she's back in her room.

How did everything I want just slip through my fingers that quickly? How did I go from being so sure I would spend the rest of my life with Olivia to wondering if I'll even see her again after today?

No matter how hard I try, sleep doesn't come. All I can see is the back of Olivia's head getting farther and farther out of my line of sight.

The next morning, as soon as I finish with my morning hygiene, I head over to her dorm room to try to talk things out. I imagine I can feel the heat

of her body against the door, but she doesn't open it. Damn, that's where we are? She can't even look me in the eyes as she flays me wide open?

I pull out my phone and text her.

Me: You're really not gonna open the door?

Her response is immediate.

Olivia: Please don't make this harder than it has to be

Harder than it has to be? What does that even mean? Years of our lives together reduced to a fight outside of a party and a damn text message.

Me: Why does it have to be hard? Just let me in

Olivia: It's not worth it

All the air in my lungs dissipates. I thought we were in this together. There's not a damn thing in this world that could make me stop fighting for her. Except her. Because if she doesn't think we're worth fighting for then what's the point?

Me: I'm not worth it?

The minute it takes for her to respond ages me by at least a decade, and the response just kills me right there.

Olivia: You're worth more than I can give you. I love you, but the whole baby thing opened my eyes. My heart's not in it anymore. I don't want this anymore. Us. I need space to figure this out

I look at the door. I wonder what she sees when she looks at me through the peephole. Does she see me as the fool I am? Does she even see me at all?

I place my hand against the door, trying to feel close to her one last time, but I just feel cold.

Goodbye, Olivia.

CHAPTER
Ten

Kai
Six months later

**Rice University Sophomore, Olivia Harding,
Drafted by Orlando's Yellow Jackets**

I read the headline on my Yahoo home page a few more times before closing out of the browser.

She did it. She made it to the pros. I had no doubt she would, but now knowing that she's officially in Orlando, almost one thousand miles away from me, everything feels fresh again.

"Hey, Kai. You ready to go?" My roommate pokes his head back into the room. His voice is edgy and his smile is tight so I quickly grab my shoes and follow him to class.

Twenty-two years old

Ever since Instagram was created, I've been in a pit of hell. Why? Because I can find out what Olivia is doing too easily. We're not connected on

Facebook anymore, and she barely even uses that but she's on Instagram a lot. Her username is InLivInColor and I'm embarrassed by how that's the first thing to pop up when I click the search bar in the app. I don't follow her but I find myself searching for her page too many times a day. Fucking pathetic.

It's graduation day at Rice. I should be excited. I'm getting my degree and I already have a job in my field lined up, but instead I'm staring at a picture of Olivia standing arm in arm with her teammate, Angelica Flores a.k.a. Clutch. It looks like the picture was taken mid laugh.

The caption reads: *InLivInColor: This pic may look normal and happy but if you look closely you can see me crying out for help because @ AngieFlores24 won't stop singing "Sexy and I Know It" in my ear*

Frustration seeps into my bones. She's moved on. Great. Good for her. But I can't seem to do the same. I haven't been able to stop replaying our last conversation for the last two and a half years. My parents have asked no fewer than fifty times what happened, but I can't bring myself to tell them the details. Maybe it's because I don't want them to hate her, even though that hasn't stopped Kylie. She gets irritated anytime she sees or hears Olivia's name, but she won't talk about it.

I just have to get through today and then maybe I can push her to the back of my mind.

Twenty-two years old

Google Homepage

Women's Professional Soccer Will Not Return in 2013

Instagram

Picture of Olivia smiling brightly

InLivInColor: Knocked down, but never out

Twenty-three years old

Instagram

Picture of Olivia in a Portland Victory Jersey

InLivInColor: Told you I'd get back up. Portland, let's get it!

Google Homepage

National Women's Soccer League Formed to take the Place of Women's Professional Soccer. See Where Your Favorites Landed

Instagram

Picture of a window looking out on a rainy day

InLivInColor: Do you ever feel like nothing you do matters? Do you ever wish you could just take everything back?

Post deleted by InLivInColor

Two days later

Instagram

ESPN posts headline that reads: G League Center, Dante Moore, Accused of Sexual Assault by Numerous Women—Dropped from League, Negotiations with Portland Raiders Halted

@InLivInColor commented on this post: *Three sad face emoji*

Five months later

Instagram

Picture of Olivia and Angie clinking wine glasses together. @AngieFlores24 is tagged

InLivInColor: You thought 174 miles could keep us apart? Never. Watch out Seattle, I might just kidnap my boo and keep her with me

@AngieFlores24 commented on this post: *secretly plots on kidnapping you and bringing you back to Seattle with me*

Twenty-four years old

Google Homepage

Portland Victory Star Midfielder, Olivia Harding, Taking Her Talents to North Carolina Meadow

Google Homepage

Seattle Reign Star Midfielder, Angelica Flores, Traded to North Carolina Meadow

Instagram

Picture of Olivia and Angie in matching North Carolina jerseys. @AngieFlores24 is tagged

InLivInColor: Reunited and it feels so good. We back in this bitch!

@AngieFlores24 commented on this post: Yesssss bitch!

Twenty-five years old

Instagram

Picture of Olivia in a bridesmaid dress standing next to Angie and WNBA North Carolina Cougars point guard, Justine Richards, both in wedding gowns @AngieFlores24 and @JusInTime are tagged

InLivInColor: The U.S. got its shit somewhat together and finally realized that LOVE IS LOVE sooo this happened! Congratulations to my beautiful sisters. I'm honored to have stood beside you as you said I do. I wish you nothing but love and happiness *Heart emoji*

@JusInTime commented on this post: We love you!

@AngieFlores24 commented on this post: Love you boo! And no you cannot come on the honeymoon

@InLivInColor commented on this post: Bitchhhh come on I just wanna lounge on the beach you won't even know I'm there!

@AngieFlores24 commented on this post: LOL vete

@InLivInColor commented on this post: Fine just leave me here. Hurry back we got a cup to win *tongue out emoji*

One month later

Google Homepage

U.S. Women's National Soccer Team Brings Home World Cup—First Time Since 1999

Instagram

Picture of Olivia on the field with USWNT, celebrating win

InLivInColor: Holy shit, is this real life??
Grateful beyond belief

Two months later

Instagram

Picture of Olivia standing between Angie
and Justine, dressed up for a night out. @
AngieFlores24 and @JusInTime are tagged

InLivInColor: You've never seen a third wheel
look this good

Twenty-eight years old

Google Homepage

North Carolina Meadow Defeats Portland Victory in
National Women's Soccer League Championship

Instagram

Picture of Olivia and Angie pouring Gatorade on
their coach's head. @AngieFlores24

InLivInColor: You earned it Coach!

Two weeks later

Google Homepage

WNBA North Carolina Point Guard, Justine Richards
Named MVP After Amazing Season

Instagram

Picture of Angie and Justine kissing
@JusInTime is tagged

AngieFlores24: Proud af to call you mine! Por siempre y para siempre

@JusInTime commented on this post: *kissy emoji* love you wifey see you tonight

@InLivInColor commented on this post: Ayeeee!! Proud of youuuuuuu. We're getting fucked up tonighttttt

Twenty-nine years old

Google Homepage

U.S. National Women's Soccer Team Brings Home Another World Cup!

Instagram

Picture of Olivia and Angie with their tongues out holding up their middle fingers @AngieFlores24 is tagged

InLivInColor: Gang

Current—thirty-two years old

Google Homepage

USWNT Midfielder, Olivia Harding, Tears Her ACL During Game Against Paraguay—Out for the Rest of the Season—No Word Yet on Plans for PT

Part Two

CHAPTER
Eleven

Olivia

"**O**H MY GOD, STOP SCRATCHING. YOU'VE HAD THAT THING ON FOR a week; it can't itch that bad."

I pause in running my nails down the side of my leg brace to glare at my best friend, Clutch. Her real name is Angelica Flores but she only answers to Angie or Clutch. No one calls her Angelica unless they're looking for a fight.

"Why don't you mind your business, Angelica?" I even make sure to pronounce the *g* as an *h*, the way her Honduran mama would. She narrows her eyes at me, but she must see the vulnerability I'm trying to hide in my gaze because she dismisses me with a small chuckle. Damn, I was really counting on that fight.

"She still scratching that thing? Somebody's nervous." I turn my glare onto Justine who ignores me to dive into the deep end of her and Angie's pool. She and Angie are the only true family I have, besides Kai's Aunt Patrice, so while I don't appreciate them giving me shit, I know it's out of love.

"I'm not nervous, thank you very much." A fucking lie. I'm nervous as all hell. In just a few days I'm going to come face to face with the only man who could possibly unravel the careful facade I've created for myself.

"Okay, so it's been what? Twelve years since you've spoken to Kai?"

"Thirteen." Thirteen painful years.

"Well, listen. I'm just gonna warn you now. I've seen the pics of you guys at prom and all that and he was cute back then but he's a grown-ass man now. Like the IG pics do not do that man justice." Angie fans herself as she describes Kai's apparent manly prowess. She used him as her PT when she fractured her fibula years ago, and I wouldn't allow her to tell me a damn thing about him or his life.

"Thanks for the unnecessary warning."

She shrugs with a smug smile.

Every fiber of my being wants to hear how he turned out. I know of Kai Morris, top-of-the-line physical therapist, but who is the man behind that? Does he still have that slight hitch in his voice when he laughs? Does he still make dumplings with his grandmom every Friday night? Does he still go for long, punishing runs when upset? Does he still have that way of projecting his calm nature onto everyone he comes across so that they want to spill their deepest, darkest secrets to him?

I don't deserve to know. He's not mine. And that's my own fault, so why did I decide to torture myself by calling him for help when my life fell apart?

One minute, I'm flying down the field, keeping Paraguay's midfielder at bay, and the next I hear the loudest fucking pop I've ever heard and I'm being carried off the field.

It wasn't even a thought to call Kai. The moment the fog lifted from my mind and I realized what happened, my fingers acted on their own accord and pulled up the number that I may or may not have stolen from Angie's contacts.

A part of me is surprised that he even agreed to do this for me. He should hate me. Shit, I hate me. But a bigger part knew he'd accept because that's just who Kai is—the golden boy. Always putting everyone else's needs before his own.

"Oh God, am I being selfish? I've been so worried about how I would feel seeing him again I didn't even think of how he would feel having to be around me. Should I cancel? I should. I can find another PT. A local one. Yes, that's exactly what I should do. There's no need for me to go home to Texas and subject Kai to my bullshit when there are perfectly capable PTs in the North Carolina area. Shit, where's my phone?"

"Oh shit, she's spiraling." Justine's voice brings my surroundings back into focus. Did I say all that out loud? Shit, I did.

I clear my throat and adjust my legs so they're just grazing the water in the pool. "Guys, I'm not spiraling. I'm fine. I just realized that I need to change some things around."

Angie rolls her eyes. "Ay, Dios mío. You're not switching PTs; stop it."

"Oh I'm sorry, I didn't know you were my mommy now."

"You can call me mami if you want." She makes a kissy noise at me while Justine chuckles. "Kai is the best in the business, and Coach has already cleared you to spend your entire recovery time back in Texas so that's not an excuse. What are you really worried about?"

Rejection.

Or even worse. Falling back into his arms and being the cause of his ruin.

Texas has too many memories and it's too close to my father, who wouldn't hesitate to ruin Kai's life if he even thought we were reconciling. I know all too well what he's capable of.

The thought of my father getting involved in Kai's life is enough to send me running for the hills.

"I don't know." I wince as the lie leaves my throat. As much as I trust Angie and Justine with my life, there are some things I can't share with them. Some things I have to take with me to my grave for their own good.

There are many things I'll never forgive my father for but taking away my ability to truly let anyone in is one of his biggest offenses.

I grab my phone when I feel it vibrating to find one of the other reasons I'll never forgive him is texting me.

MDR: You sent extra this month, how come?

I type out and delete five messages before I settle on something simple.

Me: Willow's birthday is coming up, right? Just thought I'd help with any party plans

MDR: You don't have to do that you know

Me: I know

MDR: You have to let it go Livvy

If only I knew how. I put my phone facedown and look at my reflection in the pool as my feet wade in the water. I'm disappointed in the face looking back at me. I am not that scared little girl anymore. I have to stop acting like it.

"I think you do know and you just don't wanna say," Angie says, bringing me out of my pity party.

Before I can respond, Justine, the only one of us actually in the pool, swims over to Angie and yanks her in the pool by her legs. Angie screams bloody murder before Justine dunks her back in the water and hops out onto the ledge, adjusting her Senegalese twists that she threw into a messy bun as she does.

Angie pops out of the water, wiping the soaked strands of her chestnut-brown bob out of her face. "Mierda! Babe, why the fuck would you do that?"

"Because, Liv clearly doesn't want you to press her right now, so you need to give her a break." She sticks her tongue out at Angie, prompting a laugh out of me.

Angie gives both of us an "oh it's like that" look before she starts splashing us both with water. I jump up when the water smacks me in the face.

Angie cracks up at the death glare on my face. "Alright, alright. I'll drop it for now."

"And they say miracles don't happen," I mumble, making my way back to one of the lounge chairs surrounding the pool.

Angie gives me the middle finger before swimming between Justine's golden-brown legs and kissing her cheek.

"Okay, so on to a new subject then. Have you talked to Tevin to let him know you'll be leaving town?"

I hit her with another one of my death glares because she is pressing all my damn buttons today.

"You know I haven't talked to that man since he couldn't stop trying to put his lips where they don't belong."

Tevin was the last in the string of casual flings that make up my so-called love life. I have two simple rules—no serious relationships and absolutely no kissing.

I'm always up front and honest about my boundaries at the very beginning, but Tevin thought he was going to be the guy to change my mind. He wasted his time. Three months ago he tried to kiss me goodbye after what had been a decent sexathon. He kissed the door instead and I haven't spoken to him since, despite his constant texts and calls.

"My, my, you are one testy bitch today." Justine smacks Angie in the arm for that but she just laughs, and I can't help it; I laugh with her.

"Okay, so clearly I taught you nothing. Let me show you how to adequately change a subject." Justine turns to face me. "So I got you a private plane to get you back to Texas."

Angie snorts. "Damn, babe, that was good. Hold on, let me get a notepad. I should be taking notes."

I can't have heard her correctly. "Jus, have you lost your mind? Why would you do that?"

She waves me off. "Well, technically I didn't. You know my wallet cannot sustain that but Tyson did. He insisted actually."

Tyson is Justine's brother. He plays power forward for the Los Angeles Tyrants. As soccer players, Angie and I unfortunately make a good deal more than Justine, but Tyson undoubtedly trumps us all. He's humble about his fortune, but he's definitely not afraid to spend it. I can't remember the last time I saw Tyson on a commercial flight or in a car that wasn't expensive and foreign. I'm not surprised at all that he offered me a private plane to fly home. He'd give anyone the designer shirt right off his back, but I am surprised Justine thought I would take it.

"I don't need to fly private, though. It's unnecessary."

"So you'd rather be cramped on a commercial flight with your crutches and leg brace when you could fly in style?"

The argument that I could just fly first class rather than charter a whole plane dies on my tongue as I realize how silly I would sound. Fuck it, if he wants to spend the money on me, who am I to stop him?

"You know what? Tell him I said thank you."

"That's my girl," Angie says with a wink.

Texas, here I come. Let's hope I make it out with the cage I built around my heart still intact.

CHAPTER
Twelve

Kai

Shane: Brooooo come on I'm available

Shane: You owe me anyway for not telling me you know Olivia freaking Harding

My jaw clenches as I reread Shane's messages for the third time. Shane is one of my best friends and one of the few people, outside of my family, that I would trust with my life. The others being my other friends—Lincoln, Isaiah, and Dominic. They have been my extended family, my brothers, since I was twenty-one years old. I don't know what I would do without any of them, but you know what I don't trust Shane with? Olivia. He may be the sweet guy but he's also a manwhore. He isn't a huge soccer fan but he watched a game with me once years ago and saw Olivia, igniting his celebrity crush. Have I wanted to knock his ass out several times as he raved about her "hotness"? Yes. Mainly because hot is a dumbass word and calling Olivia that is an insult to her beauty. It doesn't even make the top five list

of words that should be used to describe her. Gorgeous, stunning, incandescent, even ethereal would be more appropriate. Have I ever shared with him my history with Olivia or that I even knew her? Hell no. What would I even say? It's not like Olivia and I were on speaking terms.

I asked Olivia to let me know when she was flying in so I could assist her, but she insisted I not pick her up from the airport. Stubborn-ass woman. In my frustration with her, I ended up telling Shane about her being my new client and how we grew up together. He's been harassing me to let him pick her up from the airport ever since. I'm tempted to let him because I don't want her having to deal with getting a cab or Uber with her crutches but fuck him. I don't want him drooling all over her.

I type out a quick response to him.

Me: I owe you nothing

He takes no time at all to respond

Shane: Hey you think she'll sign something for me? What's her favorite dinner food?

Shane: Better yet what's her favorite breakfast food? *wink emoji*

I almost launch my phone across the room.

Me: You're not taking her to dinner and you're damn sure not making her breakfast

Shane: Mmm I think that should be her choice, no?

I'm going to kill him. I should hit up Lincoln's wife, Ciara, to find out the best ways to dispose of a body. She writes thrillers for a living and she kills people off in some interesting ways in her books.

Olivia's not even here yet and she already has my brain scrambled. I need some air. I throw on a T-shirt and shorts and grab my running shoes then head toward my door.

I poke my head into Po Po's room to make sure she's resting comfortably before I head out. Po Po is my maternal grandmother. She has Coronary Heart Disease but we thought she was managing that well with

a heart-healthy diet, medications, and exercise. Then, she had a stroke two years ago and my parents and I decided it was best she didn't live alone anymore.

My parents would never put her in a nursing home; it's just not how either of them were raised. My paternal grandmom passed away when my dad and aunt were just teenagers, so I never met her. But their dad took on the care of his late wife's mother until she passed, because he couldn't stand the thought of putting her in a home even though she wasn't blood. Blood doesn't always make family.

My dad spent my whole life working sixty-plus hours a week as an anesthesiologist, and my mom worked her ass off to get her accounting firm off the ground. They did all this while making sure Kylie and I received equal amounts of love and attention. They had finally gotten to a place where Dad dialed back to a normal forty-hour workweek and Mom's firm ran like a well-oiled machine so that they could take vacations and enjoy the life they built. I couldn't let them give that up, especially knowing what I knew, so I volunteered to have Po Po stay with me. I can't be with her twenty-four-seven, but I have a nurse, Lily, come in to check on her and administer her medications while I'm at work.

Po Po used to be one of my favorite human beings on the planet. That is, until I found out that she heavily objected to my mom, her Chinese daughter, marrying my Black father. I don't know the full details of how my dad came into that information but the implication was clear. How could she claim to love me when she didn't accept half of me? I never confronted her about it, but the discovery changed our relationship forever.

Sometimes, the resentment I feel toward her is so heavy I don't think I can carry it, but I have no choice now. After her stroke, her speech recovered for the most part, but she still struggles to get her words right from time to time and the stress from that aggravates her CHD. What good would it do to confront a sick old woman about how deeply she hurt me?

I quietly close Po Po's door and make my way outside. The bullshit starts to melt away with every crack of the concrete beneath my feet. I

can't hear anything but the music in my earbuds and my harsh breaths. I can't see anything but the beautiful buildings in my neighborhood. I can't feel anything but the vibration of my bones.

I make my way back home, but before I go in I pull out my phone to text Olivia. Her flight is due to take off soon so I hope she sees my message.

> **Me: I know you don't want me picking you up from the airport but can you please let me send a ride for you?**

I stop midstretch when I see her response come through.

> **Olivia: Depends, what are the chances of you showing up and kidnapping me if I don't agree?**

> **Me: Who told you? *runs to hide the zip ties and duct tape***

> **Olivia: LOL**

> **Olivia: Look you don't have to try to be nice to me, Kai**

> **Olivia: I don't deserve it**

My heart seizes at that.

> **Me: You deserve nothing but the best in this world, Olivia.**

> **Me: It's just a ride, nothing more**

Five minutes go by before she answers.

> **Olivia: Okay.**

> **Olivia: Thank you.**

I let out a sigh of relief and send a text to Shane letting him know he can pick Olivia up but to keep his hands and eyes to himself. The asshole has the nerve to ask me if I want him to drive blindfolded too. I put my phone away and head inside before I cuss him out.

> **Shane: The eagle has landed. I repeat the eagle has landed.**

Twenty minutes later.

Shane: Package has been secured.

Jesus. Why am I friends with this guy?

Me: Bro, stop being so weird about it

Shane: Just thought you'd want live updates. Gotta go, I've got precious cargo in the car

What a jackass.

The next day, I'm at my office waiting for Olivia to arrive. We agreed to meet here so I can see how her knee is looking and assess where she is. Physical therapy is going to be limited at the beginning to allow for initial healing, but I need to see what we're working with now.

She let me know when she arrived safely yesterday and that was the extent of our conversation. I don't know what to expect from her, but I'm ready for anything.

A knock on my office door has me standing at attention. Faith, my office manager, lets me know that Olivia is here, so I rush out and there she is. My past, my present, and my future looking me right in my face.

Her chocolate eyes are still giant pools of wonder that I can easily get lost in, though they look more tired than they used to. She has on a white crew sweatshirt and a pair of matching athletic shorts, leaving her perfectly toned legs on display. Her hair, currently pulled back into a sleek low ponytail, is still so dark it almost resembles ink, but you can catch the glimpses of natural copper in certain lighting. There's not a single blemish on her walnut-brown skin. She's absolutely perfect.

"Hi Olivia." *Hi* seems like such an inadequate greeting for everything I want to say to her now that she's in front of me, but I don't want to scare her away.

She seems to relax at my greeting. "Hi."

"Want to come back to my office with me?"

She nods, tucks her crutches beneath her arms, and makes her way toward me. I turn my back and lead her back to my office, giving me the reprieve I need so she doesn't see the revelation on my face. The revelation that Olivia Harding has always been and will always be one thing above anything else.

Mine.

CHAPTER
Thirteen

Kai

"COME ON, OLIVIA, YOU GOT TEN MORE IN YOU." I GENTLY TAP HER injured knee, encouraging her to continue with our straight-leg exercises.

"Ten?! You can kiss my whole ass." It takes everything in me to hold back my laugh at the adorable scowl adorning her face right now. It's the same one she used to give me when I'd wake her up before her alarm for no real reason.

Physical therapy with Olivia these past few days has been a special kind of torture. Being able to see her up close and touch her—but not the way I want to—has really fucked with my head.

I knew she looked great when I saw her last week but she looks better than great; she's as gorgeous as she was when we were younger. Her lithe body still feels so smooth and enticing beneath my fingertips.

"With pleasure," I reply. The scowl slips from her face for just a second but long enough for me to see the reluctant desire there. I've been crossing

the line from the moment we started our work together, slipping in comments I'd never say to another client for obvious reasons but I don't care. I'm trying to stir a reaction out of her. Push her to see if I take up as much space in her head as she does mine. With the displeasure planted firmly back on her face, I put her at ease with a chuckle. "I'm just kidding. Seriously, come on. The Olivia I knew would never let these exercises kick her ass like this."

She folds her arms over her chest so I know my taunt landed. "Yeah well, I'm not the Olivia you knew."

I don't show her how much her comment guts me. I want to scream "whose fault is that?" at her but I don't. I just get down to her level and lean forward until our faces are inches apart, the slight hitch in her breath spurring me on to whisper, "Bullshit." Her eyes widen and I can tell she's about to tell me off, but I push forward before she can. "I'm sure you've changed since I last saw you. I'm sure you've grown; I know I have. But at your core, you are still the same badass who took my world by storm, so yes, I do know you. And you know me. For as long as we're on this earth and even after that, our souls will recognize each other so don't give me some bullshit about you're not the same, Olivia. You have always been and always will be one of the strongest women I know, and you do not back away from a challenge so lay your ass back down on this mat and get it done."

Her eyes blaze with frustration and determination and her gaze drops to my lips for so long my dick starts to twitch, but then she pushes backward, away from me, until her head hits the mat. I slowly rise from my position, subtly adjusting myself in the process and watch in awe as she powers through the rest of our straight-leg raises and quadriceps sets without complaint.

About an hour later, after we're done with our session, we sit down in my office to recap our plan for her recovery. I try to concentrate on the notes I need to send to her coach, surgeon, and training staff but my focus keeps drifting to the way she keeps shifting her hands in her lap. The therapy sessions are somewhat easy, but we at least have something to distract us from the weird situation we're in. It's what comes after—the talking—where we can't seem to find our balance. We used to be able to have entire

conversations without words, and now we have no idea how to talk to each other. What a gut punch.

The bright side is that this is the first session where she hasn't asked afterward how long treatment is going to take. My answer hasn't changed since she first reached out to me, and I think she's finally accepted that as badass as she is, she can't rush her recovery. To get her back on the field safely and at the level she was at before, it's going to take about a year.

A year of seeing her every single day after having been denied the pleasure for thirteen years straight. I'm still trying to wrap my brain around that. If we're going to survive this year we're going to have to break this tension. Eventually, we have to talk about what happened between us all those years ago, but we're not ready for that. For now, we can at least try to bridge this gap between us. She was my best friend before she was the love of my life, and I'd like to get that back if nothing else.

"So, how are you?"

She stops fidgeting with her hands and looks up at me. "Oh, um, I'm okay. I feel like I can put a little more weight on my leg so that's good."

I drop my hand off my mouse and scoot my chair out so I can rest my arms on my knees. "That's great, but I didn't ask how your knee was. I asked how you are."

"So, is this a psychological therapy session now? Because I gotta tell you, I did that already."

"Such a smartass," I say under my breath. "You're stuck with me for a year. Unless you'd like to find someone else. I can refer you to my boy Ollie if you'd like, but I'd prefer to keep working with you myself. I thought maybe we could be friendly during this, but if you'd rather we keep strictly professional and not talk outside of our sessions, say the word."

Ollie is a colleague and good friend of mine. He mostly works with the Austin Legends but he takes on other clients too. In fact, I just sent a client his way to clear my schedule for Olivia. He resembles Adam Brody a little bit and he's just as nerdy. I'm sure Olivia would love him just like she unfortunately liked Shane, but I'll be damned if I actually send her his way so I hope the offer doesn't backfire on me.

What feels like an eternity passes before she takes a deep breath and her shoulders visibly relax. "I'm okay, Kai. Really. Life is good. How are you?"

Thank fuck. "You know, I can't complain."

Her bow-shaped lips part and a small chuckle escapes them. "Really? 'Can't complain' is still your favorite response when someone asks how you are?"

I just offer her an easy smile and a shrug to keep from blurting out the truth. That I used to say 'can't complain' when people would ask how I was because I could never really complain about anything when I had her by my side to get me through it. That the phrase hasn't been my go-to canned response since the day she left. That it just slipped out now because even though we're broken and may very well be past the point of fixing, it's still true. I can't find anything to complain about when I'm staring into those eyes.

She shakes her head in disbelief. "Well, that's good then. How's the fam?"

"They're good. Kylie is still a spoiled brat. Surprise, surprise. Mom and Dad are living their best lives. Po Po lives with me now."

Her smile widens with excitement. "Oh, I know you two get into all kinds of trouble then. Partners in crime."

I blink away the painful thoughts that enter my mind. That might have been true a decade ago but not anymore.

"She's sick now. She's got heart disease and she had a stroke a couple years ago."

Her jaw goes slack. "I'm so sorry to hear that." A look of guilt crosses her face, and I hate it because it's unnecessary. There's nothing for her to feel guilty about.

I laugh off her comment but I know she sees the hesitation there. "Okay, I have a question that's been eating away at me."

Nervous energy sets into her shoulders and I almost feel bad. Almost. "Umm, okay."

"Do you still have the same pregame ritual?"

Sweet laughter fills the room making my chest tight. "What you want me to say? Don't fix what ain't broke," she teases.

"I mean, are we sure it ain't broke? I can't help but think if you had someone to be your Monica the routine might...flow better."

She holds her hand up in offense. "Excuse you, if I had to choose I would definitely be the Monica in that duo, but luckily I don't have to choose because both parts are mine. And what are you trying to say about my routine?"

Olivia Harding is a lot of things—gorgeous, smart, athletic, talented, and compassionate to name a few—but artistically inclined is not one of them. The girl is tone-deaf as hell and can't dance for shit, but she swore up and down she ate her performance of "The Boy is Mine" up, and it made her feel better so I cheered her on. Her energy was so infectious I couldn't help but to be swept up in it. Swept up in her. She went on that day to have the best game of her life. From then on, she had to perform that song before every game, same hoodie and all. If there's one thing all athletes are, it's superstitious.

"Oh nah, I'm not saying nothing about it. It's just you would think the way you fly up and down the field, you wouldn't run out of breath trying to do both parts of that song."

The fist comes flying at my arm so fast I don't even have time to block it. I pretend that the punch hurt while she looks shocked that she even allowed herself to touch me before giving in to her laughter. "Shut your ass up. It's hard to do both of their ad-libs by yourself! And don't you tell me I needed a partner. That's the point of a ritual, jackass. You gotta do it the same way every time."

I pick up a piece of paper off my desk and wave it like a white flag. "I hear you, I hear you. Don't bite my head off; I was just trying to be your music video producer."

Her eyes dance with humor as she narrows them into slits at me. "Mm-hmm, why don't you produce some results on this knee instead?"

Before I realize what I'm doing, I wrap the end of her ponytail around my fist and give it a small tug before removing my hand and sliding back over to my desk. "Patience."

She doesn't say anything about my actions, but the increased rise and fall of her chest and the heated pools of her eyes tell me all I need to know.

"R-right," she stutters.

We spend another fifteen minutes discussing her recovery plan and tentatively catching up on the last decade plus of our lives.

We stand so I can walk her out, my palm resting against the small of her back, and I feel the shiver run up her spine but neither of us acknowledges it. "Hey, I meant to ask you, how is your dad? You're staying with him right?" Judging by her reaction, I know that was exactly the wrong question to ask. Her eyes shutter closed and she shrugs my hand off her back, giving me a wide berth. What the fuck just happened?

"He's fine, I guess. No, I'm not staying with him. Thanks for the session."

Her dad is a piece of shit, but I didn't expect the mere mention of him to make her look like she wanted to throw up. I just assumed she would be staying with him while she's in town. I know for a fact she doesn't have a place of her own here.

"Oh, well, okay. Who are you staying with?"

She avoids my gaze again. I don't like this. "I'll see you tomorrow." She rushes off, faster than she should with her knee.

Concern gives way to the confusion and frustration seeping in my bones as I'm left to remember the last time Olivia walked away from me with little to no explanation. Letting her walk out of my life was my biggest mistake. Though I know her storming off doesn't mean she's leaving me again, considering she's stuck with me for PT, I'll be damned if I let this go.

I catch up to her and grip her by the elbow. "Hey, what are you doing?"

"Leaving."

"Fuck that, we're not done here."

"I'm pretty sure we were."

"You shut down on me when I mentioned your dad. I wanna know why."

She scoffs. "Trust me, you don't."

"Olivia." Her name is a command on my tongue, and her back straightens at the tone.

She lets out a deep sigh. "My father and I aren't close and you know this."

"I know that, but that back there was different. You never used to react like that to his name. Did...did something happen between you two?"

I know I have no right to ask considering I had the opportunity to tell her about me and Po Po earlier. But something feels wrong here. If he hurt her, I'll kill him with my bare hands.

I'm gutted when her wounded eyes meet mine. "No, Kai. Nothing happened. I've just tried my best to put strict boundaries between us since... well, since leaving. I just don't like talking about him."

She's holding back on me but I'll accept it for now since I feel more confident that he hasn't physically hurt her. The emotional scars he's left on his daughter are no better, but I don't have a way to protect her from those. I can only hope she'll let me help her heal them again. "Okay, if you say so. But my other question still stands. Who are you staying with?"

Her stare becomes distant once again, and I hate watching the coldness take over the eyes that were once the key to my happiness and freedom. "Why would you assume I'm staying with anyone?"

"Because you shouldn't be staying alone during the beginning stages of your injury. You're going to need assistance with certain things."

"I've been fine so far."

"Fuck, you are still the most stubborn woman I've ever met."

"Oooh, now I'm stubborn. Earlier I was the strongest woman you've ever met. Funny, how things change."

I know she's teasing but it doesn't sit right with me. I grab her chin and pull her head up until she has no choice but to see the sincerity in my eyes. "Don't twist my words. The two are not mutually exclusive, Olivia. You are both incredibly strong and a giant pain in the ass, and I wouldn't change a damn thing about you."

She wraps her tiny hand around mine but doesn't pull out of my grasp. "Dammit, you can't say stuff like that to me."

"Why not?"

"It's too much." She finally pulls away from me. If she only knew. It's not even close to being enough.

I decide that now isn't the time to press the issue, so I go back to my original point. "You shouldn't stay alone."

She sighs in exasperation. "Who should I stay with then?"

"Me." There isn't even a moment of thought before I answer. The only person she should stay with is me. I don't really have the room for her considering Po Po has my spare bedroom, but I'd make it work. She could take my room and I'd sleep on the couch. I'd sacrifice every comfort available to me to make her life easier.

"No." She shakes her head vehemently against the idea. "No, that's not happening. Just drop it, please. Okay?"

I nod my head slowly, letting her slip into her car and drive away. Am I actually dropping it? Absofuckinglutely not. I'll just have to go about it in a different way.

"So what do you need?" my sister, Kylie, asks before taking a huge bite of her enchiladas.

"How do you know I need something? I can't just take my sister to dinner?"

She stops midchew, narrowing her eyes at me. "Sure, but you always act like you're gonna make me pay for half when we both know you're just gonna pay. When you straight-up offer to buy without argument, I know something's up."

I cough into my hand to hide my laugh because she's got me. I don't ask Kylie for much, but when I do, I bribe her with food first. Right now, we're at her favorite Mexican restaurant.

"Okay, fine. I've got a proposition for you."

Her eyebrows lift before she shifts back into her seat and leans back, throwing her arm on the back of her chair. "I'm listening."

I roll my eyes. Always with the dramatics, this one.

"Umm, Kylie?"

I turn to the voice that just interrupted me. I find a guy about my height but leaner with tan skin and light-brown eyes watching Kylie with intensity. She turns to him, unbothered.

"Oh, hey Ethan. How are you?"

"I'm fine. I texted you earlier to see if you wanted to meet up, but I see you already had an invite." He tries to hide it but I see the way his eyes look me over head to toe before he huffs his disapproval.

Kylie and I share a look as she chuckles. "Yeah. Ethan, have you met my brother, Kai?"

Ethan's eyes widen. He clears his throat and then offers me his hand. "No, uh, I haven't. Good to meet you, man."

"You too."

"Well, I'll just go. I'll text you later, Kylie."

She taps her fingers against the table. Ethan turns to leave but Kylie calls him back. "Hey, Ethan?"

"Yeah?"

"Are we dating?"

"What?" He looks over at me like I can save him, but there's nothing I can do for him. He was screwed the minute he approached our table.

"I asked if you and I are dating? Are you my man?"

His fists clench, but not in anger. It's more like he's trying to avoid wiping his palms against his pants. "We've never talked about it, no."

"I thought so. Then, don't ever try to check me like that again, okay?" She doesn't even wait for him to respond before giving him her back. "I might text you later." She dives into her enchiladas again, and Ethan walks away with his head down.

I wish I could say this is the first time I've been confused for Kylie's date but it's not, and unfortunately, I'm sure it won't be the last. That's just what happens when you and your sibling don't look alike. Our mom is Chinese and our dad is Black. Kylie favors our mom with her high defined cheekbones and thin lips. I don't favor either parent really, but I do have my dad's strong jawline. Kylie's skin tone is bronze whereas I'm more brown-skinned. She has a button nose whereas mine is wider. Her natural hair holds a loose wave whereas mine is coarse and has a tight curl to it that I let grow out. Kylie is what our Aunt Patrice calls racially ambiguous. People have no idea what ethnicity she is, and she gets the irritating "what are you mixed with" question often. The question gets under my skin every time because though

Kylie actually is mixed, the question implies that it's the "other" part of her that makes her beautiful. As if being Black couldn't be enough. I, on the other hand, never get questioned about my blackness. People either think I'm Black or Hispanic. Now that we're grown, people tend to assume we're a couple before finding out we're brother and sister. It used to bother the shit out of us but now we just brush it off.

"So, are you gonna text him later?"

"Hell no. What a fucking creep." I'm not surprised. Kylie is a serial dater. It takes a lot to keep her attention and the minute a guy pisses her off, he's out of there. I agree though; that guy was a fucking creep. "So, back to your proposition."

I wipe my mouth with my napkin. "What do you think about moving into my place for a year?"

"With you and Po Po? Umm, no thanks. You only have the two bedrooms."

"I won't be there so you can have my room."

She leans in closer. "And where will you be?"

"I'm going to stay with a client to help them during their recovery."

She drops her fork. "No."

"No?"

"That's what I said. You think I'm stupid? I know your "client" is Liv. Olivia. Whatever."

I roll my neck to prepare for the battle that's coming. "Yeah, okay. My client is Olivia. What's the problem? The two of you used to be close."

"That was before she up and left you to pursue her stardom." She crosses her arms across her chest. Our server makes her way over to grab our plates and see if we need anything else. Kylie orders another margarita and waits until she leaves before continuing. "She abandoned you. She abandoned us. So of course we're not close anymore, and I don't care to help her."

"Kylie."

"No, Kai. You know I'm right. You tried to hide it but you were devastated when she left, and no one but me gets to make your life miserable, so fuck her." You and Po Po.

"Kylie, let me be clear. I love you and I love that you want to protect me but one, I'm a grown-ass man so I don't need you to defend me and two, I'm not gonna let you disrespect her so let that be your last fuck her." I appreciate her being overprotective of me. I can always count on her for that even though I can't count on her for much else. I even understand her anger with Olivia. They haven't spoken in the last thirteen years either, and I know that really hurt because she really looked up to Olivia. But I don't care what wrong she's done, I'm never going to let anyone disrespect her.

Her eyes flash with rage. "You still love her?"

I fold my hands over each other. "I don't think a single day has gone by that I haven't loved her, but that's beside the point. Right now she's strictly my client, and I need to help her so I'm asking you to have my back and step up for Po Po." Po Po has a nurse that comes over to check on her every day while I'm at work, but she needs someone to be there in case anything happens overnight, which is why she moved in with me in the first place. "You can stay there rent free which gives you a chance to save up for a new spot. It's a win-win, Kylie. Come on."

Kylie has a place with a roommate, but they had a big falling-out and she's been looking to get out of there ever since. The server drops off her margarita and she sighs heavily before taking a heavy sip. "Fine. But understand, I'm doing this for you and Po Po. Not her."

"Noted."

"Promise me one thing." She holds her pinky out and I grab it with my own.

"What?"

"Don't let her break your heart again." I can make that promise. Because I'm not letting her get away from me this time.

A few hours later, after Kylie and I have explained to Po Po what's going on and I've packed a few bags, I'm standing at Olivia's door waiting for her to

answer. I had to bribe Shane's dumb ass to get him to give me the address where he dropped her off that day.

She answers the door in a pair of baggy sweatpants and a tight tank top that does nothing to hide her dark nipples. My dick twitches in my pants. She looks from me to my duffle bags with alarm.

"What the hell are you doing here?"

"Hey roomie."

"Excuse me?"

"You wouldn't come stay with me. So, I'm staying with you."

"Like hell you are."

I step into her space, and to her credit, she doesn't back down. "Never been to hell but I can tell you that this is happening." I toss my duffle bags in the house without taking my eyes off her. "You cannot stay by yourself in the beginning stages of your recovery. So you have two options. You can let me in so I can unpack and get comfortable and then we can work together to get your ass back on that field, or I can throw you over my shoulder and move you out of my way so I can unpack, get comfortable, and help you get your ass back on that field." Let's be real, I don't need to stay with her for a full year. She's only going to need assistance for another couple of weeks, but I'm hoping by then she won't want me to go. I'm taking too many liberties here, but I can't find a single fuck to give. She's here. I'm not giving up until I can say I've tried absolutely everything. She'd be well within her rights to call the cops on me to remove me from her property, but I'm hoping her love of soccer will win out here. It has before.

I know the moment her eyes shutter that I've won. She steps aside, and I walk right in and pick up my bags.

"Don't get cocky. I'm letting you in here because I want my career back." She doesn't have to remind me. I'm well aware that I come second to soccer.

"Understood."

"Also, I don't know where this demanding side of you came from, but this is my house. Well, it's my house for as long as I'm renting it. So don't think you're gonna come up in here and boss me around all the time. I'm not having it."

Her command makes me smirk. She has no idea. I toss one of my bags over my shoulder and lean down to whisper in her ear. "I've changed a lot over the last thirteen years, Olivia. I look forward to us getting reacquainted." I start walking down the narrow hallway, leaving her behind. "Bedrooms this way?" I don't wait for her response, but I swear I hear her curse under her breath.

CHAPTER
Fourteen

Olivia

WHO IS THIS MAN AND WHAT HAS HE DONE WITH THE REAL KAI Morris?

The Kai I knew let everything roll off his back, but this guy won't get off my fucking neck. He's so fucking pushy. And I can't lie…it's sexy as hell.

It doesn't help that he's sex incarnate. When he was nineteen he was athletic so he had muscles, but now he is a well-defined machine. The sleeves on his shirts emphasize his hard-earned biceps, and the veins in his forearms pop with every movement. He used to wear nothing but white or black tees, but now he walks around in casual short-sleeved shirts, leaving the buttons undone far enough for me to see his muscular chest with the smattering of hair there, looking like he should be on a beach vacation somewhere. The cross he wears around his neck is hard to look at though. I knew the moment I looked at it that it was the same one I gave him all those years ago. I'm not even particularly religious, but it was the last thing my mom gave

me before she left. She said I should pray before every game. I didn't then and I don't now. I gave it to Kai because I couldn't bring myself to get rid of it, but I couldn't keep it either. I thought maybe if he prayed for me God might actually listen. I can't believe he kept it.

The ear jewelry is new too. I didn't think I would be attracted to a guy who wears earrings, but Kai wears the shit out of them. He wears one small hoop in his right ear and a cuff on his right helix. They're understated but make him stand out. I wonder if he's pierced anywhere else.

And that right there is exactly why I need him to get out of my space right now. I can't go there with him ever again. He still doesn't know the whole truth about what happened when I left. He deserves better than me and the complications I bring. I can't promise him anything but a broken heart and a ruined career.

I walk down the hall to my guest room where Kai is already making himself at home, putting his clothes in the closet.

"You're unpacking like you're welcome here. How long do you plan on staying?"

I catch the smirk spread across his face but he doesn't turn in my direction. "Let's play it by ear."

Oh hell no. "Let's not. I don't need assistance. I'm giving you a week then you're outta here. Period."

A hum of disapproval fills the room but he's otherwise silent. I know what he's doing. He wants to bait me into showing my ass, but I won't give in. No matter how badly I want to grab the clothes he's holding out of his hands and toss them in my front yard.

"Do me a favor?" he asks so casually it makes the hairs on the back of my neck stand up.

"What?"

I watch as he throws his empty duffle bag on the top shelf of the closet and then points to it. "Can you grab that bag for me?"

I roll my eyes so hard I think they're going to get stuck in the back of my head for a minute. Okay, so I'm still limping heavily and I can't reach

any high shelves because it puts too much strain on my knee, but there's an easy solution for that. I just don't put anything on a high shelf.

"Better yet," he continues, "where's your crutch? Since I noticed you're still limping you should be using your crutches but I haven't seen them."

"Oh fuck off, Kai. I'm not grabbing shit. So obnoxious." I turn to walk out and find my damn crutches when suddenly I'm in the air. I'm pinned to Kai's chest while he carries me bridal style out of the room. "Umm, uh, what are you doing?"

"Where do you wanna go? The couch, your room, or the kitchen?" He's exerting zero effort in carrying me right now, and all I want to do is melt in his arms, but instead I find myself trying to wiggle free. Bad idea because he just grips me tighter so I can feel every ripple in his muscles, and the scent of his cologne wraps itself around me like a warm hug. "The sooner you tell me the sooner you can get down."

Jesus. "My room." I need some space from this man.

He glides down the hall to the master bedroom and gently deposits me on my bed. We both seem to notice my crutches sitting by my nightstand at the same time, causing him to shake his head before grabbing them and setting them beside me.

His stare pins me in place. "I'm just trying to help you, Olivia. I'm not your enemy."

No, you're not. But you're the one I can't trust myself with. "I know." His hand traces a path from my brow line to my jaw with reverence before he drops it. I don't dare breathe because if I inhale his scent I'll lose all self-control.

"So stop fighting me every step of the way. Like I said, let's play it by ear to see how long you might need me here to serve you. Okay?" Oh hell. I will literally agree to anything to get him to leave my room before I straddle him and tear his clothes off. I nod my agreement. "Good. And use your damn crutches. Unless you want me to carry you everywhere. I have no problem being the throne you sit on." I have absolutely no response to that.

The next day, Kai has another client to work with so I'm left to my own devices. Angie has been blowing up my phone since I told her Kai is now staying with me, so I decide to finally read and answer her texts.

Angie: Holy shit he just steamrolled his way into your house?

Angie: That's sexy af

Angie: Tell me he's staying in your bed

Angie: Helloooooo

Angie: *inserts gif of little boy tapping his fingers, waiting*

Angie: Ay dios mío

Angie: Are you getting dick right now? Nasty girl. Tell me everything

Me: Dry spell still very much active

I chuckle when I see the bubbles pop up immediately. She must've been waiting for my message.

Angie: Disappointing

Me: I don't want Kai's dick so it's actually the complete opposite of disappointing

Angie: Justine says and I quote "why do heteros waste so much time acting like they don't want to fuck?"

Me: Justine can kiss my ass

Angie: She says she loves you too

Me: Forreal what am I gonna do? He can't stay here. It's too much

Angie: Sorry boo can't help you here. I agree with him that you shouldn't be staying by yourself

Me: Traitor

Angie: Call it what you want. My advice is either deal with your shit head-on or start wearing a fucking chastity belt because that's the only way you'll keep the goods away from that man.

Me: I'm perfectly capable of keeping the goods away from him

Angie: Bitch please I don't even like dick and I'd get on my knees if he asked

Me: Why do you always have to do the most?

Angie: Why do you always have to do the bare minimum?

She texts again when I leave her on read for five minutes.

Angie: Mhm exactly and just out of curiosity how many times have you masturbated since being back in Texas?

Three times. Once after I saw him for the first time, once last night, and once this morning when I heard him showering.

Me: None of your business

Angie: LOL *sucia*

Angie: Good luck boo

Ugh, what good is she? I toss my phone on the couch when there's a knock on the door. I grab my crutches and make my way across the room. Someone should really create some more comfortable crutches because these suck.

Panic settles into the very marrow of my bones when I move my curtains to the side to see Jason Harding waiting for me on the other side of the door. How the hell did he find me? I figured I'd run into him eventually, but I'm not ready to deal with him yet. The banging just gets louder, so I take a deep breath and yank the door open.

"Hi Dad."

"Liv. When were you gonna tell me you're back in town?"

I shrug in response, causing him to huff. I can see the wheels turning in his head. "You gonna invite me in?"

I debate telling him no and slamming the door in his face, but I know

he'll just come back. It's better to get this over with while Kai's gone. I don't need the two of them seeing each other. I step aside to let him in, giving him as wide a berth as possible.

"Nice place," he compliments.

"Thanks. What are you doing here, Dad?"

"We haven't talked since your accident." Oh, you mean right before I went into surgery when you called me not to check on me but to tell me my game was sloppy that day which is probably why this happened and walk me through what I needed to do to get started with recovery? I wonder why we haven't spoken since. "I wanted to check on you, see how PT is going. You never told me who you're working with." For very good reason.

"Nope, I didn't. PT is going great. Thanks for stopping by."

"Don't try to rush me out, girl." His words take me back to when I was twelve years old, trying to please him. I hate that he's still able to reduce me down to that. I've long given up on the hope that I could make him happy, but I still do what I can to not make him angry because when he's angry, it takes forever to pick up the fragments of my life he shatters in his wake.

My fists tighten as he walks farther into my house. My skin crawls with every brush of his hand against something that belongs to me. He picks up Kai's coffee mug and my hackles rise. My soul screams to demand he put it down because he has no right to touch his things. He doesn't even deserve to exist in the same space as Kai. Instead, I keep my mouth shut because I can't afford to clue him in to the fact that Kai is staying here. Shame coats my insides as I once again don't stand against my father in defense of the only man who has ever put me first.

"Can I get you some water or something?" I'm so disgusted with myself. He shakes his head. "No, I'm not staying. Just checking in. So who are you working with for PT?"

He hasn't once asked how I'm doing. He's only concerned with me getting back on that field. I don't even think he sees me anymore. I'm just a means to an end. "I'm working with Kai Morris." There's no point in hiding it from him. He'll find out eventually; I might as well stay ahead of it.

He blinks in disbelief. Satisfaction coils in my gut as the panic sets in his gaze. "You're not serious."

"I am."

Four steps. That's all it takes for him to make his way from my kitchen counter to my personal space. There's a silent battle of wills between us, and I take pride in my small victory when he looks away first.

"Why would you be working with him?"

"Because he's the best."

"You can't afford to get distracted from your goals."

"I'm not distracted."

"That boy does nothing but distract you."

"He's not a boy anymore, Dad. Just like I'm not a little girl anymore. I can handle my own recovery without your input."

His eye twitches. "I'm the reason your career has gone as well as it has, so you should be thanking me instead of being a little shit." Right. He's the reason. Not my natural talent and sheer determination. I'm done with this conversation.

"Loosen the reins. I got this. Kai and I are long over. You made sure of that, remember? It's just PT." I won't let him do to Kai what he did to Dante.

He looks me over as if he's waiting for my nose to grow before checking his watch. "I'm running late for a meeting, but we'll talk about this later, Liv. Answer your phone when I call you."

I limp after him to hold the door open. He reminds me once again to expect his call before hustling out to his car. I wave him off then close the door and lean my forehead against it.

A part of me is pissed at my father's audacity, but another part of me is glad for his pop-up visit because it just solidifies that I need to keep Kai in a strict friend-only zone.

CHAPTER
Fifteen

Olivia

MY GOOD KNEE BOUNCES UP AND DOWN VICIOUSLY AS I WAIT FOR Kai to finish up his notes after our session.

I hate this office. The walls are too white and the air is too thin. Every time I sit in this damn chair I feel even further from my goals.

"Tell me what's up," Kai demands.

"What do you mean?"

He doesn't look at me nor does he stop typing his notes. "That knee is going crazy over there and you're really quiet. What's bothering you?"

When I don't answer, he scoots his chair over until he's right in front of me, pulling my chin up so I'm forced to look in his eyes.

I've never been so conflicted by someone's touch. I want to fall into him and not come up for air until our bodies can't be separated, but at the same time I want to get far, far away from him until my life transforms from the bright technicolor I crave back to the safety of the dreary gray I've grown accustomed to.

Being this close to Kai is dangerous. His sage-and-peppercorn scent floods my senses and ignites a fire inside of me.

"Olivia." God, the way he says my name, I feel it in my core. What is happening to me? "It's only been six weeks. You're exactly where you should be at this stage. You're not walking with a limp. You don't need the crutches anymore. There's no swelling. Your quadricep activation is getting better and it'll continue to get better as we go. So what's up? What's upsetting you?"

I bite my bottom lip to keep my thoughts from spilling out. My grip on reality is slipping by the second.

"I told you; I think we should be increasing the frequency of our sessions to speed up the process."

He leans back in his chair. "And I told you that we're already meeting every day. I'm not going to push you harder than your body can handle to get you back on that field. You and your health are more important."

I haven't been more important than the game of soccer in a long time.

I wipe my hands down my face. "You're right. I just—"

He cuts me off. "I'm sorry, what did you say?"

"What?"

"Did you say I'm right?"

I press my pointer finger into the wall of muscle he calls a chest. "Shut your ass up. I've said you're right before." I start to pull my finger back, but he lays his hand on top of mine, keeping it there.

"Mmm, I don't recall."

"Well that's probably because it doesn't happen often."

"I can think of multiple times where I was right and you wouldn't admit it."

"Name one," I challenge. My hand is still pressed firmly against his chest, but I don't dare think about that or look down at the sight.

"How about when we were sixteen painting Old Man Underwood's house with the aerosol cans, and I told you to press and release quickly not press and hold?"

"Ahh, I can see how you misunderstood. You weren't right, you were right adjacent."

A deep chuckle escapes his mouth. "Right adjacent, huh?"

"Yeah, see if I had just held it for a second less, the can wouldn't have blown up in my face."

We fall into a fit of laughter, but the accelerated rate of his heartbeat pulsing under my palm causes the laughter to die in my throat. Space. I need space.

I clear my throat and he releases my hand, scooting his chair back over to his desk to finish his notes. The air in this room is thick with want and regret, but neither of us says a word.

"So, any other concerns?"

A lot, actually. But none that you can help me with. "No. You're...well, I won't say the 'r' word because that would be twice in one day and we can't have that, but I will acknowledge that I need to trust the process and stop with the pressure."

He presses his lips into a thin line, but his eyes still crinkle with laughter.

We wrap up our session and I pack my stuff to leave. Kai's staying behind because he has a session with another client, so I'm headed out solo this time. As I walk by him to leave, I swear I hear him mumble, "I'll see you at home." Slick motherfucker.

Goddamn it! I could kill that big oaf.

My box of Frosted Flakes is now on top of the cabinet that sits above the fridge. Seeing as I can't reach that fucking spot, I know I didn't put it there.

Normally my breakfast would consist of an omelet, some sort of fruit, and maybe a protein shake, but today all I wanted to do was eat a big-ass bowl of my favorite sugary cereal and veg out on the couch. Is that too much to ask? Apparently so for Kai All Up In My Business Morris. Ever since that walk down memory lane in his office last week, I've been distancing myself from him, but every step back I take, he takes two steps forward.

He's everywhere! I like to have a cup of tea every night? He's there at seven thirty p.m. on the dot to deliver it. I buy ingredients to cook chicken

alfredo? He cooks it for us before I have a chance. I drop a glass in the living room? He picks me up and puts me on the couch so he can clean it up. It's annoying! He's so damn nice and helpful, and if I'm not careful he's going to help me right out of my panties and I can't have that shit. Doesn't he understand my self-control is hanging on by a damn thread?

I make one more weak attempt to reach the cereal box. Man, I really need to get a little step stool. Wait, what? No. I don't need a damn step stool. He needs to stop putting stuff on high shelves or get the hell out of my house.

I'm so deep in my thoughts I don't even hear him enter the room until it's too late. His chest molds to my back so there's not an inch of space between us, and he reaches above my head to grab the box, every part of him overwhelming my senses. His scent invades my nose. The feel of his length against me sends a shiver down my spine. "Here, let me," he says as he pulls the box down and places it in my hands.

I turn around to face him but of course he doesn't give me a damn break and back up. He stays right in my space. A growl rips from my chest and my brows furrow as I slam the cereal box on the counter next to us. "I bet you're expecting a thank you, but you're not gonna get one because you know what? If you hadn't have put the fucking box up there in the first place, I wouldn't have had to struggle."

He seems utterly amused with my anger and that just pisses me off even more. "I didn't mean to put it up there. I'm sorry." I start sniffing the air, and he looks at me in complete confusion. "What are you doing?"

"Oh me? Nothing, I just smell bullshit." He cackles at that and throws his hands up in surrender as he takes a couple of steps backward. He crosses his arms across his chest waiting for me to continue. "You're doing too much and it's irritating my soul."

"What am I doing?"

"You call it helping; I call it getting on my fucking nerves! You're picking up this, bringing me that."

He chuckles again and as much as I love that sound right now, I want to shove it right back down his throat until he chokes on it. "If I remember correctly, the whole reason I'm here is to help you."

"But I never asked you to do that, and if I remember correctly, I told you I wanted you out after a week."

"Why don't we talk about what's really bothering you?"

"Don't do that."

"Do what?"

"Dismiss what I'm saying. I'm telling you what's really bothering me and it's you all up in my space."

"No, see, I would never dismiss you, Olivia. I'm always listening to you and I hear what you're saying, but your problem is that you know I'm also hearing what you're not saying loud and clear."

I tilt my head to try to process what he's even saying. "Look, I'm not about to sit here and argue with you. You said yourself my recovery is going well and I really don't need help anymore, so you can just go pack your stuff and go home."

He rubs his hand against his chin in thought. "Okay, I can go home if that's what you really want."

"It is."

"But do you wanna know what I think?"

"Not even a little bit, no."

"I'm gonna tell you anyway." Figures. I take a deep breath and motion for him to get on with it. "I think you miss me as much as I miss you, and you don't know what to do with that so you're pushing me away. You've been running from me for the last thirteen years, but now you have to face whatever it was you couldn't face back then, and it scares the shit out of you. But here's the thing. If you'd just take your wall down one damn inch you'd realize that there isn't a war I wouldn't fight, dragon I wouldn't slay, or mountain I wouldn't climb for you. You don't even have to ask. All you have to do is let me in."

And therein lies the problem. Kai is too good for this world. I know he would do anything for me, and I would do anything for him. It's why I've stayed away this long. It's why I should've stayed away. Fuck. I can feel the tremble in my hands getting stronger, so I fold my arms across my chest. "I haven't been running away from you."

He scoffs. "Out of everything I said, that's your takeaway?"

"It's the only takeaway I care to address. Everything else is irrelevant."

Anger flashes across his features. "Irrelevant?"

"Yes, Kai. Irrelevant. I didn't ask for a fucking heart-to-heart. I am not your problem to fix. I don't need you to slay any dragons for me, I don't miss you, and I don't need you. I—"

I don't know when it happened, but sometime during my rant, Kai moved. And before I know it, his lips are crashing down on mine.

They're as soft and intoxicating as I remember. His kiss is like that first shot of liquor after a hard day at work. It's a shock to the system, but then the liquid trickles down your throat and settles in your gut, warming you up from the inside out and making you forget all your troubles. I've been sober for a long time. So long that this one drop is enough to pull me under the waves of its influence where I can drink until I reach the end of the bottle.

His tongue glides along the seam of my bottom lip, demanding entrance, and I can't tell which way is up so I give in. The second our tongues meet I know this is the moment where I relapse.

My hands wind their way around his neck and settle deep into his curls. He grips my hips and pulls my body farther into his. His kiss swallows every moan and groan out of my mouth for its own, consuming me until there's nothing left. There is no me and him. There's only us and this moment.

This. This is how addicts are made.

This is why I haven't kissed a single man since the last time Kai's lips touched mine. Why settle for a cheap substitute when nothing's going to taste as good as your favorite drink?

A whimper escapes as his hands grab my ass and haul me up his body until my legs wrap around his waist, but the chill from the fridge door against my back is the cold shower I need to bring me crashing back down to reality.

When my eyes fly open, it's not Kai I see but another man with good intentions and kind eyes. A man who also wanted nothing more than to fight my battles. What am I doing? What happened to Dante was devastating. If the same thing happened to Kai, I would never recover. I would never want to.

He freezes when he realizes I've stopped kissing him back, and the hurt on his face flays me wide open. He sets my feet on the ground and waits for them to stop wobbling before he steps back.

He's about to speak, but if I hear his voice my resolve will crumble, so I close my eyes and put my hand up to stop him. I don't open my eyes again until my walls are firmly back in place. My middle finger rubs against my thumb as I wave my hand in his direction.

"You do not have permission to kiss me." I keep my head high as I storm to my room, and once I'm safely behind that door and my music is blasting to drown me out, I slam my face into my pillow and I scream. I scream and punch my mattress until my mouth goes dry and my hand grows tired.

"He kissed you?" Angie asks. Kai left the house. His stuff is still here so I'm guessing he left to put some much-needed distance between us. So I called Angie to fill her in on the clusterfuck that is my life.

"Yep." I nod along even though she can't see me.

"Was that your first kiss since—"

I cut her off. "Since the last time we kissed, yeah." I know it's a big deal—considering my hard and fast rule about absolutely no kissing—but I don't want to talk about the kiss. The last time we kissed our lives were completely different. We were nineteen and I had a baby in my belly. Too much has happened since then. He still doesn't know the whole truth about the abortion I had. It's too painful to think about and yet I can't get his lips off my mind. I've got a hangover that has no cure, and I need to be talked off the ledge before I reach for the bottle again.

"How was it?"

"Soul-snatching. Heartbreaking. Blissful. And also never happening again so I need to move past that. I need to focus on what happens next."

"And what's that?"

"Surviving the rest of my time here."

"How are you going to survive when you're barely living?"

Living is for the brave. That isn't me.

I change the subject and she allows it. We talk about the home renovations she and Justine are trying to get done and her mom's recent return trip to Honduras. We keep chatting until I hear Kai come back. His movements are loud and precise, as if he's alerting me to his every whereabout so I can easily avoid him. It's a kindness I don't deserve but take full advantage of anyway, only coming out for food when I know he's in his room.

If I really wanted Kai out of my house I know he'd leave, so I'm left to grapple with what kind of person I am that I won't let myself have him but I also won't let him go.

I used to think I was nothing like my father, but every selfish decision I make calls that into question. I am the daughter of a woman who didn't want me and a man who only views me as a gateway to his lost hopes and dreams. A product of pure selfishness. Was there ever any hope for me?

I pull out my phone and reach out to the man I actually have the courage to speak to right now.

Me: I don't think I'll ever be able to convey how sorry I am to you

He answers moments later.

MDR: Liv. It's been years. Too many years. You've gotta let it go

Me: I don't know how

MDR: I don't know either but I'm not gonna keep telling you that there's nothing to be sorry for. You warned me and I didn't listen

MDR: Is this about him?

Am I that transparent?

Me: Yes

MDR: Let him in, Liv. Let him help you

Me: That would make me a monster

MDR: How so?

Me: I know better now. I can't let what happened to you happen to him

MDR: Something tells me he's the one that would survive the storm

MDR: I gotta go but while we're talking I'll say this again, stop sending me money

Me: Now you know that's not gonna happen

MDR: Never say never Liv

CHAPTER
Sixteen

Kai

THAT STUBBORN WOMAN IS GOING TO BE THE DEATH OF ME OR THE death of my dick, whichever comes first.

Do I regret that kiss? Not one bit. Kisses like that could start and end wars. Seven weeks with her and I'm already tired of pretending like her very existence doesn't set my soul on fire. Like I'm not starving to devour every inch of her.

My timing was all wrong though. She's nowhere ready for all that.

But fuck, she tasted so good. Her lips have always been made for mine with their penchant for giving as good as they get. She smelled like coconut, tasted like honey, and felt like home. And the sounds she made? Fuck, I missed those. The sounds of her coming apart from my hands and mouth. I could drown in her. If she hadn't pulled away I wouldn't have stopped until my aching dick was driving into her wetness.

I have no idea what got in her head yesterday, but I'm glad she stopped us from going further. Sleeping with her would've been a mistake. Let me

rephrase. Sleeping with her would've finally given me back the piece of myself I've been missing for the last thirteen years, but seeing the regret I know I would've seen on her face would've been a gut punch I wouldn't recover from, so I'm grateful it didn't happen.

Olivia used to be a warrior. She still is. I can see it in her eyes in those brief moments where her guard is down, but something is holding her back. She used to be the girl that didn't give two shits what anyone had to say about her, the girl that made the varsity soccer team during her freshman year tryouts, the girl who pushed me to stand out among a crowd that only wanted to fit in. I don't know what happened to her, but it kills me to see her light dimmed when it used to be able to light an entire stadium.

Yesterday, I gave her a reprieve because I knew she needed it. She was right; I stole a kiss from her and that was wrong. Fine. If I want her back for good then I need to take a step back and focus on rebuilding the friendship first. Once I have that then it'll be time to take back what's mine.

We don't have a therapy appointment today so I'll leave her alone for a little longer, but her time is running out. I have a few errands to run and then she'll have to face me. As I'm pulling out the clothes I'll be wearing today, my phone starts blowing up. I look at it and roll my eyes when I see it's the guys.

Linc: Ding dong

Linc: You hear that boys?

Isaiah: Nah, what's that bro?

Linc: It's the sound of Kai's timer running out

Linc: Time to tell us why you're shacking up with your client, Kai. And why you've been so quiet since she showed up

Isaiah: *inserts gif of Michael Jackson eating popcorn in the *Thriller* video*

I shake my head reading their texts. Last year, when Isaiah was going through all his bullshit with his now wife, Nina, I told him how I had been in love and almost had a baby once. I'm not sure if he's figured out that Olivia

is the woman I was talking about, but I'm sure he suspects by now. I'm going to have to tell the guys everything about her eventually, but I don't know if now is the time. I'm enjoying being on my own little island with her.

Shane: I mean, have you seen her?

Shane: I'd neglect you assholes for her too. She's even more fine in person

Like I said, I love these guys. I would die for any of them. But I will fuck Shane up. And when I'm done fucking him up, I will rip his arms from his body and bitch-slap him with them if he doesn't stop talking about Olivia like this.

Me: Shane, don't make me kill you

Dom: Is this the part where we act like we don't think he's fucking his client?

Linc: Yep and this is the part where Kai denies it

Linc sent his text at the exact same time that I sent mine.

Me: I'm not fucking my client

His reply comes immediately.

Linc: Told you

I chuckle as I throw my shirt over my head. Fuck these guys.

Shane: Wait, so should I be shooting my shot or no?

Me: Stay away from her

Isaiah: Your honor, I'd like to submit Kai's sus-ass texts as Exhibit A

Isaiah: *inserts gif of Will and Carlton from *The Fresh Prince* slamming briefcases on a courtroom table and sitting down*

Isaiah: He's definitely fucking his client

Shane: Gonna need a clear yes or no here. She's fine as hell

Me: Linc, will Ciara give me tips on how to get rid of a body?

Linc: She says for legal reasons she has no idea what you're talking about

Isaiah: Exhibit B, your honor

Me: Who tf is even the judge?

All three texts come in at the same time.

Linc: I am

Dom: I am

Shane: I am

I put my phone away because I don't have time for these jackasses. They'll get the full story soon enough. For now, I'm going to check in on my parents.

They still live in the house I grew up in, and every time I drive up this street, no matter how hard I try to resist, my eyes always drift over to the house of the girl that wrecked me. Her dad moved after she left college, so at least I don't have to deal with possibly running into him.

When I walk up the pathway to our front door, I hear Deborah Cox's "Nobody's Supposed to Be Here" crooning from the open window so I already know they're in there cleaning. I let myself in to find Mom dancing in the kitchen while she mops the floor and Dad singing along while he vacuums the living room carpet.

This has always been a Saturday morning tradition in my house. No matter how tired my parents were from working long-ass shifts the night before, as soon as Kylie and I heard the old-school R & B or gospel music playing, we knew it was time to get up and clean. Dad said he and Auntie used to do the same with my grandparents when they were growing up and my mom was happy to pick up the tradition.

Mom twirls in a circle, mop in hand, and startles when she sees me.

"Kai, sweetie. I didn't hear you come in."

"Sorry. Didn't mean to scare you." She waves me off as she walks over to pull me into a warm hug.

She tries to get my dad's attention, but she's drowned out by the vacuum and he's focused on his vocals.

"Xavier!"

He freezes and turns the vacuum off. "Lisa, baby, you know this is my part." He turns around with his hand extended to her but then sees me. "My boy!"

"Hey, Dad," I say as he smacks my hand and pulls me into an embrace. "What are you doing here?"

I turn to my mom with the bag I carried inside held out to her. "I went to T-Mart and got you Sachima, Mom." She beams a megawatt smile at me before snatching the bag out of my hands, patting me on the cheek, and running back to the kitchen. Dad's smile follows her the whole way.

T-Mart is an international supermarket downtown. It sells food and snacks from many different Asian cultures such as Chinese, Korean, and Japanese. My mom's favorite snack growing up was Sachima, and we used to take a family trip to T-Mart every month so my mom could pick up some goodies. Now that Kylie and I are grown, we don't make that trip anymore, so I try to stop by and get her stuff from time to time.

I don't actually speak much Cantonese, much to Po Po's chagrin. I love my family and I love learning about my culture. Po Po would always tell me stories about Guangzhou growing up and about her Buddhist beliefs, even though my mom and dad are both Christian. She and Mom even taught me how to make a few recipes, which I loved, but I've always felt more comfortable with my Black half than my Chinese half. I'm not ashamed of it by any means, but I guess I just don't know how to embrace it fully. Maybe it's because I look more Black or maybe it's because the kids at school were always quicker to accept me as Black—or assume I was Hispanic—than as Chinese or even as mixed race. So, learning another language was not on the top of my priority list. I often wonder if that's why Po Po didn't want Mom marrying Dad in the first place, but I can't bring myself to ask. She never pressured me to learn, but I could tell it hurt her.

"So come on, sit down. Tell me what's up." Dad leads me over to the same leather couch that used to drive me crazy as a kid. Do you know how hot and sticky leather couches get during the summer?

"Not much, just working."

"Mm-hmm."

He gives me that look that tells me he knows what's up. "So, Kylie told you, huh?"

"The question is, why didn't you?" Snitch.

I brush my hand through the curls on top of my head. "I don't know. There's nothing to say really."

His thick eyebrow lifts in question. "Olivia Harding comes back to town to work with you and you're living with her, but there's nothing to say?"

"I guess I've just been trying to wrap my head around the fact that she's really here."

"More like you've been trying to keep her all to yourself in your own little world."

"That too."

He huffs out a laugh while clapping me on the shoulder. "So, how is she?"

I proceed to fill my dad in on Olivia's progress through therapy and how I'm having a hard time getting through to her. He's quiet throughout, nodding his head at the right moments.

He takes a moment to collect his thoughts. "Did you know that your mom and I broke up once?"

I'm a little taken aback by his question. I've always known my parents to be a strong unit. How did I miss this?

"When was this?" I ask.

"Mmm, you were about six, and Kylie was two."

Six? How did I not remember my parents being broken up when I was six? And why is he telling me this now?

"What happened?"

"Well, you remember me working sixty-hour weeks when you were younger? That was honestly great work-life balance compared to what I was

doing when you were that age. I was never home. Your mom was tired of raising you two by herself and not being heard by me. I lost sight of what was important. She had me leave the house and we were separated for six months."

"You lived in a different house from us for six months?"

"Yep. It only took me one day to realize the mistake I made. The rest of the time I had to earn my place back by your mom's side. Coming home to that empty apartment every day was hell on earth."

"So what did you do to get back home?"

"I had to put in the work. Prove to your mom that I heard what she was saying and was willing to make the necessary changes to get my family back. I took a sabbatical from work to focus on you kids and attend couples counseling with your mom. We agreed that when I returned to work I'd be doing fewer hours. Granted it was still a lot, but I found a schedule that worked so that I always made time for family. She wanted to quit her job as a CPA to start her own accounting firm, so I gave her the support she needed to do that. It took a lot of work and compromise, but we found the perfect balance for us."

I'm not even sure what to do with this information. "Why are you telling me this?"

"Because I want you to understand that if you really want something, you have to be willing to work for it. To give it your blood, sweat, and tears."

Ahh. He's telling me not to give up on Olivia. He doesn't have to tell me twice.

"I got you, Pop."

"I know you do."

I spend another forty-five minutes catching up with my parents before I head out to run the rest of my errands.

By the time I get back to Olivia's house, it's almost dinnertime. As I'm about to walk into the house, a familiar Audi R8 pulls up into her driveway. What the fuck is Shane doing here?

"Why are you here?"

He laughs and I'm trying to figure out where he heard a joke. "Our girl invited me over for dinner."

Our girl.

My fists curl up by my sides, itching to collide with Shane's nose. If he weren't my boy he'd have already caught these hands. And did he say she invited him? That means they exchanged numbers that day he picked her up from the airport.

Don't kill him. Don't kill him. Don't kill him. I mumble the mantra to myself a few more times.

"I can see the wheels turning in your head, man. I gave her my number just in case she needed anything while she was here." He pauses. "And I do mean anything." As if he knows it's coming, he dodges my fist as soon as I swing. "I'm just joking, man! Kind of. But really, today's the first day I've heard from her since I picked her up from the airport. She thought it'd be cool to have a 'family' dinner."

In other words, she wanted a buffer between us for tonight. Clever girl. It won't work, though, because I don't give a fuck if Shane's there or not. I would bend her ass over the kitchen table and let Shane watch, that's how badly I want her, so she can fuck around and find out if she wants to.

I motion for him to follow me to the door. I push the door open, and he steps up to head inside when my arm flies out to block his path. "Let's get one thing clear. You keep your hands to yourself, your feet to yourself, your eyes to yourself. Hell, you even keep your laugh to yourself. Just keep your overall white-boy charm to a minimum. You got me?" Shane and his blue-ish eyes, perfectly coiffed hair, and sharp jawline can focus his efforts elsewhere.

"Oh, you are so fucked," he whispers as he ducks his tall, lanky ass under my arm and inside the house.

Don't I know it?

"Shane, hi!" Olivia shouts when she sees him. She reaches her arms up to wrap around his neck for a hug, and he lifts her off the ground for a split second. I'm convinced he has a death wish.

"Thanks for the invite, baby girl." This motherfucker.

She laughs and explains to me that she thought it would be nice for me to have a friend over as a token of her appreciation for staying with her during her recovery. She's so cute when she lies. I call bullshit with my

smirk, and she returns the smirk tenfold before shrugging and going back into the kitchen.

"Shane, make yourself at home," she calls out to him as she bends over to pull something out of the oven. It smells delicious, but I can't tear my eyes away from the curves of her ass to see what it is. She has on a pair of tight black leggings that hug her like an old friend and a gray cropped sweater that leaves the toned expanse of her stomach exposed. Damn, I want nothing more than to wrap my arms around her and watch her melt into me.

I make my way over to her just as Shane pops into the kitchen.

"I don't think so. You cooked so put me to work. What do you need?" he asks, his eyes shooting over to me in amusement.

"Let me grab you a beer, man." I grab a beer from the fridge and uncap it. Olivia isn't drinking a lot of alcohol or caffeine during her recovery, so I pull out the pitcher of iced tea from the fridge, pour her a glass, and place it on the counter by her. I tug on her elbow slightly and am satisfied by the goose bumps I feel on her skin before I brush past her and slap the bottle into Shane's hand. "Go sit the fuck down," I whisper to him.

He looks past me to where Olivia is. "I've been told I can't be helpful, beautiful, but I want you to know I do have impeccable manners."

I've decided I'm going to kill him. I'll miss my friend but he's gotta go.

He laughs the whole way to a seat at the small dining room table.

I make my way over to the kitchen cabinets to grab a few plates while Olivia silently slices the lasagna she made.

"You know, we used to be best friends before we dated. Do you remember that?"

She's hesitant at first, but she finally turns toward me after a moment. "Your point?"

"We didn't use to need buffers between us to eat dinner together."

She maintains eye contact with me as she grabs the plates out of my hand and then turns away to start scooping servings onto each one. "Yeah, well, until you learn to keep your lips to yourself, maybe we do." She walks back over to the cabinet to grab glasses for water and I follow her.

When she turns around to face me, she jumps when she sees how close

I am. Before she can skirt around me, I place my hands on the counter behind her, boxing her in.

She refuses to meet my eyes but I'm a patient man, so I wait until she finally does before I speak. "I could've saved you the effort, then. You were right. I stole a kiss from you and that was wrong. But I won't be stealing another one."

"Good."

"I won't need to because you're gonna give it to me."

"Excuse you?" She takes in my smug smile with scornful indignation.

I lean in a little bit closer and her gaze falls to my lips briefly. "I didn't stutter. You're going to initiate the next kiss we share. You know why?"

Her only response is a lift of the head and a narrowing of her eyes, so I continue. "Because next time, I won't be stopping until you're coming apart beneath me and screaming my name, so I need to be sure it's what you want."

"Then I guess you'll be waiting forever then, huh?"

I rock my hips forward so my knee falls between her thighs. She gasps at the connection. "You should know by now I'd wait an eternity for you, Olivia." Her lips part slightly and the rise and fall of her chest gets deeper. Her body is trying to tell her mind what it wants, but I know she's not ready to listen so I lick my lips, tap the tip of her nose with my finger, and push myself away from her. "When you're ready," I remind her. I make my way back over to the island where the plates of lasagna sit. "Smells delicious; let's eat."

I grab them and balance them on my forearms. I don't hear her moving, so I turn back to her to find her in the exact same spot, looking dazed. It isn't until I come back to the kitchen to grab the glasses of water she started to fill that she snaps out of it.

Dinner isn't awkward. Shane and Olivia banter back and forth like old friends, and I find that it doesn't bother me, though I'm still going to crush him for his incessant flirting. I actually like that she's taken to my friend so quickly. It tells me that she'll love the rest of them just as much.

You could cut the sexual tension between Olivia and me with a knife, but there are more than a few moments throughout the night where my Olivia shines through. My friend Olivia. She gives Shane as many embarrassing

stories about my teenage years as she can while he tells her equally embarrassing stories about my adulthood. A shadow of grief creeps into her eyes while he tells her about my college graduation that he and the boys crashed. She does what she can to cover it up, but I see it before she can hide behind her smile. I know the cause behind those shadows. She should've been at that graduation. She should've walked across that stage with me or at the very least been in the crowd. I don't know how to get her to let the past go. Whatever moments we missed back then don't matter now. All that matters is now. I need her to choose the now.

After dinner, Shane convinces me to go with him to meet with the guys. Olivia all but pushes me into his car. I agree only because it's time to get the conversation about my past with Olivia out once and for all, and I know those assholes won't wait any longer. She walks behind me to pick up my plate, but I place my hand on top of her wrist to stop her. "You cooked; we'll clean."

"I'm capable of loading the dishwasher."

"No one said anything about capabilities. It's called good old-fashioned home training." My fingers trace a path up her arm, and I watch the light layer of hair there stand at attention from my touch. "I'll lock up behind us so you can go relax if you want."

She snatches her arm away from me like I burned her. "Umm, yes. Okay, yeah. Yep. Got it. I'll just...I'll go."

I snicker under my breath and stand to grab the dishes when I feel a brush against my stomach. I turn and Olivia's hand is brushing against my stomach as she leans forward to grab one of the glasses on the table. My dick is immediately swollen.

"I'll just help you carry some stuff into the kitchen." She leans up until her lips graze my ear and whispers, "Two can play that game." She drops her hand and strolls into the kitchen where Shane is already rinsing off his dishes.

There's my girl.

CHAPTER
Seventeen

Kai

Twenty-four.

That's how many cold showers I've taken since my intense moment with Olivia a few weeks ago. It's been torture.

I start my day with one to tamp down the unbridled need festering inside of me, and it works for a while. I'm cool enough to ignore her coconut scent floating around every corner of every room in the house and the gentle hum of her tone-deaf singing I hear coming from her shower every morning. But then we get to my office and I have the freedom to touch the smooth surface of her skin and my resolve is tested all over again.

Being a man of my word has never been such a challenge. I promised her that I wouldn't cross her boundaries again. That our mouths wouldn't touch until it was her who united them. I promised myself that I would give her the space to reconcile in her heart what both of our bodies so desperately want. But every day I go without sinking inside her makes me want to break that promise and shatter it beneath the weight of our bodies.

Still, I knew I was playing the long game here, and I'll play it for as long as it takes. I didn't fight for her when she left the first time. I accepted that she didn't want me anymore, that I was in the way of her dreams. I was complacent. That won't happen again.

The bright side in all of this is that while she hasn't come around to me romantically, she's more than come around to me in a platonic sense. We've gone from her awkwardly shuffling around me to being willing to spend hours in my company. On Friday nights, we cook dinner and watch movies together. Arguing with her over which movie to watch has become the highlight of my week.

A small grunt of pain escapes Olivia's lips, bringing me back into the present. I take a moment to observe her form and know immediately what's wrong.

"You're overcompensating."

She brings her injured leg up from its split-squat position until she's standing upright. "What?"

"Your form is all off. You're overcompensating with your unaffected leg to take the pressure off this leg."

Before I've even finished my sentence, I've moved so I'm standing directly behind her, the heat from my chest encroaching on her back. My hands fly to the sides of her waist and a gasp falls from her lips, so quiet I almost missed it, but I don't miss how her back goes ramrod straight and the tension sits in her shoulders. I give her hips a squeeze and her body seems to relax against its will. My right hand leaves her waist, and she shudders as if she can't stand the loss of my touch. My lips curl up into a secret smile with the satisfaction that I know I affect her. I settle my hand against the back of her leg, then trail it down a dangerous path to her injured knee and tap it. "Extend this leg back."

She does as I say with no objection, and I swipe my thumb across the inside of her kneecap, watching her body reward me with another shudder. It's inappropriate. I shouldn't be doing this. I would never touch another client this way but fuck if I can stop it. I move my right hand back up to her waist, holding her in the position I want her. Once she's in her stance,

I maneuver so I'm standing in front of her. Her breath catches as our eyes meet. "Like this?" she grits out.

"Just like that. Now hit your split squat." She does so with measured confidence, but it's me who falters once she's in her full squat because of course she's eye level with my dick. She's always looked so good on her knees for me. I see the moment she notices our awkward position because her eyes bulge and fly up to my face. One of us should move. I should step back and she should stand up, but we don't. Instead, she does something to tug at the fraying thread of my willpower—she licks her lips. A growl rips from my chest before I can stop it. My hand acts of its own free will and reaches out to cup the back of her neck. Her teeth trap the plump swell of her bottom lip behind their cage, urging me to pull it free. I'm seconds away from doing so but manage to stop myself.

Fuck, this woman.

Dropping my hand to my side, I grant myself a moment of relief by taking a big step back from her. "There, didn't that feel different from how you were doing it before?" The fact that I'm even able to remember what we were doing is a miracle.

Somehow I throw my PT hat back on and pay close attention to how she lifts herself back up from the squat, noting she does it correctly. "Yep, definitely feels different," she mumbles.

"Good. Now go ahead and do three more sets of five." I don't even wait for her response; I cross to the other side of the room before I say fuck all to my promises.

Later that day after I've had my twenty-fifth cold shower, Olivia and I are back on solid ground. We're sitting in the kitchen talking about how I still play *Super Smash Bros* to this day. I tell her that I mostly play with Lincoln and Isaiah's nephew, Malcolm, and that I've rest-smashed him with Jigglypuff quite a few times. She's still salty about me doing that to her precious Samus when we were kids.

She's telling me her friend Justine got her hooked on the *Dark Pictures Anthology* games when I get a text from Kylie.

Kylie: Hey favoritest big brother. I need you to come home today. I have something to do and I don't know when I'll be back but it'll definitely be after Lily leaves

Kylie: I'm sure she'd love to see you anyway it's been a while

My jaw tightens at her attempt at a guilt trip. I've been taking care of Po Po for years now with no help from Kylie. I've arranged my entire schedule and life around my grandmother's needs, never doing anything for myself unless my parents are able to come stay with her. Kylie's been at it for ten weeks; she can deal.

"Woah. What happened?" Olivia asks.

"What do you mean?"

"Just a second ago everything was good, and now you look like you wanna murder something."

"I'm good. That was just Kylie. I need to go check on Po Po tonight."

Her mouth opens then clamps shut. A look of resignation crosses her face. "Oh, okay. Is she okay?"

"She's fine. Kylie's just not going to be home, and we don't like to leave her unattended." God, if Po Po knew how we talk about her like she's a child incapable of being left to her own devices, she'd have all of our heads.

If our relationship hadn't taken a dive off a cliff, I'd probably do more to ensure she's happy instead of just comfortable. Thinking about that makes me feel like the biggest piece of shit ever. Holding on to all this animosity is exhausting.

"You should come with me," I blurt out.

Her eye twitches. "I don't need a babysitter."

"When did I say you did?"

Tightening her grip on the kitchen island, she leans forward. "You only want me to go to keep an eye on me which is dumb. I'm sure I don't need to tell you why it's dumb."

I start to respond, but apparently her rant isn't over. "You think I don't

realize that you don't spend any time with your friends? Shane told me how close you are with the other guys. What are their names? Dom, Lincoln, and Isaiah? Yet I've never seen them and I know you're not going to see them because if you're not with another client, you're with me. You don't have to rearrange your life around me. I'm fine."

I'm not.

Trust me, the guys have given me enough shit about basically ditching them for the last few weeks, but I just want to soak up as much of Olivia's time as I can. I want her forever, but I've already learned the hard way that my love isn't enough to keep her here once our year is up.

"Let's get one thing clear, okay? I'm well aware that you don't need a babysitter. I'm not spending all my time with you because I feel obligated to. I'm doing it because I want to. I've missed you. I've spent the last thirteen years of my life wondering about the woman you turned out to be, missing the sound of your laugh and the peace that settles over me whenever you're around, so if you think I'm going to spend the time I have with you with my friends who I see every fucking day, you've forgotten who I am. You are my priority. That will never change."

She visibly swallows and I think she's about to retreat, but she gives me words I didn't realize I wanted to hear so badly. "I've missed you too. So much."

I want to pull her into my arms so I do. I rest my head on top of hers as she wraps her arms around my middle, squeezing like I'm the only life-line she has.

"So, come with me?"

She nods silently against my chest, and I plant a kiss on her forehead.

The ride over to my place is my favorite kind of loud. Olivia sings along with the radio at the top of her lungs and both of us laugh at her attempt at runs.

Nerves flash across her face the moment I put the car in park. I don't know if the nerves are because she's seeing my grandmom for the first time

in a long time or if it's because it's the first time she's seeing my place. Either way, I can't resist the urge to reach across the middle console and grab her shaking hands. "You okay?"

"Yeah, I'm fine." Her voice is too high and she won't meet my eyes.

"Oh, I know what your problem is. You're worried Po Po will assume you've stolen my virtue since I've been at your house."

She gasps and turns her head so quickly that it causes her to choke on her own spit. She swats my arm away when I try to pat her back, which only makes me laugh harder. "I hate you. And I will gladly tell Po Po that your virtue is still intact."

"Unfortunately." That earns me a shot to the ribs and a chuckle. I'll take it.

When we get into my apartment, it's entirely too quiet so I call out. "Po Po, I'm home."

Relief slams into my chest when I hear her shuffling around in her room. "Ahh, my little wolf is home." I wince at the nickname. I used to love when she'd call me that as a kid. Now it just hurts. Olivia rests her hand on my shoulder with her eyebrows raised in question, and I silently tell her everything is fine.

Po Po walks around the corner and stalls when she sees Olivia. "My little tulip," she shrieks. "I heard you were home but I can't believe my eyes." She struggles to get those words out but no one bats an eye. She walks up to Olivia and wraps her up in a tight hug. For someone whose strength has significantly declined over the years, it looks like she's squeezing the life out of Olivia, but the harder she squeezes the more Olivia visibly relaxes and sinks into the hug.

"It's so good to see you, G." G for grandma. Since Olivia didn't have grandparents growing up—her dad's parents passed away before she was born and her mom's parents weren't involved in her life—she adopted Po Po as hers as much as Po Po had adopted her. I realize at that moment that I haven't told Olivia what I know about Po Po for the same reason I haven't told Kylie—I don't want them to lose her like I did.

Po Po releases Olivia from her hold and lightly taps her cheek, her eyes shining with appreciation. "I'm so glad you've come home to us."

Olivia ducks her head bashfully. "It's just for the year while I'm going through physical therapy."

She receives a bright smile in response. "We'll see." Turning on her feet, she heads for the kitchen, still speaking to us as she goes, our cue to follow. "Sorry if this one dragged you with him to...to umm..." Her voice strains in frustration but I've learned to give her a minute to find the word she wants. "Babysit. To babysit me. He and the rest of the family think I'm incapable of staying by myself."

"Po Po, it's not that we think you're incapable."

She stops walking abruptly, causing Olivia to almost collide into her. "I know, I know. It's that you worry I may have another stroke or a heart at-tack while no one's with me. How sweet of you." Her sarcasm sucks the air out of the room.

Olivia bounces on the balls of her feet. "Don't worry, he didn't have to drag me. Nothing could keep me from you."

Po Po's hands clap together, appeased. "Oh, you know what we haven't done in a while?" Considering she and I haven't spent any real quality time together in years and Olivia hasn't been around, the options are endless. "We haven't made dumplings."

I'm already shaking my head no before she even finishes her statement. I can't do this with her. "No, Po Po. We're not making dumplings tonight."

"And just why not?" Her question is met with silence because I have no answer. Not one I can share without years of resentment flying out. Po Po studies me and sighs in defeat. "Alright, my little wolf. No dumplings. I'll have that unseasoned chicken you insist I eat, but come fix something for my little tulip, okay?"

She turns to continue her walk into the kitchen when Olivia grabs her hand and walks with her. I take a minute to catch my breath before joining them.

I whip up some salmon, brown rice, and vegetables for all of us, and yes, I do put more seasoning on mine and Olivia's than on Po Po's but the

woman has CHD for God's sake. I won't feel bad for adhering to the diet the doctor told us to follow.

I stay quiet the entire time I'm cooking, letting the two of them catch up on all the years they've missed. Focusing on the task at hand helps me to calm down my nerves.

Once it's time to eat, I continue to let the two of them dominate the conversation. It's bittersweet seeing them together again.

Once dinner is done and the dishwasher has been loaded, we hear keys jingling in the doorway. "I'm home!" Kylie calls out.

"Ya Tou, welcome home. I thought you'd be later." Ya Tou. Po Po's nickname for Kylie. Ever since I discovered Po Po's truth I've gone over every interaction we've ever had with a fine-tooth comb. I can't help but notice that my nickname was English while Kylie's was Cantonese. Was that because Kylie looks more Asian than I do? Was I not worth a Cantonese nickname in her eyes?

I hate how one discovery sent everything I held dear into question.

"Yeah, I thought I would be too but that's okay. It smells good in here. What are we...having?" She stumbles on the last word when she enters the kitchen and sees Olivia standing at the sink. "Oh, hi. I didn't realize we had company."

"Hi Kylie."

"Olivia." Fuck.

"Come in, let me fix you a plate." Po Po taps the chair next to her at the small kitchen table.

"No, no. You sit. I was joking. I'm not hungry. I'll just get some wine and get out of your way."

"You're not in the way, sis."

She looks Olivia up and down. "Right." She grabs the bottle of red wine from the counter and a glass from the cabinet. As she pours, she asks, "So, Olivia. How does it feel to be back here?"

Olivia clears her throat. "Umm, different."

"Yeah. I bet if it weren't for that injury you'd have never come back, huh?"

"Kylie," I warn.

"What? It's just a question." Her gaze never leaves Olivia as she sips her wine.

"Honestly, you're right. I probably wouldn't have come back here if it weren't for the injury." That hurts to hear but it's not unexpected. "But that has nothing to do with any of you and everything to do with me."

"Not surprising. Everything was about you."

"Alright, enough."

I see Olivia attempting to wave me off from the corner of my eye, but I ignore her. Kylie looks at me with defiance in her eyes. "I'm looking out for you, Kai."

"I'm not gonna tell you again that I don't need you to do that. Dial it back. Now."

"Fine."

"Fine."

Kylie tops off her wine glass and turns to leave when Olivia calls her name. "I just want you to know I'm sorry."

Kylie stops long enough for Olivia to know she heard her and then continues on her way.

We say our goodbyes to Po Po, with Olivia promising her to come see her again and then we ride back to her place in silence.

"I'm sorry about Kylie."

"Don't be. I deserved it. And don't try to tell me I didn't. I abandoned her just like I abandoned you. You're just a saint who won't let me take responsibility for my actions."

I'm not a saint. I just want her more than I want to be mad at her.

"I'm not stopping you from taking responsibility for your actions, Olivia. Anytime you wanna give me the real reason you ran out of town, I'm here to listen. Because I know you well enough to know that there's more to the story than you just wanting to go pro." One minute we were planning our lives together and the next she was telling me that I was holding her back and taking off without me. I refuse to believe that the switch happened out of nowhere. I'm not a fool; I know she owes me an explanation. But at the

end of the day, I still want forever with her, so I'm willing to wait for that explanation until she's ready to put in the work to get us there.

Her cheeks hollow out but she stays quiet. Too quiet. Before I can reach across the seat and touch her, she's out of the car and walking to the house.

A couple hours later, sleep eludes me so I find myself outside on the front steps, listening to the sounds of the country night.

The door opens, but I don't turn to watch her come out. She lowers herself onto the step next to me and passes me a plate with a peanut butter and jelly sandwich on it.

Eating our sandwiches in companionable silence, I've never been more at peace.

CHAPTER
Eighteen

Olivia

I OPEN MY DOOR TO FIND KYLIE'S SIGNATURE LONG, DARK HAIR FACING me. When she spins around, her smile immediately falters. Disgust drips from her every pore.

"Shit," she whispers. "Kai made it seem like he'd be here and you wouldn't."

"Umm, sorry to disappoint."

Her scowl somehow deepens at that. "Right. Well, I'm dropping this off for him. Don't know why he didn't just tell me to bring it to his office but okay." She holds up a small duffle bag but drops it on the ground when I go to grab it from her.

"Thanks, I'll let him know you brought it."

"Okay, bye."

"Kylie, wait!" She slowly turns back around, her shoulders practically touching her ears. "Do you want to come in for a minute?"

"Why would I want to do that?"

Good fucking question. "Just…could you?"

She chews on her bottom lip for a moment, looking back to her car like she's ready to make a run for it, but then she claps her hands, yells 'fuck it,' and follows me inside.

I offer her a seat but she makes no moves to get comfortable. She barely moves past the entryway.

"So, yesterday was awkward. And that's my fault."

"Okay."

I have no idea what to say to her. I don't know how to fix this, but I hate that she looks at me like I'm the worst person she's ever met. "I'm sorry," I offer.

She rolls her eyes and shakes her head. "Yeah, I'm sure that was enough to get my brother sniffing around your pussy again, but it doesn't work with me."

I would love to explain to her why I made the choices I did, but I know they won't offer her any comfort, and I can't bring myself to share those things with her before I've shared them with Kai. As much as I adore Kylie, it would be wrong of me to come clean to her first.

"I get it. I do. I don't say I'm sorry because I expect you to forgive me. I would like you to, but I realize that's not even possible without an explanation."

"Which you're not willing to give," she interrupts.

"Not yet."

"Right. Everything on your time."

"I want to make things right with you."

"Did you know Tylah and I had a huge fight that ended our friendship my junior year of high school?"

"No, I didn't."

"Yeah, you wouldn't because you left without ever looking back."

I looked back. At times it felt like all I did was look back on my old life and wish I'd never left it, but I thought I was doing the right thing.

"I never ever forgot about you. I thought about you so many times."

"And yet you never reached out. Do you know how much that hurt? I

don't know why you and Kai broke up. He never gave us the details, but I didn't realize he and I were a package deal. I would've never turned my back on you just because you and my brother were over, no matter what the circumstances were. But you, you just took off and left us all guessing. At least Kai got the benefit of an official breakup. We never heard from you again."

"You're right. That was shitty of me and I regret it every single day."

"Good. Was it worth it?"

"Was what worth it?"

"The fame and fortune you left us for."

Fuck, of course she thinks I left because I valued money and fame over her. I haven't given her a reason to think otherwise. "It wasn't about that. There was so much more going on."

She waves her hand in dismissal. "Was it worth it?"

I let out a heavy sigh. "No."

She nods and wipes a rogue tear from her eye. "Good. Listen, for some reason my brother wants you in his life again and that's fine. I won't stand in your way. But if you hurt him again, you and I will have a serious problem."

"I don't want to hurt either one of you ever again."

She opens her mouth to speak but the words never come. She chews her bottom lip again and closes her eyes for a moment. When she opens them, I see the steely resolve she's put up against me. "A friendship with me isn't on the table, so you'd do best to focus on the sure thing—Kai."

She moves to open my door but hesitates. "Hey, Kylie?"

"Yes?"

"I still have your friendship bracelet. I never forgot you."

Her grip on the door handle tightens, but she still doesn't turn back to look at me. "Good for you. I burned mine."

She doesn't close the door behind her. She just runs to her car and races off.

Hours later when Kai gets home, I tell him about the bag Kylie dropped off. "Why didn't you have her drop it off at your office?"

He scratches the back of his neck. "I may have had it in my head that if

you two saw each other maybe you could at least start a conversation. Maybe that's what you need to move forward."

I pull him into a hug, and he settles his head on top of mine. "That's sweet. I appreciate the gesture but it didn't go well." I recap the conversation we had, and he looks pained by the idea of me never reconciling with his sister. "She's not you, Kai."

"What does that mean?"

"It means you accepted me back with open arms, no questions asked. I still don't know why but it means a lot that you have. Kylie isn't willing to do the same and that's fair. That's actually the more logical response. She needs time and she needs answers. Answers I haven't given her. Or you. You can't force her to accept me. She might never accept me again, and that's my cross to bear."

"I get that. I just know how much you meant to each other. I want you to have that again."

"Time will tell, I guess."

"Fair. I'll leave it alone."

"Thank you. And thank you for trying. It really was a sweet gesture."

"Hmm." He leans down, our lips mere inches from each other. If I just tip my head up a little more, we'll connect. Ah fuck. I drop my eyes to the floor.

"I'm, um, gonna go take a shower."

The disappointment in his sigh hits me in the gut. "Okay, Olivia."

I have to get my shit together before I cause any more damage.

CHAPTER
Nineteen

Olivia

"I DON'T NEED THE CONTACT INFO FOR ANOTHER PT. I ALREADY HAVE one."

"One that's not doing a damn thing for you."

"What are you talking about? As far as I know you haven't attended a single session, so you haven't seen how much I've improved."

He rolls his eyes. I hope they get stuck in the back of his head. "Take the card, Liv." He holds up a business card for a physical therapist who I've worked with before, and he's good, but nowhere near as good as Kai. The card dances on his fingertips as he checks his phone. His arrogance irritates me. He knows I'll take the card without hesitation because even at thirty-two years old, my father's word is final.

I swipe the card out of his hand, letting the thick cardstock slide between my fingers. It feels wrong. It feels like a betrayal. So, I take three steps to the right and let the card fall where it belongs, in the trash.

"I'll be watching, Liv," he says to my back because I'm already walking away.

I really should thank my father for the ridiculous conversation we had in the park the other day. My conversation with Kylie already had my wheels turning, but the conversation with my dad was the final straw. The man is clearly unhinged. It's tearing him up inside that Kai is back in my life. I thought if I kept it strictly professional I could keep Kai safe from him, but he clearly doesn't want me involved with him in any capacity. So, if he's going to lose his mind regardless, I might as well get what I want. And what I want is a six-foot-three, broad shouldered, brown-skinned man whose smile brightens my day.

Kai has never wavered with me. He deserves to be put first.

Today, we're going to spend a few hours with his circle of friends. I reached out to Shane to organize it since Kai acts like he has no friends when I'm around. Kai and I have been circling each other, isolating ourselves in a world where only we exist. But a world where we exist outside of our problems isn't sustainable. Our adolescent hearts are still tethered together, but our adult souls are strangers. I want to fix that. I want to know who Kai is outside of me. I want to allow Kai to know this new version of me, maybe even to love it too.

"Are you sure you wanna do this?"

I zone back in to find Kai watching me, concern swimming in the depths of his irises. We're parked outside of Sasha's, a coffee shop run by his friend's sister of the same name. I'm not sure how long we've been parked, but his worried glance tells me too long.

"Why? You think your friends won't like me?"

"You make a lasting impression on everyone you meet, Olivia. I know they'll love you. You just seem like you're in your head about something."

"When am I not?"

"Well, talk to me. What do you need?"

For you to be mine again. "Absolutely nothing," I say, tracing a line up his thick bicep. He shudders under my touch which sends a thrill down my spine. "Let's go so I can meet Shane's friends."

He playfully pinches my side. "Shane's friends, huh?" I laugh until the butterflies in my stomach simmer down.

When we walk inside, I'm taken aback by the vibrant aesthetic. It's a perfect blend of bright colors standing out against the white of the walls and tables. It looks like a place you could spend hours in without realizing it. There's a reading nook in the back corner. I'd love to bring Justine here so we could chill and read our smutty books.

Kai's hand caresses my lower back as he leads me over to Shane, who is talking to a gorgeous Black woman. She has on green-and-white wide-leg pants with a white crop top, which makes me like her immediately because even though it's November, it's still Austin, Texas, so it's hot as fuck here and I appreciate her for wearing a very summer outfit. The tight curls of her dark afro are perfectly picked and her brown skin is flawless. Her face looks bare of any makeup except for the heavy lining of her eyes, which gives her a sultry vibe. When she sees Kai and me approaching, she turns her body to face us, and her eyes light up with Kai and slightly fall when they see me. I let it slide because I recognize the look all too well. She's wary of me. If I had to guess, she knows about my history with Kai and is cautious about my intentions with him now. It's respectable. As long as she keeps it cute, I'm fine with it.

"Liv, my girl!" Shane shouts, his arms already stretched out in front of him to wrap around me. Kai blocks Shane's arms and pushes them down by his sides. The move is aggressive but I can tell he's smiling as he does it.

The two of them dap each other up and communicate silently before Kai crushes the woman into a hug.

"Hey, Sasha."

"Hey, Kai. Nevaeh has been asking for you."

"Aww, I gotta get over there to see my girl. We need to have a standing date like her and Shane."

Shane has told me that Nevaeh is his 'best bud' outside of the guys. "You wanna be like me so bad. That's my little buddy, get your own," Shane interrupts.

"Boy, fuck you." Kai turns to me. "Olivia, this is Sasha. She runs this place. She's Lincoln and Isaiah's older sister but really she's the big sister for

all of us. Sasha, this is Olivia. My client and…friend." There's a pregnant pause before he says friend, and I shift to put all my weight on my good leg.

"Nice to meet you, Olivia."

"You too, Sasha. This place is gorgeous."

"Oh, thanks." She looks around the place as if she's seeing it for the first time, like she's trying to see it through my eyes and she's proud of what she sees. "Can I get you anything? A muffin, a donut, a coffee?"

I take a peek at the display behind her, and I zone in on the row of cinnamon rolls. I haven't had anything that sweet in a long time but shit, it looks delicious.

"I actually would love one of those cinnamon rolls."

She smiles before moving around the counter to grab one and warm it up for me.

Before anyone else can speak, the bell above the door chimes and we turn to see a gorgeous Hispanic man with tawny skin walk in. His brown hair has a slightly shaggy look, and he runs his fingers through it before shoving his hand into his pocket as he walks over to us.

The men share a greeting and Sasha receives a hug, but his hands go back into his pockets as he's introduced to me as Dominic and I'm introduced to him.

"Good to meet you, Olivia." The deep baritone of Dominic's voice adds to the gruffness of his greeting. I see what Kai meant about him being more reserved than the rest of the group.

The door chimes again and a man and very pregnant woman stroll in. The woman's stomach is perfectly round beneath her blue T-shirt dress. Intricate tattoos run down the entirety of her left arm, and ombre-blonde box braids drop to the middle of her back. She's stunning. The man on her arm is just as fine, and I can tell right away that he's one of Sasha's brothers. They have the same eyes. Based on his brawny build, I'm willing to bet this is the firefighter brother, Lincoln, making the woman his wife, Ciara.

Another couple walks in, Isaiah and Nina I assume from the process of elimination, and Isaiah has an adorable baby girl strapped to his chest. This entire crew is ridiculously good looking.

Introductions are made and we move to a couple of the tables pushed together to get out of the way of any incoming customers. It's interesting watching Kai interact with these people. The closeness between them is obvious to any passerby. It reminds me of my friendship with Angie and Justine. The kind of bond that goes deeper than blood, straight to your very essence. Kai has told me that he met the guys when he was twenty-one, though he won't tell me how. He said it's some sort of closely guarded secret which sounds dumb to me but that's neither here nor there. I'm just happy that he found them when he did, because if his years after we broke up were anything like mine, I'm sure he needed them.

Just then, baby Bianca, who's been asleep against Isaiah's chest this whole time, wakes up and starts screaming at the top of her lungs. Isaiah sways side to side and rubs her back to try to comfort her but she won't settle. Nina starts to reach for her but Kai gets there first, holding his arms out for her. As soon as Isaiah puts her in his arms her cries go from a loud roar to a low whimper and my chest aches. Of course he's a damn baby whisperer. I've seen and been around babies plenty of times since I made the choice not to have mine, and it's never bothered me, but I've never seen Kai with a baby before. And to see how good he is with her breaks something deep inside of me. That should've been us. He should've had the chance to hold our baby and soothe them back to sleep. We should be worrying about the stresses of raising a teenager right now. My hands become clammy and my neck feels hot. I try to excuse myself to the bathroom, but the words are stuck in my throat so I just run off without warning.

I splash water on my face the minute I get into the bathroom and try to calm my breathing. There's a small bench in the bathroom which comes in really handy since I don't want to sit on the floor, even though it looks immaculately clean, and I desperately need to get off my feet.

My head is in my hands when the door creaks open, and I try to conceal the tears falling but I know it's no use.

A handful of paper towels are held in front of my face, and I look up to find Ciara watching me with sympathetic eyes. Nina and Sasha are on either side of her, comfort rolling off them in waves.

"You okay, boo?" Ciara asks.

"Oh yeah, I'm fine. I just got a little warm."

Nina sits down beside me and pats my hand. "We may not know each other, but I do know a freak-out when I see one. You don't have to share, just know we got you."

They got me. Normally a statement like that from anyone besides my girls would have me rolling my eyes, but for some reason I believe her. "Why?"

Sasha sighs, drawing my attention to her. "Listen, Kai is family. I know he introduced you as his 'client and friend' but it doesn't take much to see how important you are to him, and I won't even bullshit you and act like we don't all know about your past with him at this point. So if you're important to him, you're important to us." The skepticism I saw on her face earlier has been completely replaced with understanding and acceptance.

"And just take it from me, once these bitches decide you're their friend, you have no say in the matter. I tried when I first moved here," Ciara adds.

"There was little to no effort to get rid of us, ma'am," Nina interjects.

"Mm-kay."

"Thank you," I whisper. My breaths come easier by the second.

"Of course. Can I hug you?"

I nod my head and fall into Nina's embrace. I'm not really much of a hugger, and I think she senses that which is why she asked, but I'm appreciative of the fact that she seemed to also sense I needed one in that moment. I'm careful to suck my tears back so they don't fall and mess up her T-shirt, but otherwise I just let myself feel all my emotions. Ciara rubs my back, and Sasha smiles at me over Nina's shoulder.

I pry myself out of Nina's arms so I can look each of them in the eyes as I let the confession fall from my lips.

"I, um…had an abortion when I was nineteen."

"I won't lie and say I didn't assume you suffered a loss when you got choked up watching Kai with Bianca. I'm so sorry for your loss," Ciara offers. Sasha and Nina echo her sentiments.

My loss. Any time I've shared that information with anyone, which has

been a whopping three times total, I've never been told that they were sorry for my loss. It's always been 'I'm sure you made the best decision for yourself' or 'I'm sorry you went through that.' Never 'sorry for your loss.' I am very pro-choice and always advocate for women making whatever decision they feel is best for them and their bodies, so I don't come from a place of judgment. In my case, however, I made a choice to keep my baby and raise them alongside Kai, but that choice was taken from me, and that's the part of me that never healed. It is a loss.

Once my eyes have been dried and the ladies have helped me make sure I look presentable, we make our way back out to the guys. A sleeping Bianca lies against Kai's chest, and the sight brings me solace instead of pain this time so I answer his questioning eyebrow with a heartfelt smile.

"What were y'all doing all this time?" Shane asks.

"Do yourself a favor and never involve yourself in women's business," Nina chides. Everyone laughs at his expense, including Shane himself, and the moment is forgotten.

Dad: Liv, I called you last night and you didn't answer. I need an update on your status

Dad: Liv, answer your phone

Dad: How is PT?

Dad: Liv, your behavior is childish.

Dad: You always have to make things difficult and you wonder why I have to take control

Dad: I'll be in touch

I exit out of the text thread with my dad because fuck him and his stupid-ass check-ins, and I open a text thread with Ciara, Nina, and Sasha. Shane gave me their numbers and said he cleared it with them first, so I'm trying to figure out a way to reach out.

Me: Hey guys, thanks for letting me be weird and cry in your bathroom yesterday.

Ugh, no. Delete that.

Me: Hey, sorry if yesterday got too heavy. Want to get brunch?

What even is that? Delete.

Me: Thank you for yesterday. You're all amazing and made me feel a little less alone.

Coming in too hot. Delete.

Why the fuck can't I draft a simple text? I feel like I'm on a damn dating site. Let me try one more time.

Me: Hey. Did you know if you put the first letter of our names together it would spell CONS? Could be a cool group name.

Ha, okay, I'm done. I exit out of my messages and put my phone away.

"Okay, good. And just remember not to bend forward from your lower back." Kai's hand graces my lower back while I'm mid-deadlift, setting my core on fire.

I'm so pissed at myself for not making my move last night. When we got back to the house after the meet-up, I was emotionally drained and I couldn't bring myself to do it, so I caught up with Angie on the phone instead.

Today, our therapy session is pure torture. His touch makes every nerve in my body tingle. The smooth tone of his voice as he guides me is like velvet clinging to my body.

"That's good. Let's move on to some heel raises and then we'll cool down for the day."

I nod my head, my mouth too dry to speak, and position myself facing the wall to begin the exercise. I barely even notice the slight twinge of discomfort in my injured leg as my heels leave the floor. I'm too focused on the cravings I feel that are too loud to ignore now. That's the best way I can

describe it. I crave every part of him. I need his smiles, his love, his acceptance, his touch, his kiss. I need to know what his beard feels like between my legs.

My balance shifts, and instead of coming straight back down on my heels, I teeter to the side. "Shit." Large hands grip my hips to prevent my fall. I hiss at the contact, not because it hurts, but because the rough pads of his fingers brush against my side beneath my tank top, and his hands on my bare skin feel so good, I never want it to stop. Instead of using his hands to fully stand myself back up, I lean into his grip and arch my back. Not too blatantly but not so subtle either. When my ass grazes his groin, he groans softly in my ear, and his right hand travels farther up my body until his fingers are spread across my stomach. He applies enough pressure to my midsection that I'm forced to arch more until my ass is planted firmly against the swell of his dick. I reach out to hold the wall for leverage, but when I feel Kai's breath on my neck, I can't fight the small moan that falls from my lips.

His teeth nip my ear for a brief moment before he whispers, "Whatever you want is yours, Olivia. But you know what you have to do to get it."

And with that he disentangles his body from mine and leaves me standing there slack-jawed while he walks over to the treatment tables and starts wiping them down. Session over.

Once I pick my jaw off the floor, I run through my cool-down stretches alone. I feel Kai's gaze on me from time to time, probably ensuring I'm stretching correctly, but otherwise he can't be bothered with me. Fucker.

I was his last session of the day. Normally when our schedules align that way, I catch an Uber to his office so that we can ride home together. I usually use the time he's shutting the place down to do extra stretches or check in with my coach, but today I don't want to do that. I want to put us both out of our misery. I should spend this time trying to think of how I'm going to tell him what I've been keeping from him. I owe him answers, but for the first time in a long time I want to live without thinking about the damn consequences.

My feet make the decision for me and carry me over to where he's

standing, looking over paperwork. He looks at me expectantly, so I keep walking until the tips of our shoes connect.

"Whatever I want, Kai?"

The curious gleam in his eyes transitions into a ravenous hunger. He nods. Just as I start leaning forward to kiss him he holds up a hand. "I want you to understand what you're signing up for if you connect your lips with mine. My self-control is a fraying thread, and every time you touch me in a way that's more than friendly or show me a version of you that wants this as much as I do, it unravels a little more. I'm a strong man but I am not invincible, so if you do this, the thread officially snaps. All fucking bets are off."

Perfect. I give him the best answer I can. I pull his head down to mine and put everything into the kiss.

The moment our tongues meet, he takes control and I let him. It feels so good to let go. His mouth assaults mine in a way that leaves no room for hesitation or doubt, only pure unadulterated need.

His hands trail down to the curves of my ass, hauling me up and planting me on one of the treatment tables.

"Kai, we can't do this here," I say even though the breathiness of my voice says that I absolutely want to do this here.

"Why not?"

"What if someone sees?"

"No one is going to see your beautiful body but me. Everyone is gone for the day."

"But I mean this is so inappropriate. You treat patients on these tables!"

He lifts my tank top and sports bra over my head and fuck if I even try to resist. "I don't give a fuck. This is my office. I can do what I want, and what I want is to pleasure your body until your voice is hoarse from screaming so much. That okay with you?"

"More than okay." I roll my bottom lip between my teeth.

"Good. Take these off." He pats my outer thigh to make me lift my hips so that he can slide my leggings off, taking my panties off along with them so I'm left fully exposed to him. He locks eyes with me to make sure I'm watching before his gaze travels down every inch of my body, scorching my

skin in his wake. My spine shudders under his assessment. I want him to burn me until I'm nothing left but embers.

When he reaches my center, he licks his lips like he's just seen a dessert buffet. I open my legs a little more so he knows that the all-you-can-eat buffet is open for business.

"I've missed you."

"Show me."

"You know what happens next, right?"

I chuckle. "I mean, I thought this was the part where you reintroduce your dick to my pussy, but if something else is about to happen, by all means do tell."

He wipes his hand against his beard. "You're funny. No, love, what happens next is I'm going to destroy you. I've craved you for years, and you've denied me for too long, so I'm not going easy on you. I'm going to completely wreck your body until only I can piece you back together."

Shit.

There are no more words to be said. He slides me down to the edge of the treatment table, picks my legs up to hold them spread open in the air, and begins his feast.

His tongue invades my folds, lapping at the wetness he's already caused. The muscles in my stomach constrict, and my head falls back in ecstasy. His tongue game is next-level. He knows exactly when to be gentle and when to be punishing, which brings a moment of irrational sadness to the forefront of my brain. He's no longer the inexperienced young man that was dedicated to finding what pleased us both but a grown-ass man who's learned with and from women who weren't me. It shouldn't bother me. I've slept with my fair share of men since leaving him, but fuck if I'm not jealous as all hell.

A sharp sting hits me, and it takes me a moment to realize that he just slapped my pussy. And I liked it.

"I don't know where you went just now but stay right here, Olivia. I'm not playing with you." I grab hold of my legs to keep them steady because they're already shaking. I'm not going to survive this man. He's my addiction and I do not want to be saved. No, I need to drink every last drop. With my

legs where he wants them, he pumps two fingers inside of me, and I start riding them shamelessly. "Eyes on me," he commands.

The sight of Kai sucking my clit into his mouth is almost too much to bear, but I keep my eyes on him because I want to please him and reward him for making me feel this way.

"You taste so good." He is filthy with his words and his tongue, and my vision is starting to blur from the effort it takes not to close my eyes. He sets a punishing rhythm of intense, quick licks that make my toes curl before switching to soft, leisurely strokes that leave my body quaking.

"Fuck!" I moan. He keeps up the delicious torture until I'm coming in waves, drenching his fingers and beard. My legs start to buckle but he slaps my pussy again, telling me I need to keep them up. I'm entranced as I watch him gather my arousal and drag it down to my puckered hole. My eyes roll back in my head as he circles the area, giving me a chance to tell him I don't want this but I do. I want it so badly. With no resistance from me, he slowly pushes in. "Oh my God," I cry out.

Once he's knuckle deep inside me, he uses his free hand to spread my lower lips open and thrusts his tongue back into my pussy. Fuck, the sensation is overwhelming in a way that makes me feel out of control but powerful at the same time. My fingers ache to touch him so I run my hands through his curls and grab his roots as he sucks my clit again. He flattens his tongue and soaks up every drop of my desire. His name falls from my lips as my second orgasm hits me, harder than the first.

He gives me a moment of recovery before he removes his finger and blows on my clit. My nerves go haywire, I'm so hypersensitized.

"Fuck, Kai. I can't take any more." I move my hand down to push his face away, and his eyes snap up to mine.

"What are you doing?"

"I can't..."

He cuts me off. "You will. I warned you already that I was gonna wreck you, so you're not done. You'll take everything I give you until I say enough because you can handle it. Do you understand?"

I nod my head.

"Say it," he demands.

"I…I understand."

"Good girl. Now move your fucking hand."

Yes sir. My hand falls away and his mouth immediately replaces it, driving me to heights I've never been before. Three fingers join that skilled tongue of his in their quest to make me lose my mind, and it's working. His thick fingers curl inside of me while the thumb on his other hand moves inside my ass, filling me more than I thought possible. I'm delirious with bliss and can't resist the urge to press my pussy closer to his face. I grind myself against his face, and he growls with pleasure, rewarding my thrusts with firm strokes of his tongue.

I didn't think it was possible for me to come again, but when he rubs circles against my clit and licks me all the way to my ass, I freeze. The pressure builds up inside of me and before I know it, I'm squirting. I coat him with my essence, and he eagerly licks every inch of my pussy and thighs to clean it up. His beard and lips shine with the proof of my release, and if I could find the energy to speak I would ask to taste some. He was right about my voice being hoarse when he was done with me because I can barely get his name out.

When my body finally stops shaking, he kisses my inner thighs and my injured leg before gently bringing my legs back down to the table, kissing and rubbing my ankles along the way.

He helps me redress myself because I'm too weak to do any lifting right now, but when he kisses me, I feel like I can go another five rounds. He laughs and lowers my arms when I try to wrap them around his neck. "Let's go home so I can tear that ass up properly."

If what he just did to me wasn't proper, I'm terrified of what I'm in store for, and I've never been more ready for anything in my life.

I don't even remember the drive home. I may have passed out; I'm not sure. I barely register that we've reached our destination before Kai pops my door open and scoops me into his arms, bridal style. Closing the passenger door with his foot, he carries me up the steps, over the threshold, and to the master bedroom in record time.

We're a mess of limbs. It takes me back to when we used to spend hours fooling around in his car in a parking garage because we couldn't get any privacy at our houses. Except now our urgency doesn't come from fear of being interrupted, it comes from the fact that if he's not inside me in the next few seconds I might combust, and not in a sexual way.

It only takes seconds for me to be naked again, but this time he joins me. I watch him remove his shirt in awe. His body is unreal. I study each of the abs on his eight-pack, because a six-pack would've been too basic for Kai, as if I'm waiting for each one to tell me its life story. He slides his sweatpants down his legs, but when he pulls his briefs down to join them, I audibly gasp.

Holy fucking shit, he is pierced down there. I'm so captivated by the barbell extending through the head of his dick, I can't even speak.

"You like what you see?"

"How long have you had that?"

"My dick? All my life. You should remember it well."

There he goes bursting the bubble of my lust. "No, smartass. The piercing."

He looks down at it with a smirk. "A few years."

"And who'd you get it for?" I know I have no right to ask and my testiness is irrational, but my curiosity just won't die. It's not lost on me that an apadravya piercing is commonly known to be a sexual benefit for a partner. Who the fuck did he get it for?

He chuckles as if he can read my thoughts. "I got it because I wanted it. It was an impulse decision."

"An impulse decision?" Kai is a go with the flow kind of guy, but he doesn't really do impulse decisions. What looks to us like he's just doing whatever he wants whenever he wants is actually meticulous planning on his part. He thinks everything through.

"Yep. I just woke up one day and decided I wanted one. That's it. Now, would you like to argue with me some more or would you like me to fuck you now?"

His words make my core hot. I'm still recovering from the three orgasms he drew out of me in his office, but I need to feel him inside me now.

"I want you to fuck me."

He reaches down to pump his shaft from base to tip twice, the thick head glistening with pre-cum. "You want me to fuck you, what?"

Oh my God. "I want you to fuck me, please. Please, sir."

"Sir, huh? I like that. Come here." He motions for me to shuffle to the edge of the bed.

He reaches down to his pants to pull a condom from his pocket, but I put my hand up to stop him. "Wait. I, um, I want to feel you. I'm recently tested and I have an IUD." I haven't had sex without protection since the last time Kai and I did that which led to our unborn baby. The thought of going bare again sends me into a slight panic, but my desire to feel him completely when our bodies reunite overpowers the sensation. He's the only one I would trust with this.

His eyes soften as he brushes his hand across my cheek. "I've tested negative recently too. Are you sure you're ready, baby? Because I don't think I can be gentle this first time."

"I don't want gentle, Kai. Wreck me again."

He wastes no time pushing into me, and the pressure against my G-spot is instantaneous, making my back arch off the bed. Fuck. What the hell was he thinking getting this piercing? A man with a dick this impressive doesn't need any further enhancements. He leans down to kiss me, tangling my moans with his.

"You were made for me," he says, peppering kisses along my jaw and chest before he leans up and throws my injured leg up on his shoulder. The slight bite of pain enhances my pleasure, but when he begins massaging and kissing my injured leg to make sure I'm okay, I almost come right there because, God, how is he so gentle and aggressive at the same damn time. My soft mewls become more frenzied the quicker his strokes become. Kai's dick is going to be the death of me, and I will gladly plan my funeral right now if it means this feeling never ends.

"Oh fuck, Kai. More."

He grins at my command. Then, he reaches his hand down to grip my throat and squeeze. I slap my hand on top of his to make him increase

the pressure and he does. He squeezes to the point that all of my senses are heightened. I can feel my heart beating out of my chest and my pussy clenching around him. My throat bulges against his hand as I try to moan.

"You want more, Olivia?" he asks.

I nod emphatically. He loosens his grip on my throat just enough for me to speak. "I want it all."

He picks my other leg up to put it over his shoulder so he can hit another angle, and my vision blurs.

Nothing has ever felt better than this. I don't have the voice to muster up another scream. The best I can do is whimper through my pleasure.

"Look at you, taking all of me like this. I told you that you were made for me." And he was definitely made for me. I bite my lip to hold in my whine. "Don't hold back on me, love. Let me hear you."

"Shit!" I scream. My vocal cords literally feel scratched now. "It's so good."

He presses his hands against my stomach to pin me deeper into the mattress, the sound of our skin slapping together filling the room.

He holds his finger up to my lips, and I suck it into my mouth without hesitation. "Your mouth feels so good. I can't wait to fill it," he says as he pops his finger out of my mouth and then presses it against my clit. I can't hold it in. I cry out my release, clenching my walls around him until he lets out a deep groan to accompany his own filling me up.

I don't remember much after he slides himself out of me. I just remember a warm washcloth hitting my sex and whispered words before falling asleep, "I'm never letting you go again."

CHAPTER
Twenty

Kai

THE SCENT OF BROWN SUGAR AND STRAWBERRIES FLOODS MY SENSES, waking up every part of me. And I do mean every part.

Waking up with Olivia's soft body in my arms feels so right. It solidifies the notion I've been carrying around all these years that I haven't been at peace since she left. Last night was nothing short of perfection. I've imagined what I would do when Olivia finally dropped her carefully constructed I and gave in to what's always been between us no less than a hundred times, but feeling her come apart again and again on my tongue and watching her eyes roll back in her head as she clenched her pussy around my dick was incredible.

I look down at my sleeping beauty—clad in nothing but a tank top, boy shorts, and a purple bonnet—and consider my next move. Olivia may have given in to her sexual needs last night, but she's still tight-lipped about our past and more importantly how we move forward. I'm happy to break her back in any way she wants, but I want more. I want to wake up to her in

my arms every day. I want my ring on her finger, my name on her jersey. I want to be by her side as she continues taking the world by storm. I want to share our story with our grandkids. I want to love her completely, in all her forms, for the rest of our lives. I just need her to want that too.

She stirs under my arm but remains asleep. Unable to resist, I squeeze her tighter against my chest, and she lets out a tiny puff of air, her lips turning up in a grin. Her legs tangle tighter with mine, and her hand rubs the plane of my chest then wanders down to the band of my briefs, slipping in and gripping my length.

"Mmm, so last night wasn't a dream," she murmurs.

"Oh, it was a dream, Olivia. But it one hundred percent happened."

Her eyes flutter open at that, and I'm undone by the emotion I see there. I can't process my next words because all my blood is flowing to where she's stroking me.

"I want to taste you."

Fuck. I massage the column of her neck and pull her lips to mine. "Didn't I already tell you anything you want is yours?"

Emboldened by my words, she pushes herself up to a sitting position and then swings her legs around to sit back on her haunches. She licks her lips as she watches me pull my briefs off, my dick pulsing with need between us.

I expected her to tease me a little bit first—kiss the head and flick her tongue down my length. It used to be her go-to move. What I didn't expect was for her to swallow me whole immediately. She sucks me to the back of her throat, pushing past her gag reflex, and hums.

"Oh fuck," I curse. She massages my balls while continuing to take me deeper. Shit, her mouth is pure heaven. A utopia I would revolve my world around. She releases me with a pop and swirls her tongue around my head, paying close attention to the barbell and pulling a groan out of me. Then she glides her tongue from the underside of my shaft to the tip and does it all over again.

When she takes all of me into the warm embrace of her throat again, I need something to hold on to so I reach down to smack her ass and squeeze one of her cheeks. She moans around my dick before sliding her hand

between her thighs to rub her pussy. I smack her ass harder, making her hum again, and I can't control myself anymore. Reaching my other hand over, I yank her boy shorts off her legs, and to her credit she doesn't release my dick from her hold. Not until I swing her legs over my face and flick my tongue over her clit.

"Mmm fuck, Kai."

"Did I tell you to stop?"

She shivers in my arms then pushes her body back so her pussy lips hit my mouth and she lowers her head back down. Good girl. I mirror her movements. When she circles the tip of my dick and my piercing with her tongue, I trace my tongue up and down her folds. When she inhales me like she's trying to drain me dry, I suck her clit into my mouth and graze it with my teeth. My fingers join my tongue, playing her like a fiddle until I can tell she's about to come. Before she can, I ease up the pressure, and her legs vibrate against my face. She hisses when I blow on her throbbing clit, and she grazes my dick with her teeth. I chuckle at her clear frustration, but I'm not ready for her to come yet. I smack her ass with both hands, massaging both cheeks before spreading them apart and flicking my tongue against her asshole. She tries to clench but I still have her spread wide.

"Jesus," she whimpers. I use her wetness and my finger to trace her rim then I pierce her with my tongue. "Ahh shit, yes." My dick falls from her mouth but she strokes me with her hand until she's able to handle taking me in again.

I take great satisfaction in all the needy whimpers and moans I hear from Olivia as I eat her ass. I imagine all the ways I can drive her body crazy. She'd look like a queen with all of her holes filled. I'd drain every drop of pleasure from every hole in her body until there is nothing left but me. I make a mental note to order a few things.

I drive my tongue up and down her butt crack while two of my fingers pump in and out of her pussy. She writhes above me while forcing my dick to the back of her throat. I hear her gag and then she removes me from her mouth and spits on the head. Her hands twist and massage the part of my dick she can't reach while her head bobs up and down. Fuck, she's incredible.

She's been so good for me; I think it's time to reward her. I finish eating her ass and kiss each of her cheeks before sucking her clit in my mouth, my tongue and fingers working in tandem. I feel her release coming the same as I feel my own.

"Come with me, love."

That's all I need to say. Her release coats my tongue and beard and mine hits the back of her tongue. We swallow each other's cream, guiding each other through our orgasms.

In a clumsy move, she rolls off of me then spins around like an awkward break dancer until her chest is flush with mine again.

"What a fucking way to start the day," she says on an exhale.

"I can't think of a better way."

She hums her agreement. "So...you eat ass now. That's new."

I choke on my laughter. Leave it to Olivia to let that be the first thing on her mind.

"You didn't like it?"

"Oh no, I fucking loved it. It just took me by surprise."

I absentmindedly draw circles on her arm with my pointer finger, keeping my gaze locked with hers. "What can I say? You're a four-course meal of fine dining. I think I'd be foolish to leave a single crumb on my plate, don't you?"

Her eyes widen then her lids lower so she's looking at me from under her lashes. "Very foolish. And you don't strike me as a foolish man."

I lower my head to nibble on her earlobe. "Glad you've caught on. I much prefer to savor every bite of my food." I lick a trail down the smooth skin of her jaw and kiss her neck. "Taste every flavor."

"Mmm. Wait, why four courses?"

Rather than answer her with my words, I trace each meal with my fingers. I reach around to press the pad of my thumb against her puckered hole. "One." She mewls and arches her back into my touch. I take my other hand and cup her sex. "Two." She's so sensitive that her mewls intensify and her head falls back. I bend down to suck her bottom lip into my mouth. "Three,"

I whisper. I move both my hands up her body, ignoring her protests, until I reach her hardened dark-brown nipples and tweak them. "Four."

"Oh, so the courses are just the places you can stick your dick." She means for this to come out threatening but her voice is too breathy to do the job. All she succeeds in doing is making my dick hard for her again, imagining sliding between her breasts, her lips, her pussy, and her ass. My tongue lavishes her right nipple until I hear a soft moan and then I suck and bite it while massaging the other with my hand.

"That was me being generous. Really, I could feast on every part of your body for the rest of my life and never feel more full. I could survive solely on the taste of you."

She swallows hard. "Well fuck, I'm hungry. What do you want for breakfast? You've definitely earned the right to make requests this morning, and we're both gonna need our strength today."

She slips out of bed and pulls her panties back on before kissing me long and hard and sashaying her way out to the kitchen.

"Yeah, so I thought I'd retire and become a fisherman. Get a big-ass boat and set sail."

"That's great, man." A boat would be cool. I wonder if Olivia would like one of the boat cruise things on Lake Austin. It's then that I realize what Jay just said. "Wait, what'd you say?"

Jay finishes his jump on one foot and then lets out a howl of laughter, his broad shoulders shaking as he does. Jay Daniels is a wide receiver for the Dallas Cowboys. He tore his Achilles tendon earlier in the year and had to have surgery. I've been working with him for the past eight months, and he's about ready to return to the game. Though he'll miss the game against the Packers in a couple weeks—and I know he's upset about that—I have no doubt that he'll be ready when they take on the 49ers in January. He's one of my favorite clients, the other being none other than Olivia.

"Bruh, you got me over here playing hopscotch and shit and you're

not even paying attention. I'm talking about being a fisherman and you ain't cracked not one joke. Only thing that could have you that distracted is a woman."

He's not wrong. I've had him doing plyometric exercises for longer than I normally would and yet I can't recall a single moment of it. I'm off my game. I can't focus on anything but getting back to the beautiful woman waiting for me at home.

"I don't know what you're talking about." I dismiss him with a smile.

"Yeah, aight," he says as I lead him to the treatment table to do some stretches. "So, who is she?"

"Still don't know what you're talking about."

"Oh shit, I tell you about all the women in my life..."

"Against my will," I interject. I don't need to know about all the women who want to play nurse with him.

He continues like I never said a word. "And you can't tell me about this one? She must be the real deal then."

Not wanting to expose my relationship with Olivia before she's ready, but also not wanting to deny how much she means to me, I give him the best answer I can. "She really is." Jay nods in approval then lets me continue his stretches. "So are you really gonna be a fisherman whenever you retire?"

"Fuck no, bro. I don't do open water like that." Laughter rises up from my chest and bubbles out, and it's not long before Jay joins me.

Once I finish with Jay, I have to get through two more client sessions before I'm able to get back to Olivia. When I walk in, she's filling a glass of water, wearing nothing but a T-shirt and panties.

She takes a sip from her glass but is startled by my entrance so she misses her mouth. A trickle of water snares my attention as it glides down her chin and slope of her neck to the collar of her shirt. A shirt that's very familiar to me. "Oh, hi."

I think I mutter a hi back to her, but I'm too enraptured by her shirt to notice. My shirt. It's my white Rice University T-shirt. I recognize it from the writing on the sleeve. "<3 Olivia". It's funny how she signed her name on

my shirt to lay claim to me for everyone to see and then she commandeered it and wore it for herself anyway. I can't believe she kept it after all this time.

"Are you okay?" she asks.

"You've had my shirt this whole time?"

She looks down at herself as if just realizing she even had it on. Her fingers tug at the ends of the shirt in a self-conscious gesture. "Oh, yeah, I... um...I wear it to bed sometimes or..." she trails off.

"Or what?" I take a step toward her, and another, until she's firmly pressed against the kitchen island.

I tip her chin up with my finger, and when her dark-brown eyes meet mine I see the storm in them. A storm of vulnerability. "Or when I'm having a bad day."

My chest tightens at this revelation. She wears my shirt when she's having a bad day. I was able to provide her comfort even when I wasn't there. The pain of not knowing if she thought of me as much as I thought of her eases, the weight slightly lifting from my shoulders and making way for hope.

"Are you having a bad day today?"

"Not at all. I just...missed you." I lean my head down to the crevice of her neck and inhale.

When I don't say anything she continues, "Is that okay?"

My laugh gets lost against the column of her throat so I lift my head up to her level. I wrap her ponytail around my fist and pull until her lips part. "Is it okay? Is it okay that I never stopped being a source of comfort for you? Is it okay that you've carried a piece of me with you all this time? Is it okay that something of mine has touched your skin for all the years that I couldn't? It's more than okay. It's everything."

Her hand graces my shoulder. "I didn't need a shirt to carry you with me, Kai."

My hand falls from her hair to the collar of her shirt and pulls until the fabric rips beneath my hold.

She isn't wearing a bra so her breasts are bared to me, and I'm rewarded with the sight of her nipples hardening into peaks. "What the fuck are you doing?"

"You don't need this shirt anymore."

"But…it's our memories." She looks down at the tattered piece of cloth and I kick it to the side, out of sight. I never thought I'd be grateful to a damn shirt but I am. I'm grateful to this shirt for staying by her side when she needed me but chose to keep me at a distance. However, she doesn't need an old shirt of mine to bring her comfort on her bad days anymore. I'm here now, and I'm not going anywhere.

"We'll make new ones. You can have all the shirts I own for all I care."

And then we make a new memory right there in the kitchen.

"You know what I was thinking?" Olivia calls to me over the running water. She's showering while I'm trimming my beard at the sink. I could be doing this in the other bathroom, and I probably should considering she likes to shower with the water set to the pits of hell, but I'd rather be where she is.

It's been four days since we started on this new path. We're strictly client and therapist when we're in my office, but the moment we walk through the door of this house we're all limbs and lips, exploring each other with fervor. We're worse than we were at sixteen when we took each other's virginities and learned the controlling sensation of lust. We're worse than we were at eighteen when a college campus gave us the freedom to have sex whenever we wanted. No, this need now? It's unrelenting. It's carnal. It's thirteen years of pent-up desire that refuses to go back beneath the surface. It's here to stay.

"What's that?"

"I thought we could get the stuff to make dumplings and go see Po Po."

Those words are enough to suck the air out of the room.

"No." It's all I can say. What else is there? *I would rather stab my eye out with a rusty nail than go see my grandmother right now because seeing her will do nothing but bring me pain and I don't want you to see that?* No, I can't say that.

"Really? But we have a free day and she's…"

I cut her off because I can't listen to her defend Po Po. "I said no."

She pokes her head around the shower curtain. "What happened between you two?"

Anger boils just beneath the surface of my skin, festering like poison. Anger at Po Po for shattering the illusion I had of a grandmom I could trust. Anger at myself for not dismissing her from my life. Anger at Olivia for expecting me to share when she still hasn't.

"If you wanna talk about something there's plenty we can talk about, but that's not one of them. Not today."

She pulls the shower curtain closed so I can't see her anymore. If it weren't for the pounding of the water running, the silence would be deafening.

And then, the water turns off. Her hand wrenches a towel from the back of the door and I make out the outline of her body being covered by it.

"Okay," she says as she pushes the curtain back to step out of the shower. "Let's talk."

CHAPTER
Twenty-One

Olivia
19 years old

GOD, HE'S BEAUTIFUL. I TAKE A MINUTE TO OBSERVE HIS HEAD OF curls, how perfectly conditioned they are after I helped him with his wash day just the other day. I look at his eyes, currently shining with laughter as he animatedly tells a story, and get lost in them. They're a deep brown, so dark that they appear black, and they're the kindest eyes I've ever seen. His sepia-brown complexion is mesmerizing with how smooth it is. It angers me that I have an entire skincare routine I follow meticulously every night, and he just washes his face with soap and water and yet his skin never has a blemish on it. But then again I can't be mad at him when he looks at me the way he does.

I look down to his chest, perfectly molded in his white tee, down to his hoopin shorts that hide his muscular thighs. He's just so damn fine— with a heart to make my knees weak and a mind to make my soul sing— and he's all mine.

He's been talking for the last five minutes but I haven't heard a single word. I'm too excited and scared about what I need to tell him.

I register that his mouth is closed and he's waiting on a reply from me, and before I know it the words are tumbling out. "I'm pregnant."

Kai's jaw drops and then he goes completely still, so still that I can hear the erratic beat of his heart and the faint sounds of people walking by my dorm room.

Just as I'm about to slap the shit out of him because he's scaring me by not saying anything, he slides to the edge of the bed, rubs his hand down his face, and grabs my hand.

"When did you find out?"

"Last night. Monet went out and got me a bunch of tests. Six tests later, I'm pretty sure this is really happening." Monet is my roommate and one of my teammates and we've grown pretty close. She challenges me on the field and she's the one who noticed I was more lethargic suddenly and ran to get tests the minute I said I missed my period.

Kai scoots closer to me and wraps his arm around my shoulders. "Why didn't you tell me? I would've sat with you while you took the tests."

"You would've watched me pee? That's so sweet."

He laughs and kisses my forehead. "You know what I mean."

"It's okay, really. I wanted to be sure before I told you."

I can't say I'm surprised that he doesn't seem surprised. We knew this was a possibility. We stopped using condoms, relying solely on my birth control, but I fucked up. Soccer and classes have been kicking my ass, and I also secured an internship with the Astros this semester. The new schedule forced me to change my time when I was taking my pill every day and that led to me forgetting to take it at all. By the time we realized I had skipped an entire week and a half of pills, it was too late to take Plan B, so Kai just said to let it ride. So, here we are.

"Okay, so how are you feeling? Have you been sick?"

"No, I'm good. I've just been really tired and peeing every five seconds. Oh, and I've had some cramping but I still didn't put it together until I missed my period. So,"—I take a deep breath— "what do you think we should do?"

He looks deep into my eyes and then he pushes away from me and turns so that our bodies are facing each other. "I...I don't know. I want to know what you think because this affects you more."

His answer is like a slap in the face. It affects me more? What the fuck does that mean?

I scoff. "You planning on going somewhere?"

His forehead crinkles. "Olivia, come on. You must be crazy if you think I would ever leave you. That's not what I'm saying."

"Then what are you saying, Kai?"

He grabs my hand again and I itch to shake him off of me, but I wait to see what he has to say first.

"I'm saying that you're the one that has to carry the baby. I can't do that for you. I love you, Olivia Harding. I'm always gonna be here, but at the end of the day it's you who is gonna be doing the heavy lifting and that's going to affect soccer. I don't know when you would have to be benched, but I imagine you can't run up and down the field with a big belly. And once you have the baby, I don't know how long it'll be before you can get back to it. I just don't want you to regret this—the baby or me—if it ends up costing you your dream."

I squeeze his hand with understanding. I do appreciate him taking my goals into consideration. If we go through with this, I'm going to have one hell of road getting back to soccer, if I even can. I don't even know if I would be able to handle coming back to school once the baby is born. The thing is I don't know if I'm severely overestimating my skills or if I'm just being young, dumb, and naive, but I truly believe that we can have it all. Since those two little lines appeared on the test, and then appeared on five more tests, I've been in preparation mode. I'm pregnant. We're having a baby. Kai majors in kinesiology with the hopes of becoming a physical therapist, and I major in sports management so that I'll have a backup plan if soccer doesn't work out. If my dad's career-ending injury taught me anything, it's that I don't want to become jaded like him, so I need to be prepared for any and all possibilities. I didn't expect that becoming a mom at nineteen would

be one of those possibilities, but we're here now and I don't regret it. I want this. Between Kai, me, and his family, I really think we can make this work.

I pull Kai's signature move and kiss him on his forehead, his nose, and his lips. "I love you too, Kai Morris. I could never regret you. I'm in if you are."

He laughs and buries his face in my neck. "Is it crazy that I'm kind of excited?"

"I'm not gonna lie, I'm kinda pumped to see what a little you and me looks like."

He wraps me up tight in a hug, and I melt into his embrace. "I'm telling you now though, if it's a boy and you try to name him any variation of David, Cristiano, Morris, or Usher we will have problems."

I choke on the laughter that falls from my lips and slip into a coughing fit. He's still so bent out of shape that I told him he's definitely in my top five of men I want to be with, but I wouldn't tell him where he falls among David Beckham, Cristiano Ronaldo, Morris Chestnut, and Usher.

"Not even a middle name?"

He narrows his eyes at me and I burst out laughing. "If you weren't carrying my seed, I'd body-slam you into this bed right now."

"What about a different kind of body slam?"

"What kind?"

"The kind where I lie down gently and you have your way with me." I barely get the last word out before he's stripping off his shorts. "I was joking. Aren't you about to go hoop with the boys?"

He looks at me like I've lost my mind. "Fuck them. Lie down, love."

You don't have to tell me twice.

A little over a week later, I'm hauling ass from my internship back to my dorm to relax before practice starts in a couple of hours. So far, I've been able to conceal my symptoms from everyone, but today the morning sickness hit me hard.

Kai and I went to the doctor to find out how far along I am and make

sure everything is okay. I'm six weeks pregnant, so in June of next year we're going to welcome our little one into the world. Holy shit.

I'm seconds from walking into my room when my dad calls.

"Hi, Dad. Can I call you later? I really wanna chill before practice."

"Actually, I want to meet up for lunch. I'm in the area."

A chill runs down my back. "You're in Houston? How come?" My dad never comes to visit me at school, and I never come home except for winter and summer break.

"For business. Meet me at Little Kitchen in twenty minutes." Since when does he want to meet me for lunch? We never hang out. My stomach drops with the thought that maybe he knows about the baby. No, there's no way he could know. Kai and I purposefully went to the free clinic so that I wouldn't have to use his insurance. It's not like we're planning on hiding the pregnancy from him forever. I was just hoping to hold it off for as long as possible. For Thanksgiving, I'm going with Kai and his family to visit Auntie Patrice. Six months ago, she had a whirlwind romance with a personal chef and decided to sell her business and follow him to Atlanta. She now has an even more successful dog grooming business there, and the two of them are dog parents to two Goldendoodles. We're planning to tell his family then. For my dad, I thought why not wait until we're back home for Christmas? I don't think he knows because if he did he would've gone off on me by now. He wouldn't be holding back. "Liv?" he interrupts my spiraling thoughts.

"Yeah, um, it's just I really did want to take a nap before practice. The internship wore me out today."

"Liv, come on. I want to see you while I'm in town." It's funny because the words suggest that I'm being given a choice here, but the tone lets me know that there's only one correct answer. I guess I'm not getting that nap after all. I just hope my morning sickness stays under control until I'm back in the safety of my own room.

I agree to meet my dad in twenty minutes, so I rush to change into denim shorts and a T-shirt and pull my hair up.

When I get to Little Kitchen, my dad is already there waiting for me.

He doesn't stand up to hug me like most dads. Instead, he points to the lemon water he ordered for me and gestures for me to sit.

"So how have you been?"

"Good. You?"

"Good. Classes going well?"

"Yep, they're fine." The server comes to take our order and even though I'm not all that hungry, I order a salad anyway to avoid suspicion.

"And how's that internship going? It's not getting in the way of practice, is it?" It's crazy to me that he doesn't see the merit in my internship. He doesn't want me to follow in his footsteps and become a businesswoman. He wants me to follow the path he couldn't finish, the star athlete path.

"No, the internship is great. I'm learning a lot."

"Mm-hmm."

We continue our awkward and stunted conversation until the food comes and then we fall silent. I don't mind the quiet; it's better than trying to force a bond where there isn't one. I would love to be able to cut the shit with my dad, but we just don't have that relationship. We never did, even when my mom was still around.

"So," he starts, "I spoke to Myra the other day." I barely sustain my eye roll. Myra is my dad's assistant and I don't like her. She's extremely nosey and likes to look down on people who don't adhere to the way she believes Christians should act.

"And how is Ms. Myra?"

"She's concerned. You see, she says that she saw you at the clinic and she was under the impression that you're with child. I told her that couldn't possibly be the case because my daughter wouldn't be stupid enough to let some boy knock her up at this age."

Oh, fuck. How the fuck did I miss nosey-ass Myra at the clinic? Was she sitting right beside us? Because how else would she know I was pregnant just for being at the clinic unless she overheard Kai and me talking? And why the fuck would she be at a free clinic in Houston when her bitch-ass lives and works in Austin?

"Did you have Myra following me?"

He rolls his eyes. "Don't be ridiculous. Not that I owe you any explanations but it was pure coincidence. She was off work for a few days and went to visit her niece who happens to work at the clinic. Thank God she stopped by to take her niece to lunch or else I feel like I would still be in the dark. Isn't that right?"

This is so messed-up. This is not how I wanted this to go. I wanted to tell him on my terms. I wanted Kai to be with me. I wanted time.

"Well?" His fists are clenched on top of the table. His rage is palpable. My father is not a good dad. I've come to realize that I don't even know him well enough to know if he's a good man, but I can say he has never put his hands on me. I've seen my dad angry before, but I've never seen him at this level, and if we weren't in public right now I would honestly be afraid that today would be the day he hits me.

I could lie to him, call Myra crazy, and feign ignorance. But what would be the point? One, I don't think he would take my word over Myra's, as sad as that is, and two, even if he did believe me, he'd watch me like a hawk from now on and would discover the truth anyway.

With that thought in mind, I rip the Band-Aid off. "You know what, Dad? Yeah, I am pregnant. Congratulations, you're gonna be a grandfather."

He's silent for a moment and then it happens—he laughs. It starts as a low chuckle that sends a chill down my spine then it becomes more boisterous, making my eye twitch in discomfort. Finally, it turns into a full-blown cackle, drawing the attention of everyone surrounding us and making me sink deeper into my seat.

Our server approaches our table with a cautious smile, and the menacing sneer disguised as a smile my father just gave me transforms before my very eyes to the megawatt charming smirk he gives her. "Sorry, hun. My daughter just told a very funny joke. She's very funny, my daughter. Tell me, what did you say your name was again?"

"Yvonne." She fidgets.

"What's your relationship with your parents like, Yvonne? Are they proud of you?"

I take a subtle look around, and everyone seems to have lost interest

in our antics. I try to communicate telepathically with Yvonne that she should leave while she can, but of course she doesn't hear me. "Uh, yeah. Yeah, I think they are."

"That's great, Yvonne. That's great. Do you ever lie to your parents?"

This gives her pause. "Umm..."

"It's okay, you can tell me."

"I mean, who doesn't?" She laughs and looks to me for validation. I don't have the heart to tell her that my validation would only be her downfall.

My father's smile never wavers. "That's so true. I was young once too. Can I give you some advice?"

"Sure."

"If your parents ask you a specific question, don't bother with the lie because they already know the truth. They're just giving you a chance to make it right. Take it."

She nods her agreement. He looks at me with his eyes narrowed into slits, before turning back to her. "I think we'll take the check now, Yvonne."

Without another word, she scurries off to the back. I only have twenty bucks on me, but I make a mental note to leave it for her for having to deal with our shit.

"Dad, I..."

He puts his hand up to silence me. "No. Your little comedy show is over." He takes a menacing pause. "How far along are you?"

My heart starts racing. "Six weeks."

"Good. I will make an appointment for you."

"An appointment for what?"

"To take care of your problem," he says with a sneer directed at my stomach.

An abortion. He wants me to get an abortion. My neck snaps back in shock.

"I'm not getting an abortion."

He doesn't speak again. Not when Yvonne returns with the check, not

171

when she returns again with his receipt. Not even when we walk outside into the Houston heat.

I've said all I needed to say, so I start to walk away when he calls my name. "You will take care of it. It is your only option."

"No, it's not. I'm keeping this baby with or without your blessing."

"You would give up on your dreams, give up on your goals for what? A mistake? Please. I did not raise a stupid girl."

"You barely raised me," I whisper-shout. "You have been my coach, my trainer, and my nutritionist, but you haven't been my dad. Kai will be a much better father than you were."

He laughs again, utterly void of any humor. "You have so much to learn about this world, Liv. And you will learn. We'll be in touch." He storms past me without a single look back.

My meeting with my dad fucks with me for the rest of the day. I knew he wouldn't be happy about me being pregnant but to demand I get an abortion? As if it's not my body? As if I don't have a say in what I do with said body? I'm disgusted.

"Goddamn it, Harding! What is up with you today?" Coach Naughton screams as yet another ball sails by me without a single attempt to stop it. The blow of her whistle puts an end to Monet's drive down the field. I haven't been able to focus the entire practice. I was worried about my morning sickness fucking me over, but it's my father's words playing on a loop in my head that have truly screwed me.

"Sorry, Coach!"

She assesses me and then benches me for the rest of practice.

I hate sitting on the sidelines. I hate disappointing Coach. I hate that I let him get to me. I feel Coach's eyes on me as I watch my teammate Yara inbound the ball to Monet and fly down the field, but I don't acknowledge her. I grip the sides of the bench, close my eyes, and lose myself to the crisp smell of the bermudagrass and the tender lick of the sun's rays on my skin.

I try to make a quick exit but Coach is quicker, demanding I stay later. I sneak a peek at my phone to find a text from Kai telling me his study group is running late, so he won't be able to meet me here to walk me back

but he'll see me in my room later. I shoot off a text assuring him I'm okay then head over to where Coach is waiting.

"Harding, what's going on? I've never seen you that out of it before." She passes off a bag of balls to me before bending to pick up another and leading me off the field.

"I know, I was just tired today. I'm sorry."

"That's understandable. I know you've got a full course load and the internship this year, but can I be honest with you?"

"Yeah."

"I think something else is going on. Soccer is who you are. Every time you step on this field you become one with it. Your passion shines through your every move, but today that was completely missing. Not saying we don't all have off days but you worried me today. If there's anything going on or if I can help in any way, you can always talk to me."

I soak in her words. I'm glad I made the decision to come to Rice to play under her. She's been everything I hoped she would be and more. I've gained a lot more confidence on the field and my agility has increased ten-fold. I know she'll be slightly disappointed when I have to step back from playing because of the baby, but I also know that she actually gives a shit about me and she'll work with me to get back in the game if that's what I want.

"I know, Coach. I know. I, uh, had an argument with my dad earlier and it messed me up, but I shouldn't have let it affect practice."

Her brows furrow as she nods. "Say no more; you know I'm familiar with your dad." She sure is because the few games he's come to have always led to tense conversations between them. "I've met plenty of guys like him; they're not unique. There are real men and then there are men who need to try to make women feel small and irrelevant to make themselves feel better about what they lack. You hold so much power inside of you, Liv. Don't ever let anyone take it from you."

My hand flies up to my eye to catch the fat tear that's gathering there, and Coach Naughton pats my shoulder gently. "Thank you. Really."

"Of course. You let me know if you ever need to talk." When we make

it to the locker room, she wraps me up in one of those soul-healing hugs. The ones where they rock you back and forth and you just want to sob on their shoulder.

I thank her again, and with renewed confidence in my power, I make my way back to my dorm to meet Kai.

"Liv."

I freeze at the deep baritone in that voice. What the fuck is he doing here by my dorm building?

Slowly, I turn around to come face to face with my father.

"What are you doing here?"

"We didn't finish our conversation earlier. I made you an appointment for tomorrow. I'll pick you up at ten a.m."

I push my shoulders back and walk until the tips of our shoes touch. "I'm not going to any damn appointment with you. I told you I'm keeping this baby and guess what? There's nothing you can do to stop that, so you can either fall in line and get ready to be a better grandfather than you were a father or you can get out of my life. Those are the options, Dad. There is no third. Now, I'm tired. I missed the nap I wanted to take today, and my feet hurt so I'm going to go cuddle with my boyfriend and rest. You can call me another time."

I turn toward my dorm building with my head held high, but I only make it three steps before his words make my stomach drop. "Then Kai can kiss his future goodbye."

Frozen in my tracks, I slowly turn to face him again. "What did you say?"

"If you don't go to that appointment tomorrow, Kai's future is over before it even starts."

"What do you mean by that?"

"While you were at practice, I was drafting a few emails and gearing up to make a few calls." He produces a folder and hands it to me. I carefully pull out the pages within and my jaw drops. He's drafted emails to numerous contacts that paint Kai as some sort of deranged boy with a habit of lying, cheating, stealing, and manipulating everyone around him, mainly

me. He looks like a concerned father crying out for help for his poor, naive daughter who fell into Kai's trap. It's a bunch of bullshit, but given that the sports industry is very much a boys' club, it's enough to make Kai a pariah. No one would hire him, and they may just try to have him committed if these emails went out.

My father is the COO of Momentum, the biggest athletic apparel company in the industry. Every single athlete dreams of brand sponsorships from them. Somehow the company gets away with having no women in leadership positions, and my dear old dad is one of three Black men in positions of power. After his injury, he went back to school to finish his degree and landed a job with them soon after in Strategy and Development. He climbed the ladder from there, working in many other departments and building connections along the way. When my mom took off eight years ago, he had gotten himself to a VP position, but I guess she got tired of waiting.

On top of that, he's also a silent investor in Propel Sports Management, the largest sports agency in the United States. He and the CEO go way back. He also has numerous connections with sports medicine doctors, physical therapists, occupational therapists, and universities across the country. Countless people in the industry owe him favors for God knows what. All it would take is one phone call or email from him for Kai to be blacklisted in the industry. I can't believe he would even think to go this far.

"Let me tell you what's going to happen, Olivia. Tomorrow at ten a.m. you will be standing in front of this building waiting for me to pick you up. You will not make another foolish attempt at arguing with me about your rights, your choices, or your silly wishes. You will go to the appointment I've set for you, and you will get your situation handled and then you will carry on as if this never happened.

"I can see the wheels turning in your mind, trying to find a way out of this, so I will do you the favor of running through what will happen should you not be standing in this spot when I pull up. I will send those emails to every single contact I have and light the match at the end of the fuse that is Kai's career. By the time I'm done with him, he'll be lucky if he can make

a dime panhandling on the street. Yes, you'll have this baby you seem to want so badly, but you will have nothing else because everything you have is because I made it so. I bought the clothes on your back, the food in your belly, and the home you sleep in. I pay for your education, your housing, and your car. Hell, without me you wouldn't even have health insurance to care for this child, unless you plan to give birth at the free clinic you seem to love so much. That coveted internship of yours might look nice on a résumé, but it certainly doesn't pay any bills. So what will you do when all of that is ripped away from you? When I retract the grace I've extended you? Oh, let me guess." He switches to a tone that is a clear mockery of me. "None of that matters, Dad, because we love each other and we'll be fine without you."

He bends the top half of his body closer to me. "Wrong. Those are the words of a privileged princess who has never experienced any real struggle in her life. You have wanted for nothing your entire life and yet you call me a monster. I've put in the work. I've bled for you and for your absent mother. I threw myself into the lion's den of corporate America. I clawed my way to the top of the ladder with you on my back and became a king so that you wouldn't have to. So that you could look down on the kingdom I made you. Imagine being the parent that stayed but still being made into the villain. Do you think Kai is still going to love you when he's living in a four by four shithole without a pot to piss in? He might at first because, as you claim, he loves you so much, but slowly that love is going to dissolve into nothing but resentment at the fact that being with you cost him his dream and he has nothing to show for it.

"You wanted this. You wanted soccer. You begged me to let you do this because it was your dream; it was all you ever wanted in life so like everything else, I made it happen." He lifts his hands to my face and I flinch away from him, but his hands still connect with my jaw, lifting my head ever so slightly. "I spent years molding you into the best version of yourself, cultivating your image to aim straight for stardom. I gave you the tools to become a legend, and you think I'm going to let that all go to waste because you couldn't keep your legs closed to the boy across the street? No.

You love to call me the villain of your story, fine, but let's not forget, I am also the author."

Strong hands wind their way around my body, one of them gently caressing my stomach. I close my eyes and snuggle into his chest to calm my racing heart. By the time Kai showed up to my room, my father was long gone but his threats still lingered in my head, infecting my every thought.

I should tell him. I should tell Kai what's going on. He knew something was off the moment he saw me, but I played it off as fatigue, so instead of working on our papers like he came here to do, he insisted we lie in bed and watch *The Dark Knight*, again, until I fell asleep.

Sleep isn't coming for me. All I can think about is my dad's words. No matter how hard I try, I can't think of a single scenario where Kai and I win. It would take absolutely no effort for my dad to ruin him. And then what? Every time I step out of line, he threatens Kai's future to shove me back in my cage? Is that any way to live? Me being afraid to make any moves for fear of triggering my dad's vindictive side and Kai having to look over his shoulder for the simple reason that he chose to love me? Kai doesn't deserve that. This baby doesn't deserve that.

"Hey, Kai?"

"Yeah?"

When I look in his eyes, I no longer see the future we envisioned together. The image used to be so clear. Graduation, the draft, the backyard wedding, the opening of his practice, the babies, the World Cup, everything. Now, I just see him flourishing without me while I fade away into the bleak existence my dad has planned for me. He's right; I begged for soccer. I wanted this. I just didn't realize the price of having that dream would be giving up the other.

"I just wanted to tell you I love you," I resign.

His mouth splits into a wide grin. "Bro, only you would get sappy during

a superhero movie. The Joker just blew up a damn hospital and you whispering sweet nothings to me."

He pinches my sides and I swat his arm. "Boy, shut up. I changed my mind. You're okay out of ten."

He chortles. "Okay out of ten. What the fuck does that even mean?"

"You heard me. You aight."

"Oooh, I'm just aight now? Okay. Talk your shit."

"I always do."

While he laughs at my smartass commentary, I take a moment to just bask in him. In that smile that I probably won't see aimed at me ever again after today. I know what I have to do. I take a look at the clock on my nightstand. Eleven p.m. Eleven hours until our lives change forever.

The next day, I'm standing in front of my building. The atmosphere is eerily quiet. It's a Saturday so there aren't a lot of people around. Everyone is most likely recovering from whatever party they went to last night. The door creaks behind me, forcing my attention to the two students walking out. I recognize the girl from my Business Communications class. Her purple passion twists stop just below her shoulders, making her golden-brown skin pop. I don't know the handsome guy with the close-cut fade she's with, but judging by the way their hands are intertwined I'm willing to bet he's her man. She catches me watching her and acknowledges me with a head nod before leading her man off in the direction of the dining hall.

Watching their hands until they're out of my line of sight, my heart pangs thinking about Kai. He's at his part-time job at H-E-B, completely unaware that I'm about to upend our entire relationship. I'm a coward. Coach Naughton encouraged me to stand in my power, but the moment my dad threatened Kai, I gave it all to him.

My dad's Escalade EXT pulls up in front of my building right on time, leaving no room for more intrusive thoughts. I hop onto the leather seats and slam the door shut, earning me a glare. No words are spoken on the way to wherever the fuck he's taking me. They aren't needed. He said all he had to say yesterday and I lost my voice.

Time goes by agonizingly slowly during the drive. My entire body is

vibrating and I don't know if that's from the nerves or the bass of "Int'l Player's Anthem" pumping through my dad's speakers. My father refuses to listen to the latest UGK album, still upset at the death of Pimp C two years ago, so I'm not surprised to hear the *Underground Kingz* album blasting now. I don't think my father is loyal to a single person on this planet, but he is very loyal to the city of Houston and all that comes with it. After all, Houston is where he was last happy. Austin was nothing but an attempt to run from the pain.

I lean my head against the barely legal tinted windows and study the roads as they whip past my face. Browns and greens transition into steel-grays and whites. After what feels like an hour, we pull into the parking lot of Planned Parenthood. When he gets out of the car, I take a minute to take a deep breath before joining him. He ushers me past the sea of idiot protestors waving their pitchforks and torches in the shape of signs and pamphlets admonishing those who would step foot in this building into the cool lobby.

I fill out the paperwork I'm given, and when a tear falls from my eye to the sheet of paper, I'm not surprised but still hurt that Dad doesn't even attempt to console me. I walked in here a young woman who had chosen the path of motherhood, but one hour later, I'm walking out a brokenhearted girl who just wanted her father to finally choose her over himself and his grief. But of course, he didn't.

This time, I don't even hear the cries of the protestors when we leave. The shrill cries of their voices feel so distant and hazy. I'm unaware of anything as we make our way back to campus. I can vaguely hear the bump of the speakers and I can vaguely make out the passing scenery, but it all feels like I'm experiencing it from outside of my body. I like this feeling. This feeling of being here but not really here—it keeps the aching burn of my grief at bay.

There's no fanfare when he rolls up to my building. There are no words of comfort nor words of malice, just a simple "have a good weekend" before I'm left to trudge my way up to my third floor dorm room.

Monet isn't here when I walk in, probably off somewhere with our teammates, and I'm relieved because I don't have it in me to talk about everything that's happened. I collapse into bed and let the world fade away.

It's been three days since the abortion and three days since I've seen Kai. I didn't want to see him right after because I knew I had to take that second pill and wait for the cramping and heavy bleeding the doctor told me to expect. I spent twenty-four hours sobbing over every painful cramp. If Kai would've seen me in pain he would've known something was wrong, and I wasn't ready to have that conversation. I'm still not ready.

He's been texting and calling nonstop, trying to make plans. I've been holding him off the best I can, claiming I'm not on campus when I am because I'm a coward.

My mood since Saturday has taken a sharp decline, which is how I find myself drunk as fuck at one of my teammate's parties on a Tuesday night. I just want to go back to how I felt right after—numb.

I make the mistake of checking my phone and responding to a text from Kai.

Kai: Olivia, I know you're back at school since you had class today. Wtf is up?

Me: Up? Nothing. Down? Me.

Kai: What?

Me: LOL idk

Kai: Are you okay?

Me: If u only knew

Ha, that's a song. Wait a minute, no it's not. The song is called "If Your Girl Only Knew." Close enough.

Kai: Where you at?

Me: A palace

Me: A partition*

Me: A partity*

Me: Dammit, a party*

Kai: What building?

Me: You gonna come find me, Kai?

Kai: Always

I send him the building and what I think is the room number of the party and go back to my cup that's ninety percent tequila and ten percent pineapple Fanta.

"Yo, Olivia," Kai calls to me. When did he get here? I look him up and down in his black sweatpants, white tee, and Crazy 8s and smile. He smiles back at me but it quickly falls when he gets close to me and smells the alcohol on my breath.

"You're drinking?" he asks.

"Nothing gets past you, baby," I coo.

He snatches the red cup from my hands and leans down to my eye level. "Don't play with me. What the fuck is going on?" His tone drops to a whisper. "You know you can't drink with the baby."

"I'm not pregnant anymore," I blurt out. His eyes widen then soften. He takes my hand, sets my cup on a table near us, and guides me out of the party and down to the common room on the floor. I stumble a couple times but he catches me with ease.

"You lost the baby?"

"I didn't lose it. I went to the clinic and...you know." I won't tell him the whole truth. I can't. But I won't have him thinking I miscarried. I don't deserve his pity.

"Oh." I wait for the hate to come. For the dreamy look reserved only for me to skew into pure hatred, but it doesn't come. Of course it doesn't because Kai is perfect. He was the perfect boy who I watched transform into an even more perfect man, and I don't even get to keep him. "I didn't realize you had changed your mind. I'm sorry. Why didn't you tell me? You didn't have to be alone."

Fuck. He is too much. I feel the buzz I had going start to wear off, and I suddenly long to have that red cup back in my hands.

"I'm leaving." His brows wrinkle in confusion at my words so I press on. "I'm leaving Rice. I'm entering the draft for WPS." It was the one condition I made of my father when I accepted his demand. I can't continue to put Kai at risk and I can't stand to be around him knowing I can't have him, so I demanded to leave school and go pro early. It's not common for women to be drafted earlier than their senior year, but I had gained the attention of a few teams after last season so Coach Naughton floated the idea to me earlier this year. I immediately declined at first, not interested in leaving school— or Kai—early, but now the idea felt like a lifeline.

"Where is all this coming from? I thought you wanted to get your de- gree first? Wasn't that our plan?"

"It's not really needed. I'll get hands-on experience being in the pros, and I'll make wise investments along the way so I'll be set."

He scoffs at my half-assed plan and I can't blame him. This is all com- ing out of left field, and I know I'm not making any sense.

"Okay, bet. So what's the new plan then? We find out where you get drafted and I transfer schools next year?"

My head draws back so fast that it sets me off balance and Kai has to catch me again. I wiggle out of his touch, putting a step between us. "Why would you transfer schools?"

"To be with you," he says, like it's the most obvious answer in the world. I wish it were.

I shake my head. "You should stay here. You like it here."

"I don't give a damn where I get my degree from. They have kinesiol- ogy programs everywhere. You tryna say you wanna do long distance til I graduate?"

"No."

He steps back into my space. "So what are you saying?"

"I'm saying, I can't do this anymore."

"Do what?"

"Us!" I yell. "I can't do us anymore because…because you're holding me back."

Hurt flashes across his features. "The fuck you say?"

I audibly swallow, working up the nerve to say what I need to say. The image of my dad's email draft in my mind is what pushes me over the edge. "I said, you're holding me back. I have an opportunity to get the very thing I've been working my whole life for, and I realized it would be silly for me to pass that up just for a piece of paper."

"I never said you had to pass up the opportunity. Even though you were the one that said you didn't want it when it first came up. I said I would go with you."

"But I don't want you to. Kai. We're young. We have so much life to live and we were about to give up the little freedom we have to step into roles we weren't at all ready for. It's just...too much. I think we need space. We need to go our own ways and see what's out there, ya know?"

"No, I don't know. What is going on? This ain't you. Matter fact, it sounds like your dad."

I cross my arms. "So what, I can't make my own decisions now?" I inwardly cringe at my attempt to gaslight him.

He huffs. "You know that's not what I said. I..." He lifts his hand to touch my face, but I pull away from him, eliciting another pained stare from him. "Olivia, baby, please talk to me. What do you need? Whatever it is, I can fix it. Just...talk to me."

Tears well up in my eyes but I wipe them away as though they mean nothing. "There's nothing to fix. I'm not trying to hurt you. I just need to do this, Kai. And I need to do it alone. You have to let me go."

At that, his hands fall to his sides and before he can say another word, I storm out and retreat to the safety of my own room.

Kai texts me once after I leave the party, to make sure I got to my room safely, but after I assure him I have, I don't hear from him for the rest of the night. The next morning, when there's a knock at my door, I don't even have to guess at who it is. I make my way over to the door but I don't open it; instead I listen to the raps of his hand against it.

"Olivia, please open up. We need to talk."

I stand perfectly still but I can feel his tortured soul calling to me. "I love you," he whispers.

"I need you," he says as his fist hits the door again.

"Don't do this," he pleads.

He goes silent and I ponder if he left, but when my phone buzzes with a text, I know he's still there.

Kai: You're really not gonna open the door?

I place my hand against the door and peer through the peephole. His hand is against the doorframe while his head is buried in his phone.

Me: Please don't make this harder than it has to be

Kai: Why does it have to be hard? Just let me in

Me: It's not worth it

Kai: I'm not worth it?

I slap my hand against my mouth to stop the gasp that threatens to escape. I don't want to destroy him, but I have to get him to accept this. With a new resolve, I send the message that will seal my fate.

Me: You're worth more than I can give you. I love you, but the whole baby thing opened my eyes. My heart's not in it anymore. I don't want this anymore. Us. I need space to figure this out

The moment I hit send, I place my hand against the door again and check the peephole. I can feel his energy change when he reads my text. His eyes fly up to the door as if he can see right through it, right through me. He looks like he doesn't even know who I am anymore. He's not wrong. This new me is a version I can't stand, but that's necessary. I just hope when he finds someone who actually deserves him that he looks back on our relationship with joy instead of hate.

His hand graces the door, right where mine sits, and then he walks away. I sink to the floor and let my sobs fall freely.

CHAPTER
Twenty-Two

Kai

"Y ou're fucking with me, right?"

After her shower, Olivia dressed in a pair of black barely there shorts and a black tank top that clings to her shape. She looks downright edible, and yet I can barely see her past the blinding rage I feel in my soul.

Did she really just tell me that the reason she completely shattered my heart and took off all those years ago was because of her dad?

She looks at me with wide eyes and parted lips, and I'm trying to figure out why she's shocked. Did she think she was gonna tell me this and shit was gonna be sweet?

"What do you mean?"

I scoff. "What do I mean? I spent years agonizing over what I did wrong. How you fell out of love with me. What I could've done differently to get you to stay. Then I finally get you back and I've lost countless hours of sleep

wondering how I can get you to love me as much as I love you this time and then you tell me that this whole time you were just running scared?"

Now it's her turn to scoff. "I was trying to protect you."

"That wasn't what I needed from you."

"Did you not hear what I said? What he said he'd do to you if I didn't listen? We were kids; we had absolutely no chance of winning against him."

I fold my arms in front of my chest and level her with a cold stare. "Okay and what about when we weren't kids anymore? Why didn't you come back then?"

"I...I..." she sputters over her words. "I didn't think you'd want me to."

"Right. You would've known if you had just fucking asked. But you didn't ask me shit through any of it. I was nervous as fuck when you got pregnant, yeah, but I was excited. When you said you changed your mind and got the abortion, I was upset but I accepted it because it was your body and I had no right to tell you what to do with it. When you broke up with me and then disappeared, I let you go because you made it seem like I wasn't what you wanted anymore. Like I was a burden and I didn't want to hold you back from accomplishing your dreams if that's what you thought I was doing. If you had just told me what was going on, I would've done what I had to do to protect you. I would've fought for you. You fucking took that chance from me."

"What were you gonna do?! He would've ruined you!"

"You think I gave a fuck?!" I give it right back to her. She is standing on one side of her bed while I am standing on the other, but it feels like we have miles more distance between us than just the bed. "There wasn't a goddamn blow he could land that hurt me more than when you walked away that day."

"You say that now but trust me, his blows hit hard."

"I'm not scared of your dad, Olivia."

"Well, maybe you should be! I've seen what he's capable of. I've seen him follow through on the threats he's made, and it is fucking devastating." She looks like she's about to say more, but she bites her lip to stop herself. She lets out an exasperated sigh before continuing. "If I hadn't done what

I did, do you think you'd be where you are today? Do you think G would have the care she needs? Would you be able to spoil Kylie the way you do?"

"First of all, don't throw G's care in my face. I pay for her nurse because I can and I want to help my parents. If I couldn't do it, my parents would be perfectly capable of doing so and you know that. And maybe Kylie's ass should be less spoiled, so you're not helping your case. Just admit you folded."

She draws her head back and drops her hand on her hip. "I folded?"

"Yeah, you folded on me. On us. You didn't believe I could protect you. You didn't give me a chance. You chose fear over me. Admit that shit so we can move forward. I'll take my apology in the form of your pussy."

"This is not a damn joke."

"Who's joking?"

"Fuck you, Kai," she says, seething. "I made the right choice."

She turns around and starts heading for the door, and that's when my blood boils. "Don't you fucking walk away from me." My voice is low with a sharp undertone, threatening to shatter the ground beneath our feet and plummet us into darkness.

She freezes for a moment but then she spins around, ready to cuss me out, but I move around the bed and back her against the wall in mere seconds. "That's your fucking problem—you're always walking away. That shit is over."

"Kai…"

I gently grip her chin, silencing her words. "No. I don't wanna look at your back again unless I'm bending you over something to drive my dick inside you, where it belongs."

She squirms beneath my hold. "You're mad at me but you're still thinking about fucking me." Her eyes roll with her question-but-not-really-a-question.

"What'd I tell you about shit not being mutually exclusive? Yeah, I'm mad at you, but I'm always thinking about fucking you."

Her hands push against my lower abdomen. "Be serious."

"I don't look serious to you?" I move my head lower so she has no choice but to look in the depths of my eyes. "I've always been serious when it comes to you, Olivia. You're the one that's questionable."

The slight playfulness falls away from her face, and I can see she needs some space, so I take a step back. Not too far though.

"I have always loved you, Kai. I am genuinely so sorry for what I did. I really was trying to protect you. I couldn't stand the idea of my father being this dark cloud that hung over you your whole life and mine. And now that I say that out loud, I realize that I was trying to protect myself too."

"So you...what?"

Uncertainty spreads over her face before she catches my smirk and mutters something about me being an asshole then says, "I folded."

"There you go." I grab her wrist and pull her against my chest. "Look, I can't say this whole revelation isn't still fucking with me. Frankly, I'm still fuming and not just at you, but if you think this changes how much I fucking love you, you're mistaken. I'm here. I'm choosing you like I always have, but you need to do the same. I can't go through this shit again, so if you choose this—if you choose me—then that means we stand together. No matter what bullshit your dad throws at us."

"I really am so sorry. It gutted me to say those words to you."

"I appreciate that. But I don't want more sorries. I want action. So what are you going to do?"

She looks up at me, her eyes glossy. "I'm scared."

"Understandable. I'm not expecting you to not be scared or worried. You're human and you've been burned before, so it makes sense. But you have to decide whether you're gonna face your fear or continue to let it own you."

"I...I need a minute."

I won't lie and say that doesn't sting, but I get it. She's been suffering silently for years. I can't really expect her to just let it all go because I say so, but it hurts all the same.

I nod and move to give her the space she needs when she grabs my forearm. "Wait, don't go. I just mean that there's more I think I need to tell you before you say you're all in."

"I've already said—"

"I know what you said," she cuts me off. "But I just want to get everything

out in the open. I've told you most of it, but there's more and I, fuck, I feel a breakdown coming."

I reach for her but she pulls away, not to slight me but because she's lost in her own head. "Give me a second. Stay right here."

She rushes out of the room before I can object. I sink down on the bed and bury my head in my hands.

What feels like an eternity passes before she calls me out to the kitchen. When I get there, she's standing by the island with her earnest eyes on me, picking her nails and shifting her weight between each leg. On the floor by her feet, there's a blanket laid out with a bottle of chocolate syrup, a bottle of strawberry sauce, a can of whipped cream, a bottle of honey, and a bottle of champagne. Where did she even get all of this? She doesn't eat half this shit.

"What's going on?"

"I thought we'd try something a little different."

I look again from her to the spread on the floor, and I have no idea what to make of any of this. I want to cover her with every single thing laid out and lick her from head to toe, but that's not what we're doing right now. At least, I thought it wasn't.

"Different how?"

A smile lifts the corner of her mouth. "Like a game, kind of. We'll take turns asking each other questions. If I choose to answer your question then I get to decide what I want to put on your body and where. Same goes for you and back and forth like that."

"I'm trying to really hash this shit out with you and you wanna play a game but you don't wanna fuck?"

"I'm trying to give you what you deserve and talk to you about everything but letting all that out in there"—she points toward her bedroom—"was a lot, and I don't think I can take much more of that. I still have things to tell you, and I have questions for you too. This will give me something to focus on while we continue to hash it out."

"Olivia, I. . ."

"Please," she quips. Fuck, this woman has such a tight hold on me that one word undoes me. All I wanted to tell her was that we didn't have to do

this at all. That she can ask me any questions she wants but I don't have to ask her any because the moment I found out she wanted me then and still wants me now, I was all in. The rest is noise we can sort out later, but I see how tightly wound she is. She needs this and I...just need her.

I scoot past her and plop my ass down on the blanket. "So how do you win?"

Her eyes light up as her shy smile transforms into a wide grin. She sits down across from me with her legs spread on either side of the array of food items.

"Well, the goal of this is to finish our conversation. The other stuff is meant to be a reward for opening up, so you lose if you try to take more than just your one lick per turn. If you try to initiate something more sexual, the game is over."

"So what I'm hearing is, there's no real loser in this game."

"That depends on how you look at it."

"Mm-hmm. Ladies first, love."

"No, no. You first."

Fine. "Fuck, marry, kill. Orlando, Portland, Cary."

She seemingly chokes on an inhale of air then shakes her head laughing. In our time apart, she's been on three different domestic professional soccer teams. I may have been a shell of myself without her, but I'm so fucking proud of her. What she's done in her career is remarkable and I want her to talk about it more.

"Hmm, kill Orlando. The only good thing to come out of that was meeting Angie. But that may have more to do with my mental state during those years than the team. Then, I guess fuck Cary and marry Portland. I know they're my current team and I love North Carolina and I love my team, but Portland was something special. I really fucking loved it there. The team just wasn't a fit for me, at all. So when the trade happened I accepted it. Angie getting traded there just confirmed it was meant to be."

I figured this would be her answer. Since being back here, she hasn't brought up Orlando once, and when she talks about her home in North Carolina, it's mostly about her time with Angie and Justine. When she talks

about Portland, though, it's with reverence. That city held magic for her, and I'm genuinely happy she had that, even if only for a few years.

"I think you would love it there," she adds.

"I'd love to go one day." I hope she takes that exactly how I mean that; I would go anywhere with and for her.

"Okay, time to claim my prize." She looks down at each item, wistfully tracing her hand along the top of every jar. She grabs the whipped cream and slowly pops the top off with her thumb. I watch as her gaze roams across my bare chest down to the navy blue pajama pants I have on and my bare feet before she shakes the can and squeezes a dab onto her finger. She leans forward just enough to wipe her finger across my cheek. My damn cheek. Her tongue is a faint whisper across my skin as she licks the cream off me.

I blow out a puff of air. That's cute, but if she thinks I'm going to be so polite during my turn she's in for a rude awakening.

She announces it's her turn and then clasps her hands together and bites her lip in concentration. "Did you ever have any serious relationships after me?"

I chuckle at the question. I should've known she'd waste no time diving right in with the big ones. "No. I've gone on dates, had fuck buddies, been in brief relationships. But anything as serious as I was about you? Nah."

She nods her understanding and then her head dips to the jars in front of us, probably trying to guess which one I'm going to pick.

"Take off your shirt, Olivia."

"What? We said not to make it sexual."

"The fact that you think we can lick food off of each other's bodies without making it sexual is adorable, but don't worry; I'm following your rules. I just need your shirt off to get to the spot I want. So take your shirt off and lie back."

After a brief hesitation, she unceremoniously rips the tank top over her head, tossing it behind her head without looking. Fuck, she's a vision. The soft coils of her hair hang over her shoulders, the tips stopping short just before her dark areolas. Her rich, brown skin looks so soft and inviting. Her eyes blaze with heat before she leans back to rest her head against the

floor. My hand hovers over each option, but I'm drawn to the honey. She already tastes like honey to me, so this will only enhance that flavor. Quickly standing up, I rush over to the drawer closest to the sink to grab a spoon then stalk back over to her.

Her eyes are closed when I drop to my knee by her side, but they fly open when I drip a steady, thick line of honey off my spoon from the top of her chest down to the elastic band of her shorts.

"What are you doing?" she squeals. "It's supposed to be one taste."

"Oh trust me, it will be." And then I flatten my tongue against her lower belly, feeling her muscles ripple beneath my touch. The sweet taste of the honey combined with the heady scent of her arousal have my dick aching, but I never take my eyes off of her as I drag my tongue up the expanse of her stomach and between her breasts. I place a wet kiss at the end of the honey trail. My dick presses against her thigh, drawing a soft whimper from her lips. I sit up and make a show of licking my bottom lip just so I can watch her squirm again.

I hate to burst this bubble of lust. I'd rather continue lapping honey off of her until she comes, but I have a feeling this next question is the whole reason she wanted to play this game, so I press on. "My turn. Same question back to you. Have you dated anyone seriously since me?"

She sits back up, still slightly dazed but focused, determined. "Yes and no. Fuck." She cuts herself off.

"Really, that's your answer? You're not gonna tell me who it is?"

"That would be another question." I take in the wide set of her eyes and the slight shake of her hands and realize that she's not evading my question as some sort of mysterious siren play. She's evading the question because she's nervous.

"Okay then, claim your prize."

Her face heats and she spends a little too much time studying the various containers, but she finally settles on the jar of strawberry sauce.

She takes a slow perusal of my chest, licking her lips as she does. She moves to sit in my lap and grabs my chin between her hands, shifting it from side to side. Without breaking eye contact with me, she dips her finger into

the sauce and drips it behind my ear. I feel a drop hit my back. "Mmm," she moans as she swirls her tongue on the spot, leaving no trace of the sticky sauce behind. She stands over me for a moment, but the minute I raise my hands to wrap around her thighs, she steps away and goes back to her seat across from me.

I don't even fully register her next question, and I'm pretty sure my answer didn't make much sense but she doesn't seem to mind or notice. I pick up my favorite jar of honey and my trusty spoon and get on my knees before her. I gently push her shoulder so she falls back on her elbows. She watches with hooded eyes as I pick up her uninjured leg, drip honey onto her big toe, and suck it into my mouth. I massage her heel as I suck until her toe curls against my teeth and I pull it free.

"You already know my next question. Who is Mr. Yes and No?"

She blows out a harsh breath. "Dante Moore."

Dante Moore was a University of Dayton graduate who went on to join the G league with the Idaho Champions. They used to be the Portland Raiders affiliate team, so it makes sense that she would've met him there. He was good, really good. He made a name for himself early on and everyone just knew he was going to get called up soon. That was until several women came forward and accused him of sexual assault.

I lost track of the story so I never knew what became of him after he was dropped from the league, but with ten accusations against him so early in his career, I knew it was a slim chance I'd ever see him in the sports industry again. Not that I wanted to because in my mind he was a disgusting creep who preyed on women.

My mind is spiraling with curiosity, but I know I need to let her have her reprieve, so I fan my hand out for her to pick her next prize. She quickly picks the chocolate syrup and slathers it over my stomach.

After I answer her next question, I pick up the can of whipped cream and stand up. "Come here." She wastes no time standing from her seat on the blanket and planting her feet in front of me. I instruct her to spin around and move her hair and then I spray a line of whipped cream down her back. On my knees, I use her waist to pull myself up as I lick a fine line up her

spine. I spin her around and swoop her legs from under her so she's in my arms and then I carry her back to the blanket and sit directly next to her.

"Can you tell me about Dante?" I ask.

Her face is laced with regret. "He didn't do it," she rushes out. "We dated when I first moved to Portland. We met at a charity event and we clicked immediately, but I wasn't looking for any type of relationship so I turned him down when he asked. But he just kept…trying. He was sweet, a little cocky, but a man of his word. And he wanted me. I was so messed-up over you, it took me so long to pull my shit together. I still wasn't together when he came along, but he thought I was worth the wait. I wasn't."

She rubs her chest, soothing the ache she must feel there. Without thinking, I reach forward and grab her by the hips, pulling her until she's straddling my waist with her legs stretched out behind my back, and I hold her. I tuck her head against my chest and just let her be. Even though we're both half naked and she's still sticky from the honey, there's nothing sexual about this moment. This is just me trying to absorb some of her pain and make it my own.

When I hear her soft but sharp intakes of air, I speak up. "Let it out, love. You've been holding this too long. I can help you carry it. Let me carry it."

She sniffs and lifts her head to wipe her tears before meeting my eyes. "Fuck, that was literally the point of this game so I wouldn't do this."

I wrap my arms around her waist. "We can turn this game around and make it the fun, flirty game you wanted it to be, trust me on that. But can we just let this moment be what it is? I don't wanna tell you what you need, but I can tell that you don't have anyone in your life that holds space for you to just sit in your emotions. And I know that's by design because sitting in your emotions is the one thing you don't want to do. But I got you. I swear to God if you'd just let me, I would kiss all your scars. I'd kiss them until you could appreciate their beauty the way I do."

This time when her tears fall, I take care to wipe them for her. "Okay. I can do this."

"Take your time."

She takes a deep exhale and then finally she lets it all go. "Dante was

persistent, and though I didn't think I deserved it at the time, it was nice to have his attention. So I gave in with the expectation that we'd keep it light. He wanted more and he told me to keep an open mind, so I did and things were nice, for a while. But then, my dad disapproved. He said I didn't need the distraction of a relationship and that Dante had to go. I warned Dante about it but he, like you, said he wasn't scared of him. And I was just so... tired. Tired of living under his thumb and giving up everything just because he snapped his fucking fingers. So I stayed. Not because I loved him, because I didn't. I liked Dante but never at any point did my feelings for him come anywhere near what I felt, what I feel, for you. So, he lost everything because of my selfish rebellion and had nothing to show for it."

"So, you're saying all the sexual assault accusations..."

"Came from my dad, yeah. I have no idea how he got ten women to come forward or what he said to them. I was able to track them down, and I tried talking to them but none of them would retract their story. And they seemed horrified when I asked. They knew who I was—Jason Harding being my father is no secret—so when I came to them it wasn't Dante they were terrified to speak about, it was my dad. A few of them even made me promise I would tell my dad that they didn't tell me anything."

I scrub a hand down my beard. "Fuck."

"Yeah. Dante was dropped from the G league and not a single person or company in the industry would touch him with a ten-foot pole. I tried to stand beside him, but he wouldn't let me. He didn't want to drag me down with him, which is laughable since it was my fault anyway. He refused to speak to me or see me until I agreed to let him sink alone. I've been sending him money every month since then."

"For almost ten years?"

"Yeah. He gives me shit and tells me to stop, but I don't know what else to do to make up for what I cost him. He does well for himself now—he works in construction—but his plan had been to take care of his entire family when he was called up to the NBA. He has a daughter now too, and I hate that when she grows up she's going to find those articles about him

and question the incredible man that raised her because he is none of the things they said."

"Olivia, you warned him about your father and the threats he made before. He chose to stay. He chose you. It's not all on you."

She laughs. "Now you sound like him."

"Then he's a smart man."

"I hear you. I do. But I can't just make my brain believe something else after spending the last decade thinking I'm horrible."

"You'll get there eventually."

"I guess we'll see. But when I say you should be afraid of my dad, now you understand why."

"I do. Doesn't change shit though."

"Ugh, and I'm the stubborn one."

"I'm stubborn when it comes to you."

"Fine. I'm going to try to work on letting you love me, and you're going to hold me accountable."

I stick my hand between our slick bodies. "Done."

She takes my hand in hers with a devilish smirk. "Good. Now, I think this whole fucking thing calls for a prize."

I chuckle and motion toward the jars behind us. "Pick your poison."

She staggers off of my lap and studies the jars, landing on the chocolate syrup. Returning to her rightful spot on my lap, she drips the chocolate syrup on my chest right over my heart, in the shape of a heart. No words are spoken as she licks me clean, but the message was clear.

"Actually, I think I should get two more since I answered two extra questions."

"Seems only fair."

"Pants, please."

Game on, love. I don't hesitate to pull my pants down where my gray boxer briefs are doing nothing to hide how much I want her. My briefs extend to my midthigh, but she pushes them up farther before taking my spoon and dripping honey on one leg and strawberry sauce on the other.

She folds her knees beneath her and leaves my knees weak as she trails her tongue so painstakingly slowly up each one.

"Delicious combo," she compliments while smacking her lips. This fucking woman.

She drapes her arms over my shoulders when she's done and dives right in with her next question. "What happened between you and Po Po?"

I'm disoriented at first, but I gather my senses quickly. Not an easy feat when she's still perched on my lap. It's a question I was expecting, and given what she shared with me it doesn't make my chest burn the way it did before. Instead, I'm grateful to finally be in a place where I can tell her this. I tell her everything about the decline of Po Po's and my relationship, and she listens intently the entire time.

"I wasn't expecting that and I'm so disappointed. I'm sorry."

"It's not a big deal."

"It is. She's your grandmom, and you shouldn't have to question her love for you, and you shouldn't have to act like you're not hurting because of it."

I smirk at the fierce protectiveness radiating off her right now. She slaps my arm but makes me promise that I'll confront Po Po about all of it sooner rather than later, not maliciously, but to protect my own peace.

"You'll regret it if you don't," she says. "Everyone is always so concerned with preserving the happiness of those headed toward death, but they forget about the ones left behind. Don't carry this with you to your deathbed. Deal with it now so that when you're both gone, the grief has no place to go but back in the ground."

I let that sit with me while I claim my prize and then come our next two questions.

It isn't until her question that I snap completely back to reality. "How many women have you kissed since me?"

Odd question considering she already asked me about women I've dated since her. "Like body count?"

"No, just kiss."

I frown at the question. "I don't know."

"You don't have a guess?"

I rattle off a number that I'm not even sure is correct. It hasn't been a lot, that's for sure, but can I put a number to it? Yeah, if I sat down to really think about it, but it just strikes me as odd that she wants to know about kissing and not sex. My curiosity is piqued so I decide to test a theory.

"How many men have you kissed since me?"

She just stares at me for a moment before that devilish grin is back in place. "Wait, are you skipping your prize?"

"No, I'm delaying it. Answer the question."

"Zero."

"Zero? What do you mean zero?"

"Exactly what I said. Not a single man has touched my lips since you."

How is that possible? "Not even Dante?"

Her smile turns sad. "Not even Dante. He knew about you and he knew I had a rule in place. No kissing. He never tried to pressure me into changing the rule, he just hoped one day I'd eradicate it."

"You had a rule about no kissing? Why?"

"Because. It's so personal. And I only ever wanted to get personal with you."

I reach behind her to grab the bottle of champagne. It pops open with little fuss, thank God, because my dick is already trying to fight its way out of my pants. "Open your mouth, love."

"What are you doing?"

"Proposing a toast."

"To losing?"

"Nope, to getting personal." With that, she leans her head back and opens her mouth wide. I stroke the column of her throat tenderly, marveling in her beauty.

Then, I pour a shot's worth of champagne in her mouth and seal her lips shut with mine. My tongue delves deep into her mouth while she swallows down the liquid and laps my tongue with hers. This is the kind of messy kiss that has our teeth clinking together and neither one of us gives a shit. This is ours.

CHAPTER
Twenty-Three

Olivia

E UPHORIC. THAT'S HOW I WOULD DESCRIBE THIS FEELING.

Even though I heavily protested at the beginning, I was never un-comfortable with Kai staying with me. But now that everything's out in the open? It's like this giant weight has been lifted from my shoulders. It's been three days since my impromptu confessions game, and I'm almost afraid that this state of bliss we've been in since is too good to be true, but I shut that frame of thinking down immediately. I promised Kai I would do better with facing my fears, so I'm going to stand in the light with him for as long as he'll have me.

I'm pulled away from my thoughts by Kai's heavy hands wrapping around my middle and pulling me into him. I lean back so that my head rests against his chest and he kisses my temple.

"You've been washing that glass for five minutes. You good?"

I look down at the sink. The glass I was washing is already clean and the water is just overflowing out of the glass and over my hands. Damn.

"I'm good. Just got lost in thought," I say, turning the water off and placing the glass in the dish drainer.

"Oh yeah? About what?"

His teasing tone prompts a playful eye roll from me. "Morris Chestnut," I lie.

I turn in his arms so he can see my face and his smile drops. "Morris Chestnut?"

"Yeah, I just discovered he has a TikTok and he looks damn good. The things I would let that man do to me."

He tickles my sides which only makes me laugh harder. When I lean forward so my forehead is flush against his chest, gasping for air, he lightly pinches my waist. "You think you're funny, huh?"

"Who's being funny? That man can hit it from the front, the back, the side, and upside down." He silently repeats "upside down" with a frown on his face so I stand on my tiptoes to kiss the furrow between his brows. "But so can you, boo."

He rolls his eyes and waves me off. "Yeah, yeah. Go sit down so I can make you breakfast."

I make no argument as I walk to the kitchen table and sit so I can watch him work. I watch the muscles in his back ripple with every move, making my mouth water. Kai's not bulky, but he's gorgeously toned and strong. My eyes soak in every inch of his shirtless chest. His deep-sepia skin is like a beacon to me. He pulls out the carton of eggs, spinach, cheese, and cherry tomatoes from the fridge and meticulously lines them up on the counter. He's always been extremely organized in the kitchen. His mom, grandmom, and aunt all taught him their different styles of cooking, and he took what he liked from each of them to create his own style.

His head bops along to the music in his brain as he proceeds to make two delicious omelets.

When he brings the completed plates over to the table and hands me a fork before kissing my forehead, nose, and lips, and sitting down, I melt inside. "This is so domestic," I tease. "Thank you."

He gives me a two finger salute in response.

I moan around the first bite of my omelet and then the next. This shit is delicious. "Damn, I fucked up. I should have recorded you cooking and put it on OnlyFans. I'm bout to get you an apron that says 'serving up vitamin D' and make you a star."

He chuckles and grabs the leg of my chair, tugging me closer. "Keep playing and you're gonna be eating something else for breakfast."

I involuntarily lick my lips and look down at his lap which is unfortunately covered by briefs and sweatpants. "That's not the threat you think it is."

His eyes darken as he leans in for a hungry kiss. His hands knead my upper thighs as his tongue meets mine. I scramble into his lap but as I throw my leg over his, my foot hits his plate, sending his half-eaten omelet to the ground. If he notices the plate clattering to the floor below us and breaking, he doesn't show it because he just keeps devouring my mouth. He grips me tighter, pinning my lap against him, and rocks his hips up to meet mine. "Fuck," I mumble. Needing more pressure against my aching sex, I meet his thrust with my own. He peppers kisses against my jawline down to the nape of my neck.

"You are fucking perfection. And you're mine." He grabs a fistful of my hair and yanks it back to bare more of my neck to him. He nips the spot under my collar bone, delivering a delicious bite of pain, then soothes it away with the stroke of his tongue.

I reach up to pull the straps of my tank top off my shoulders, and Kai wastes no time grabbing my right breast and sucking my nipple into his mouth. He sucks and tugs at both of my nipples with slow, measured attention, switching back and forth between nipping at them to sucking hard and slow. His hand trails between our bodies to press against my clit with the heel of his hand. I whimper against his ear, and he pulls his mouth from my nipple to take my mouth in yet another hungry kiss. And when I fall over the edge, his tongue swallows the scream of his name.

"God damn, you always know how to start my morning off right."

He picks me up with zero effort and carries me over to perch on top of the counter. "I gotta live up to my reputation, right? Serving up vitamin D."

He hands me my omelet and points down to the fork lying by my thumb on the edge of the plate. "Eat," he commands.

I clench my thighs together to hide the burst of arousal between my legs at his gravelly voice. "Oh I see. Well, if you wanna be technical, and I do, I haven't been served my D yet."

"That's because your clumsy ass knocked my food over. Did your foot black out and think my breakfast was a soccer ball?"

I bend my head down to hide my giggle. He grabs a broom and starts cleaning up my mess.

"For real, though. I'm so sorry. Do you want to split mine with me? I feel bad you didn't get to finish."

"Nah, don't worry about it. I'm hungry for something else anyway."

I look into his hooded eyes and shiver in anticipation.

I spread my tongue across my bottom lip. "I know what you mean. This omelet was delicious but I'm starving now. If you know what I mean."

By the way he drops the broom, scoops me into his arms, and carts me off to the bedroom I'm guessing he does know what I mean.

After Kai and I finish feasting on each other, I finally manage to check my phone and find two notifications. One is my calendar reminder to send Dante another deposit. The other is a group text with Ciara, Nina, and Sasha.

I wince as my hands automatically start to send Dante his monthly e-check. Both he and Kai are right; I do need to get my guilt over this situation under control. Dante has told me countless times that he doesn't need the money I send him, but I don't know what else to do. For so long it felt like the only thing I could do, as inadequate as that felt. Now, I'm looking to change that.

I complete the transaction to Dante, not ready to disrupt the routine just yet, and switch over to my texts.

Ciara: I need a writing break. Lunch date today?

Nina: Yessss, I need a drink. Or three.

Ciara: Aww what's wrong boo?

Nina: Adulting is ghetto

Ciara: So true

Sasha: I was gonna go back to the shop after my doctor's appointment but…drinks sound better so let's do that

I exchanged numbers with the ladies the day we all met with an agreement that we'd meet up but that has yet to happen, so I'm excited about having some girl time.

Me: Thanks for inviting me. I'm down

Ciara answers a minute later.

Ciara: Oh shit, she's alive! We thought you suffered from DBGD

Me: What's that?

Nina: Death By Good Dick

Ciara: Ayeeee you just get me boo

Nina: *Inserts a gif of Snape from *Harry Potter* saying 'Always'*

Me: *inserts gif of woman spitting out her drink from laughter*

Me: Hold up how did you know Kai and I are fucking?

Sasha: I mean you were fucking each other with your eyes the whole time we were hanging out that day. It was only a matter of time before you were fucking with your private parts

Ciara: *Crying laughing emoji*

Nina: LOL why are you like this?

Sasha: I know no other way

Angie and Justine would love these women. I have to make sure they never meet because I'm not up to being dragged endlessly all the time.

Me: On second thought, I'm too busy for lunch today

Nina: Blah blah blah see you soon

Ciara: WE RIDE AT DAWN BITCHES

Sasha: ...

Ciara: Sorry, always wanted to say that

They send me the location and official time for lunch so I start getting ready. Once I'm dressed in my favorite jeans, a crop top, and a flannel shirt, I head to find Kai on his computer on the couch.

"Where you off to?" he asks.

"I have a lunch date with the Cole women."

"Oh Lord, let me make sure my phone volume is up."

I raise a questioning brow at that and he chuckles. "Why you say that?"

"Because I already know you're gonna be calling me to pick you up when they ply your ass with bottomless drinks. You've had maybe two drinks since your injury, so I know your tolerance is shit."

I smack his chest. "First of all, it's lunch, not brunch, so the drinks aren't bottomless. Second, Ciara's pregnant ass won't be drinking, so I wouldn't need you anyway, sir."

"Yeah, okay. Keep it up. Just don't be on no 'can I sing to you' shit when I pick you up."

Against my will, I burst into a fit of laughter but manage to pull it together to glare at him before walking out of the house.

At lunch, I'm not surprised by how open the ladies are with me considering how they immediately accepted me the day we met. I learn that Ciara moved to Texas as an attempt to get away from a stalker. She ended up meeting Lincoln when he took care of her after she sustained a concussion and that Sasha's daughter, Nevaeh, got caught up in the stalker's plot. I also learn that Nina and Isaiah's baby is the result of what was supposed to be a one-night stand, and their relationship was almost ruined by his nasty ex. They all fought so hard to end up with the love of their lives, which only makes me admire their relationships more.

What does surprise me, however, is how willing I am to be open with them in return. Before I realize what I'm doing, I find myself unloading all of my past with Kai on them, every detail.

Once I finish, everyone's shock and rage is clear on their faces. Sasha is the first to speak up, rolling her neck before she starts. "I'm gonna say this and I mean this with the utmost disrespect. Fuck your bitch-ass daddy."

"Agreed. I don't know if we've known each other long enough for me to tell you how many ways I've researched how to kill someone but...do with that information what you will." I don't let on where my thoughts go at Ciara's suggestion, but they get very dark for a moment.

"Yeah, your dad has earned his place next to my parents in the shitty-ass parent hall of fame." Nina's parents passed away in a train accident last year, but that didn't stop her from speaking her mind about them and the neglect of their children.

"Believe me, I'm right there with y'all, but I'm trying not to give him too much of my energy. I'm trying to stop thinking so much and just let myself be happy with Kai this time."

Nina grabs my hand. "Good. You deserve that. You both do."

"Can I be honest for a second?" Sasha asks.

Nina's eyelids lower. "When have you ever not been?"

Sasha sucks her teeth. "Anyway, Liv, I wasn't sure about you at first."

"I could tell."

"Yeah, sorry. My face speaks my mind even when I don't. But I hope you understand that I didn't know a damn thing about you before you showed up. Then we found out that you broke Kai's heart years ago and all our minds were spinning. I look at those guys like my extra brothers so I don't like when people fuck with them. I remember when I met Kai, he seemed so...sad. He was always laid-back and chill, but he just had this lingering sadness about him. Over time, he seemed to find his joy again, but the minute I met you I knew I had it all wrong. He wasn't truly happy until you came back."

I take a sip of my lemonade—since I decided not to drink after all—to distract myself from the tears trying to fight their way out of my eyes. I

hate that I put Kai through all those years of torment, but I know I'll never be the source of his pain again.

We move on to much lighter topics, and I feel so at home with these women.

Ciara and I agree to go rock climbing together when I'm a little more healed and she's a little less pregnant. When our food is done and the bill is paid, we continue sitting and talking until Ciara checks her phone and abruptly says it's time to go.

"Damn, bitch, what's the rush?" Sasha asks when Ciara hurriedly stands from the table.

Ciara looks sheepish as she makes eye contact with all of us. "Lincoln just got home."

"So?"

"So, I need some dick, okay?"

Nina chokes on the last sip of her drink. "Umm, what?"

"Look, y'all. Pregnancy has made me horny as hell, and now that Lincoln's home from work I gotta get it in. Like now."

"This whole damn lunch was your idea, ma'am. You said you needed a writing break."

"Yeah, I did. And I also needed a distraction from the fact that Lincoln wasn't home to break my back."

"Oh my God, thirsty-ass bitch." Sasha rolls her eyes.

"And proud of it. How you think I ended up pregnant in the first place? Sorry, your brothers have addicting dicks that continue to knock us up," she says with a shrug.

"Now, see. That was unnecessary."

Ciara chuckles as she shuffles out the door without a look back at us. Nina drives home the fact that Ciara wasn't lying about the Cole brothers' addicting dicks, and Sasha flips her off, making my laughter impossible to contain.

They head to the bathroom and I let them know I'll wait for them outside. I make my way out not too far behind Ciara, and as if she senses my

presence, she turns and runs back over to me. "Hey, Liv. Sorry, I wanted to give this to you earlier, but I didn't want to make a big show of it."

She passes me a card and when I look down at it, I see it's for a therapist. My eyebrows peak in confusion so she quickly explains. "You've been through a lot. I know what it's like to bottle that shit in. My best unsolicited advice? Don't. That's my therapist, but if you don't wanna go to her she has plenty of recommendations. No pressure, just…extending a hand."

"Thank you, Ci. I appreciate it."

"No problem, boo. You're family now. Now, off to my dick appointment with my husband. Byeeee."

I twirl the card around in my hand, studying the elegant lettering. I saw a psychologist when my ACL tear happened, but that was mostly concentrated on determining whether I had a fear of reinjury, which could lead to that very thing happening. I don't have a fear of reinjury, but I do have a fear of laying my demons out in front of a stranger. I bit Kai's head off when I thought he was hinting at therapy for me, but I honestly don't know why. Actually, I do. Just another case of letting Jason Harding's way of life influence mine. Maybe if he had gotten therapy for all the shit he went through he could've stopped the trauma with his generation, instead of letting it bleed into mine.

"Go on a date with me," Kai whispers in my ear, making my stomach flutter.

I'm lying on my stomach but I still shy away from him, a smile firmly planted on my face. I look around to the other PTs working in the open area where we're working on strength training to make sure no one is watching us. "Kai, aren't we supposed to just be therapist and client when we're in your building?"

He releases a dry chuckle. "Olivia, at no point in time have we ever been *just* anything—let alone therapist and client." He steps away and continues to guide me through the hamstring curls I'm doing. It takes me

a moment to ignore the pulsing between my thighs to keep up with the exercises.

"So, what are you thinking for this date?"

"You let me worry about that. You just need to trust me."

That night, the grin on my face is downright maniacal as I look at Kai painting the male equivalent of my canvas, completely focused on the task at hand.

When Kai asked me on a real date, I'm embarrassed to admit I was nervous. I was nervous because I knew being seen in public in an intimate setting could get back to my dad and that would possibly set him off.

I'm not proud of letting that be the first thought to cross my mind, but I am proud of the fact that despite that, I said yes anyway. And being here with Kai, at a couples' paint and sip event, makes it all worth it. I'm impressed by what he put together for us. He knows that my ideal dates involve food and adventure, but with my injury I can't really do the things I would normally consider adventurous. This paint and sip is an excellent improvisation. The canvases we're painting are called the *This is Me* set. My canvas is a naked Black woman with her knees up to her chest and her arms across her breasts with the words "I am" painted across her forehead and words like "enough" and "blessed" painted all over her body. Kai's is a shirtless Black man only shown from the waist up, likewise with the words "I am" painted across his forehead and words like "kind", "safe", and "enough" painted all over his body. I know it's no coincidence that Kai chose the designs he did, but neither of us mention it out loud. We let the moment speak for itself.

The vibes of this place are immaculate. The room we're in is bright white but the walls are decorated with the paintings of past customers. Not only is it date night but it's also old-school R&B night so our instructor's melodic voice is accompanied by the sweet sounds of Whitney Houston, New Edition, Sade, Brian McKnight, and so many others. A few of the people at the event sing along with the songs when our instructor, Emerald, isn't talking and one of the couples even gets up to dance when Keith Sweat's "Nobody" starts to play. The man next to us whispers

something in his woman's ear, and whatever he said makes her giggle intensely. I notice that instead of painting the picture with long, black, curly hair to match the instructor's painting, she's painting hers to have burgundy locs to match her own. Her man has altered his painting as well. Instead of the short twists and full beard depicted in the original, his reflects his own long, dark locs, thin mustache, and light chinstrap. The woman notices me admiring their altered drawings and introduces herself as Chenille and her man as Quentin.

Kai brought a cooler that held a charcuterie board and sparkling wine for us to enjoy while painting. Chenille and Quentin brought assorted chocolates, cheese, grapes, and white wine. Chenille offers to share her chocolates with us, so I offer her a choice of our snack options and she takes me up on the cucumbers. This prompts the couple across from us to join the group. The shorter man, who I learn is named Jalen, offers to share the beer he brought while his partner, Sean, offers their praline pecans. Before I know it, the six of us have our own party going on. While our instructor walks around to check on everyone's progress, Chenille leans in to ask how long everyone has been together. Jalen and Sean answer together for five years, married for two. Chenille and Quentin answer one year. When the question comes to us, I debate how detailed we should be and then I remember that Christmas is around the corner. That means it's been three months since I've been back in Austin. Three months. I came in with every intention to keep my emotional distance from Kai but in three months' time I'm now going to sleep with my legs wrapped around his waist and waking up with his face between my thighs every morning. I chuckle at the complete lack of willpower I have against this man, but then I hear his answer to Chenille's question. "Well, Olivia has owned my heart for twenty years."

Quentin lets out a low whistle while Chenille's, Jalen's, and Sean's eyes widen. "Shit, really? You don't even look old enough to have twenty years under your belt. I know we don't crack but damn," Sean says, looking between Kai and me as if he's trying to find signs of aging on us he may have missed before.

Kai turns to me and gives me those three kisses I love so much. "Yeah, well that's what happens when you meet the love of your life at twelve."

Chenille swoons at Kai's words and honestly, same.

Quentin chimes in next. "You knew she was the one at twelve?"

"I don't think I can say that because at twelve I really didn't understand what love was, but I did know that there was no one quite like her and I would do anything to keep her around." At that, Quentin leans over to dap Kai up.

"You got a good one there, girl," Chenille compliments.

"Don't I know it?"

Paint night ends with Emerald complimenting all of our paintings, Kai and me taking a group picture with our new friends, and us exchanging numbers with them before leaving. When we walk outside, I wrap my hand in Kai's and take a moment to look up at the sky and breathe in the cool Austin air.

"Tonight was perfect," I tell Kai, my eyes still closed, head still facing the sky.

"It's not over yet, love." He refuses to tell me anything else; he just drags me to the car and places our paintings on the backseat. A sudden urge to have his lips against mine hits me, and I don't fight it. No, I grab him and pin him against the car and take what I want. In a matter of seconds, Kai has reversed our positions, me pinned to the car with my leg hiked up to his waist. His calloused hand against my bare thigh sends chills up my spine. "What do you want, Olivia? If you want me to fuck you up against this car right here and now, say the word."

Fuck, his words hit me right in my core. As much as I do want him to take me against this car, the open parking lot doesn't offer enough cover to not get arrested for public indecency, so I reluctantly push him away so we can get going.

Our next stop is a place I recognize. It's a karaoke bar called The Right Note that I always wanted to visit when I lived here. By the time I was old enough to go inside, I would've rather cut off my right foot than use it to step into this city.

The bar has low blue lighting with a spotlight on the dark slate stage. The red leather couches are lower to the ground with glass coffee tables in front of them. It gives off more of a lounge feel than I was expecting, but I love it.

When we walk in, a light-brown-skinned, bald-headed man is killing "I Wanna Know" by Joe. He looks to stand at about six feet tall and he has on designer jeans, a fitted, long-sleeved navy blue shirt, and one of Momentum's most popular shoes—the Momentum threes in the blue, gray, and white colorway. The women in the audience are going crazy over him, and he's eating this shit up like he's a real performer. Kai and I laugh as we make our way to a couple of empty barstools. We order wings just as Joe Jr. finishes up his song, and we continue cheering everyone on throughout the night—the mother and daughter duo who sing Gloria Gaynor's "I Will Survive," the woman I assume to be close to my age butchering Selena's "Como La Flor," and the group of college girls singing Destiny's Child's "Bills, Bills, Bills." The whole time, Kai stays in constant physical contact with me. Whether it's his hand squeezing my thigh, his arm wrapping around my shoulder, or his lips bending down to whisper in my ear, some piece of him is always touching me and I live for it. My body is so in tune with him at all times.

"Okay, y'all. Next up, Kai and Olivia want to sing 'The Boy is Mine.' Give it up for them!"

What the fuck? I shift in my seat, sure that I heard the emcee wrong, but when I turn and meet Kai's expectant eyes, I know I didn't.

"Kai, what the fuck did you do?"

He doesn't bother responding with words. He just stands up and holds his hand out for me to grab. Damn, I want to be mad at him. I really do. But the appearance of that damn gorgeous dimple makes all my anger dissipate. Fuck it. I grab his hand and rush around him so that I'm leading him to the stage instead of the other way around.

"Good song choice. Ready to be my Brandy?"

He smirks as he adjusts his mic stand. "Ready to be whatever your fine ass wants me to be."

The song starts up and my nerves melt away immediately. This shit is fun. Kai actually sounds pretty decent and then there's me. I've got a voice made for a mute button and I know it, but I couldn't care less. Kai and I are milking this performance for all it's worth, getting in each other's faces singing about a boy we each claim as our own. The audience is torn behind plugging their ears at the sound of my voice and enjoying the fact that Kai is giving this performance his all with me. Enjoying the show wins out, and when it's over, we receive a standing ovation, but when I offer to do an encore an emphatic "no" sounds from the crowd. Kai kisses me long and hard before we step off the stage, earning another round of applause.

"I didn't think you were actually gonna get up there with me," he confesses when we make our way back to the bar.

"Wrong, bitch. The fearless Olivia is back."

"Nah, fearless Olivia would've let me fuck her in that parking lot."

"I said fearless, not stupid. Your dick is good, baby, but I'm not trying to go to jail over it." I would probably go to jail behind his dick but I'm not going to tell his ass that.

"You saying my dick isn't jailworthy? What about my tongue?" The question is emphasized by the trail of his tongue on the spot behind my ear. "What about my hand?" he asks while his hand disappears under my skirt.

"Shit," I hiss.

"What's wrong, love? You need me to stop?"

I should say yes, because even though we're at the back of the bar and no one is paying attention to us because they're enthralled by the group of men singing a Backstreet Boys song, anyone could see us. But God, I want to say no because he feels so good.

"Answer me, Olivia. You want me to stop?" His voice is harsh in my ear, filled with primal need.

"I...I...fuck. No," I whimper.

"No, what?"

"No, I don't want you to stop." As soon as the word stop leaves my

mouth, that's exactly what he does. He stops. His hands and lips leave my body in a rush, and I'm immediately cold in his absence.

He leans in close but doesn't touch me again. "Go to the bathroom, take off your panties, and wait for me."

I wobble as I step down from my stool, but he steadies me and sends me on my way.

When I get to the bathroom, I check to make sure no one else is there and then I step out of my blue lace panties. I shove the panties in my small purse and wonder what the hell I'm thinking doing this but wanting nothing more than for Kai to ruin me in this bathroom.

The air shifts the moment Kai steps into the bathroom and locks the door. He stalks over to me, his eyes looking slightly unhinged. He traps me between him and one of the sinks.

"Are you enjoying our date, Olivia?"

I swallow hard and shift my weight from leg to leg. "It's the best date I've had in a long time."

"Good. Me too. You've been driving me crazy in this fucking skirt all night." He takes a long perusal of my body, clad in a black satin skirt with a high slit and a white off-the-shoulder crop top. I don't get dressed often, but I wanted to show out for our date tonight and I guess I did that based on his appraisal.

"You like it?"

"Don't ask questions you already know the answer to. Where are your panties?"

I point down to my purse and he holds his hand out for them. As soon as they're in his possession he spins me around to face the sink.

"You know, I've been trying to be gentle with your leg. Not put you in certain positions, stuff like that."

"Fuck the leg," I say, cutting him off.

His answering grin is downright sinister as he uses my panties to tie my hands behind my back. The panties are barely there but they're enough to tie around my small wrists. He pushes my skirt up to reveal my bare ass, and I shiver when the coolness of the AC grazes me. "My thoughts exactly.

Now, you claim my dick isn't jailworthy so you better be quiet, love. Or else I'm gonna have to gag you with these."

The sensation between my legs demands attention, and he answers its call by dropping to his knees. His mouth on me is hot, wet, and magnificent. He expertly switches from hard, punishing sucks to soft, languid strokes. Back and forth between sucking and licking before dipping his tongue into me and slurping up everything my body has to give him. I pull at my restraint, not actually trying to get away, but trying to get my hands on something, anything, to anchor me back down to this earth because Kai is trying to suck the life out of me. I have to bite down so hard to contain my scream that I feel the copper taste of blood fill my mouth.

The pressure is too much but so fucking good, and when his tongue makes its way up to my asshole and dips inside, my knees buckle. His right arm wraps around my waist to keep me balanced and keep the sink from impaling me, while three of his fingers on his left hand spread me wide open.

A loud moan escapes my mouth and Kai tsks against me. "What did I tell you?"

"T-t-to be quiet," I stammer.

"You gonna do what I say?"

"Yes."

"Yes, what?" His thumb presses against my clit, and I barely manage to fight off the moan.

"Yes, sir."

"That's my good girl." His fingers continue to pump inside of my pussy while his tongue continues to work my ass, and I can feel myself losing control. I clench around his fingers and he bites my ass cheek. "Don't run from it, Olivia. Give me what's mine."

Fuck. His fingers curl again and I can't hold back anymore. I collapse against the sink, my release coating his fingers, and he shoves his face back to my pussy as if he doesn't want to waste a single drop.

My legs are shaking and my heart is racing but I need more. I need him to fill me.

"I need you. Now."

He lines his dick up with my entrance. The cool touch of his piercing elicits a sharp intake of air from my chest. And then he stops. The silence is a second too long before he whispers, "Nah."

"Nah?" The fuck?

"I'm gonna need to hear you say this dick is jailworthy before I give it to you."

We stare at each other in the mirror for a moment before we burst into a fit of laughter. "I fucking hate you."

"Is that right?" He slaps his dick against my pussy and my eyes shutter closed.

"I want to. So, so bad."

He chuckles. Maniacal bastard. "So, tell me what I wanna hear."

"You. Are. Annoying," I cry out, each word punctuated by my attempts to get his dick inside of me.

"Not the magic words, Olivia."

Shit. He slips the tip in but quickly removes it, and at this point I'll say whatever the fuck he wants. "Your dick is jailworthy."

"One more time for me."

I glare at him over my shoulder, but I comply and say it again, and my last word is slightly cut off as he slams into me and the sound of our skin slapping together fills the room. He unties my hands and places a soft kiss against each wrist before gripping and kneading my ass and stroking me harder. My hands fight for purchase on the edge of the sink as I throw my ass back to meet his strokes. *Slap slap slap.* It's all I can hear outside of my heart beating out of my chest.

He leans down and lays wet kisses down my spine and back up. When he comes back up he bites my shoulder blade hard enough that I know he'll leave a mark, and the thought of his mark on me has my walls clenching around him, pulling a thick groan from him. He soothes the bite with a lick and then reaches back to grab a fist full of my hair and force my head up to the mirror. "Look at me when you come," he demands.

That's when everything goes black. I free-fall into ecstasy, chasing a

high only he can give me. We come together and I slump over in his hold, feeling nothing and everything at the same time. My ears are ringing and my entire body is vibrating with pleasure, but everything outside of this moment, outside of us, feels faint and distant.

We both release a soft groan when he pulls out of me and spins me around, then my ass is hitting the cold hard edge of the sink.

"Jesus, Kai. What are you doing to me?" I can't take anymore but fuck if I won't accept whatever he's about to give me.

"You're not getting these back." He points to the panties he threw on the ground when he untied me, picking them up and shoving them in his pocket. "And though the thought of my cum running down your legs makes me hard all over again, I won't make you leave here like that, so I'm going to clean you up." His way of cleaning me up is shoving his face between my legs again and tearing another orgasm from me before finally wiping me down. I can barely walk out of that bathroom let alone care to check if anyone sees us leaving.

The next day, I'm doing some stretching, some for my injured leg and some for my deliciously sore center, and Kai is about to go for a run, but he catches a glimpse of the FaceTime call coming through my phone and stops in his tracks.

"Ummm, why is Auntie calling you?"

Shit, I forgot to mention to Kai that I've kept in touch with Auntie all these years.

"Okay, so very short summary, we never lost touch. I've been in contact with her since leaving Houston. I just asked her not to tell you, and I also asked her not to tell me about you. I'm so sorry; I should've told you that." When I left, I intended to cut everyone off, but I just couldn't let go of Auntie. Back then I think that she was looking for a daughter as much as I was looking for a mom. She and Kai's dad lost their mom when they were

teenagers, so she understood my loss better than anyone I knew and so we clung to each other.

I flash sympathetic eyes in Kai's direction. "Hey, Auntie," I greet when the FaceTime call connects.

"Don't think because you're thirty-two that you're too old to get knocked upside the head," she glares.

"What did I do?"

"First of all, it's been weeks since I heard from you and second, when I did speak to your ass not once did you mention you and Kai were back together."

My eyes bulge at her words just as Kai steps over into the frame.

"Nephewwwww!" Patrice calls out, waving to him. "Oooh, y'all are shacking up too? See I knew y'all would find your way back to each other eventually."

"Back up, Auntie. How did you know Kai and I are back together?"

"No, let's back up a little further, Auntie. Why didn't you tell me you were still in contact with Olivia?"

Her eyes narrow at his accusatory tone. "Because I'm grown and don't have to tell you a damn thing."

For a brief, blink-and-you-miss-it second the clear frustration on Kai's face gives way to hurt. He covers it up so quickly that I assume Auntie missed it, but her next words prove she saw it. "You had a support system, sweetie. You had me, your mom and dad, your grandmom, and Kylie. Liv didn't and she's my baby girl. I needed to be there for her."

Kai huffs but squeezes my shoulder in understanding.

Auntie explains to us that she saw the Instagram post about us and had to call me to get in my ass about keeping our status from her when she was the one rooting for us this entire time. I'm too baffled by her words to even defend myself. Not that I could anyway. She was right; I should've told her. My focus goes back to the Instagram post as her voice fades away to the background, hammering away at Kai for not telling her.

Who the fuck would care enough about Kai and me to post us on Instagram? I open the app on my computer, and sure enough there's a post

from early this morning on the *Rumor Has It* gossip blog page. There are two pictures. The first is of Kai and me walking out of the paint and sip place, his hand on the small of my back, me smiling up at him, with our paintings on prominent display in our hands. The second is a picture of us in that parking lot, his face in my hands as I reach up to kiss him. It's a good thing I didn't let him fuck me in that parking lot because it seems that something worse than being arrested for public indecency would've happened; the Internet would've seen my bare ass. The caption reads:

> @RumorHasIt: Rumor Has It physical therapist to the stars, Kai Morris, is fixing more than just soccer star Olivia Harding's injury. They're supposed to be working together after a devastating torn ACL benched Harding for the rest of the season but they're looking a little familiar to me. If I were her I'd let Kai work me out too *wink emoji*. What you think, y'all? Budding love or winter fling?

Black spots line my vision as I stare at the words on the screen, reading them over and over again, trying to make sense of them. I've been a professional soccer player for thirteen years, and I've been featured in the media a few times for my skills or to highlight my teams. The details of my personal life have been featured on social media exactly once in my life and that was when I was seen leaving a club with a well-known basketball player. I faded right back into D-list territory when it was later reported that the same basketball player turned out to be none other than Tyson Richards and that Justine, Angie, and two of Tyson's teammates were with us as well. As far as I know, Kai has never been talked about on gossip sites, so why now are we big news and first thing the morning after our date? This has my father written all over it—that much is obvious—but what I can't figure out is why. Why would he bother exposing our relationship to the world? Was it just his way of letting me know he knows? He's normally more direct than that. What's his play?

I keep scrolling the comments until I come across one from Tevin, the

man I ghosted after he tried to kiss me instead of adhering to my boundaries. It reads:

@TheRealTevin: definitely a fling. Ol girl doesn't know the meaning of love.

What a fucking dick. Just like a man to place blame at the woman's feet for their refusal to simply be a decent human and not deliberately make her uncomfortable. I can't go after my father publicly, not now. He's too much of a loose cannon to attack now but Tevin? Oh, I have time for his ass.

My fingers fly across the keyboard, typing a response.

@InLivInColor: Guess I was waiting for a real man to show me what that looked like

Kai and Patrice's voices come back into focus. I completely forgot they were even here. Patrice makes me promise to call her to update her more later and then rushes off the phone when her hubby whispers something nasty to her that I wish I didn't have to hear.

Kai pushes the top of my laptop with his middle finger, obstructing my view of the screen. "Where are you right now? Because I'm hoping I don't have to go searching for fearless Olivia."

Concern mars his features, and I grab his face between my hands. "She's right here. I'm not worried about him and his bullshit."

"Good. There's no reason to be."

Not true, but I stay quiet because I understand the sentiment. This time, I'll be ready for whatever Jason Harding has to throw at me.

CHAPTER
Twenty-Four

Kai

I FORCE MYSELF TO STAY IN PLACE INSTEAD OF PACING THE LONG, narrow hallway. Pacing makes me appear nervous and I am far from nervous. I'm fucking thrilled with what's about to happen.

When Olivia told me about everything her dad did back then, I wanted to track him down immediately. I was able to contain my ire for a few days because Olivia needed me more and she is and always will be my priority. But now? Now that he's sticking his nose where it doesn't belong and causing Olivia even more pain? He's going to have to face me.

I've been waiting in this corridor for ten minutes. It's clever, really. I showed up at his office demanding to see him, and when his assistant asked if I had an appointment I let her know that he'd see me and to just give him my name. We both know he'll see me, but he's determined to make it look like he's the one in control by making me wait. He might even think if he makes me wait long enough, I'll give up and leave. He'd be mistaken.

The door opens behind me and I hear his heavy footsteps heading my

way, but I don't give him the satisfaction of turning to face him. I wait for him to step up to my side. "Kai Morris, it's been a long time, son." Son. My lips slip into a sneer but I school it back into indifference before I turn to face him fully.

"Jason." He's older now. Where he used to have a low cut fade, he now is bald. His beard is now mostly white while his mustache and bushy eyebrows have a salt-and-pepper tint to them. The lines around his eyes and forehead are more pronounced, probably from all the damn scowling he spent his life doing. He still looks sharp though. I understand why people are intimidated by him, but I'm not one of those people.

He holds his hand out for me to shake and when I don't reciprocate he lets out a dark chuckle and then motions for me to join him in his office.

"What brings you by today?"

"I think you and I are long overdue for a conversation."

He casually leans against the edge of his desk, and I stay standing behind the chairs positioned in front of the desk. "Is that right? What about? I assume it's something to do with your client, or should I call her your girlfriend now? Or maybe her original title, my daughter."

Or what about her damn name? This motherfucker is so insistent upon disrespecting her at every turn.

"I'm not here to clarify my relationship with Olivia to you. I'm here to clarify the parameters of your relationship with her going forward."

At my statement, a twisted grin spreads across his face. He doesn't take me seriously and that's fine by me. If he doesn't see me coming, it makes it all too easy to eviscerate him.

"By all means, please spell it out for me. I'm genuinely interested. What are the rules for my relationship with the child I raised?" He nods his head in mock interest but the sarcasm drips from his words.

"Simply put, there isn't a relationship. She's done with you and more importantly, you're done with her. You don't watch her, you don't have her followed, you don't threaten her, you don't utter her fucking name. You had your chance to be her dad and you chose to be whatever the fuck you call yourself being instead. So now you get to forget she exists and leave her in

peace. It's the least you can do for her." He didn't deserve to call himself her father. He didn't even deserve to call himself a man. A man is supposed to care for his daughter, be her first example of true love. He's supposed to be the person she can come to no matter what. All the things I would've been for my child if I'd had the chance, but he squandered his and not only that, he also failed at his mission. He wanted Olivia to be just like him—cold, calculating, only caring about succeeding in her field and nothing else.

She isn't any of those things. She's warm, compassionate, funny, considerate. She's bold and powerful but she doesn't use that against people. She uses her power and bravery to lift people up. She cares so much that she's too often willing to sacrifice her own well-being for the good of others. Olivia thinks she's weak because of how she handled the situation with her dad, but the very fact that she is the incredible woman she is in spite of him is a testament to her strength, not her weakness.

"The least I can do? Please. If it weren't for me, she wouldn't even have a career. Her lazy ass was too busy sniffing behind you to prioritize what was really important. I *made* her see what was important. I gave her the career of her dreams, son. And I could take it away with the snap of my fingers. This little knight in shining armor act you're putting on to appease your sense of justice or to impress my fickle daughter is…nice. It's honorable, even. But no matter what sob story she wants to tell you about how her daddy is just so terrible, the facts remain that she'd be lost without me and she'd do well to remember that."

I'm not a man that is quick to anger. It's just not an emotion I allow myself to access often. Maybe it's because I have a younger sister that can often push me too far so I've had to learn to temper my thoughts quickly. Or maybe it's because I deal with clients who are often angry about the circumstances that led them to me and I'd rather try to bring them peace than fuel their fire. People may fool themselves into thinking just because I normally keep calm means that I can't hold my own. They'd be wrong, but I keep that close to my chest. The only place I like to come out the gate with aggression is the bedroom. Jason Harding is the one person who can push me past my limits, though, because he often dances right across my trigger

point—Olivia. I don't tolerate any mistreatment of her, even from herself. Listening to this fool disparage and threaten her makes me want to beat his ass so savagely he'd be unrecognizable to anyone with the misfortune of knowing him.

I step into his space and he immediately goes on high alert, though he tries to appear nonplussed. I lower my voice to a low growl. "You'd do well to remember that I'm not the young boy that grew up across the street from you anymore. You'd be wise to consider that you don't know me or what I'm capable of before you proceed further."

He smirks. "You're taking a big risk for her. Is she worth it? As I remember it, she didn't do the same for you back then. How sure are you that she wouldn't leave you out in the cold this time too?"

The smug look on his face tells me he thinks he's hit a nerve. The truth is, he may have a little. I have no doubt in my mind that Olivia loves me and wants to choose me. My worry is that she'll revert back to trying to protect me by doing something else stupid. My smile never wavers. I let out a natural, relaxed laugh and press on. "Like I said, you don't know me anymore, Jason. And I'm not going to put the pieces together for you. I'll just let you hang yourself with your own rope. Understand this though, I will go to war behind that woman."

If he has any reply to that, he can say it to my back because I'm already out the door.

"Oh my God, that sounds delicious. Do you think you could share the recipe with me? I may have to try them for Christmas this year."

"Gladly. I'm gonna miss making them with Angie and Justine this year, so I can even come here and make them with you if you want."

My mom grabs Olivia's hand in excitement. "Wonderful."

Olivia just finished telling my mom about how she makes *rosquillas* with Angie every year to take to her family. Apparently, she normally gorges

on them this time of year because the season is over and they always make a big batch for Christmas.

It's nice seeing Olivia with my parents again. She was worried about how they'd receive her because of how things ended with us, but I told her that they were more upset that they hadn't seen her in the three months she'd been back than about that.

Her fears subsided the moment we stepped inside my parents' home and my mom wrapped her up in a tight hug. Tears sprang to her eyes when my dad told her they'd missed her, called her baby girl, and gave her a kiss on the temple. They've had so many questions about her life in the last thirteen years, but they've been careful not to bring up her dad since I texted them a heads-up about the situation. My dad gushed his pride for how far she's come in the pros, and my mom wanted to hear all about North Carolina since she's never been there.

Now, while she and my mom exchange recipes, I pull my dad aside to give him the details I'd left out in our phone conversation. I give him the full rundown of my encounter with Jason and he listens intently the whole time.

He lets out a low whistle when I'm done. "Whew, I knew that man was a cold motherfucker but that's what he had to say about his own daughter?"

"Yep."

"Some people shouldn't reproduce. Okay, so what do you and Liv need? You've gotta be prepared for backlash."

"I'm on it already. I've got a friend looking into him, and I'll see what I can use." I may not have the money or power Jason claims to have, but I've been in my career a long time. I've made friends along the way. Friends with resources and who are willing to do me favors not because of fear but because they respect me and I respect them.

"And you'll let me know if you need any help? I know how protective you are of Liv and we are too, so anything we can do to give you both peace of mind, we'll make it happen."

"I know, Pops. I appreciate it. I'm good right now though."

He nods his head along with me, mulling my words over. Once he's

satisfied that I'm telling the truth, he switches gears. "And how are things going with Liv? You guys are together together or still figuring things out?"

I laugh at his use of "together together" then turn to see my mom and Olivia still chatting away in the living room. "We're together. I'm all in. She says she is too."

"But you have doubts?"

"Nah, not doubts about that. Just trying to make sure she understands she doesn't need to protect me like she thought she was doing before. If she disappears on some superwoman shit again I think I might lose my mind."

"I think you're both on some superhero shit when it comes to each other. Be patient with her. You can't blame her for feeling just as protective of you as you are of her. It's how it's supposed to be. You've just got to communicate. Remember your goal is the same—to be together. You can figure out how to protect each other without sacrificing your relationship. Martyrs don't make good partners."

When Christmas rolls around, I brace myself for the day. My parents won a cruise trip through a radio contest, and they were going to turn it down since it would mean they wouldn't be home for Christmas until I convinced them to go. Kylie and I are grown; we don't need our parents to sacrifice a trip on our behalf. This does mean I'll be spending Christmas with Po Po without them as a buffer though. She and I still haven't had our much-needed sit-down, but I figure the holidays are not the time.

I expect Christmas dinner to be awkward but it really isn't. Po Po is having a good day. She doesn't complain about the food she can't eat, and she only stumbles over her words a couple of times. She seems content, even with our limited interactions. Olivia squeezes my thigh under the table to remind me that she's here for me.

To my surprise, Kylie seems to be more open to Olivia's presence this time. There have been no snarky comments or passive-aggressive behavior. She seems a little more reserved than she normally is, focusing most of her attention on Po Po and me, but not in a malicious way. I think she's still sorting through her hurt toward Olivia, and likewise I think Olivia doesn't know

how to approach Kylie. That's something the two of them are going to have to manage themselves, as much as I wish I could fix it for them.

"Surprise! Merry Christmas, family!" A voice cuts through the condo and the distinct tone brings a smile to my face. Olivia, Kylie, and I all rise from our seats to greet the unexpected guest.

When we step into the living room, Auntie is stepping through the door. The last time I saw her, her hair was in two French braids that went all the way down her back. Today she has blonde twists that I now know are called Havana twists through Olivia's fawning over them and the floral jumpsuit she's wearing. Seeing how tightly Auntie and Olivia cling to each other is beautiful. I don't know how I missed the fact that they were still in touch all these years. Part of me wishes I had known but another part is just grateful they had each other. As much as I hate that it's taken us over a decade to come back together, I know the timing is how it was meant to be. Olivia wasn't ready to step out of her father's shadow before. Reconnecting any sooner would've only gotten us both hurt again.

Auntie's husband, Curtis, steps in behind her carrying two carry-on bags. I dap Curtis up while I wait for Olivia, Kylie, and Auntie to finish loving on each other so I can get my hug. She gives me a sloppy kiss on my cheek, and I know I'm going to have to wipe her plum lipstick off of me.

"What are y'all doing here? If you would've given me a heads-up, I could've picked you up from the airport."

She shakes her head. "Then that would've ruined the surprise, now wouldn't it, nephew? Xay told me he and Lisa were spending Christmas adrift at sea, so we decided to hop on a plane."

She loops one arm through Olivia's and the other through Kylie's and guides them to the kitchen where Po Po is still sitting down but smiling in her direction. "Patrice, it is so good to see you," she greets.

Auntie breaks away from the girls to go over to Po Po and lean down for a hug and a kiss. "Hi, Maggie. You're looking fierce, girl. Is that the glow of a man I see?" I watch Auntie for any signs of animosity toward Po Po, any hint that she knows what I know. I don't see any which throws me for a loop because my dad tells his sister everything. So why wouldn't he have

told her about Po Po's reaction to him? Maybe he was worried she'd beat Po Po's ass, which isn't a stretch. Dad has said that she took her role as his older sister very serious, and she got into a lot of fights over him growing up.

Po Po giggles, which is something I don't think I've ever seen her do, but shakes her head. "No, no. Even though Ya Tou's been trying to get me on that hanky-panky site."

My eyes fly over to Kylie who just shrugs. "I was trying to convince her to let me make her a profile on Hinge."

"Who needs Hinge when you have me? I have a network of silver foxes I could introduce you to. Ooh, let's see, there's—"

Curtis cuts her off. "Trice, don't play."

She waves him away and leans closer to Po Po, but still keeps her voice loud enough for everyone to hear. "Curtis is very sensitive about the fact that his daddy and all his friends are fine as hell. I got you though."

"How's Mr. Anthony doing by the way?" Olivia's voice is casual as she asks, but my eyes narrow in suspicion.

Curtis huffs. "Man, go head."

Olivia and Kylie fall into a fit of laughter before Kylie finally pulls it together to speak. "Honestly, Unc, your daddy has no business being that fine."

"You're not allowed to say that shit—excuse me, Maggie, I mean stuff. He's family. And you're barely legal."

"I'm very legal. And I hate to keep reminding you of this but we're only related by marriage." Kylie tries to hug him but he stiff-arms her.

Auntie and Kylie continue teasing Curtis while Olivia snuggles up to me. I turn to whisper in her ear. "You know I'm gonna have to punish you for that later, right?"

"I'm counting on it."

⚕

Every year, Shane and I volunteer at the children's hospital the day after Christmas. We volunteer often throughout the year, but the day after Christmas is the one day we make sure we're there at the same date and time.

This year is no different despite Auntie and Curtis's visit. Auntie and Olivia plan to spend the day together while Curtis meets up with an old friend.

Shane doesn't have a good relationship with his family at all. He moved to Texas for college and never left, hoping to put as much distance between him and them as he could. He's never said it, but I think his tumultuous relationship with his family is why he volunteers with kids in any capacity he can. It might even be part of the reason he's so close to Nevaeh.

After running around helping wherever needed all day, I'm walking down the hall when I spot Shane in Dylan's room. Dylan is a sweet ten-year-old girl who has been in and out of the hospital, battling kidney disease caused by systemic lupus erythematosus. I'm not surprised to find Shane in her room. He has a soft spot for her.

"Hi, Kai!" she greets excitedly.

"How you feeling, sweetie?"

"Good. I got to see a puppy today!"

"Is that right?" I look over to Shane because I know he had something to do with her getting to see the puppy today.

"Yep," she answers proudly. "And guess what else?"

"Hmmm, you were crowned queen for the day?"

"I'm a queen every day, silly."

"Oh right, my mistake. I'm fresh out of guesses then. Help me out."

"I heard you have a girlfriendddddd." Her voice is light and airy as she sings girlfriend and Shane bursts out laughing.

"Yeah, I told her you stole my crush but that I'm okay with it."

"Well, she was my crush first so it was only right."

"I guess."

"Is she pretty?" Dylan asks.

"She's beautiful."

"Is she nice?"

"Very."

"Does she like dogs?"

"She loves them."

"Okay, I like her."

"That's all it takes?"

"I'm easy to please."

"Me too, Dyl. Me too."

We spend some more time with Dylan until she gets tired and we go off to help with other things. On my way home from the hospital, my office manager, Faith, calls me to inform me that one of the clients I booked to start next month decided she doesn't want to work with me after all. I find it a little strange but it's not like I haven't had clients change their minds before, so I hang up and head home.

With the Christmas weekend behind us, Olivia and I are back to her normal physical therapy schedule. She's my last appointment of the day, so she'll take an Uber here and we'll drive home together afterward.

When Olivia arrives, Jay and I are wrapping up his session. He makes a point to smile in her face and personally invite her to see any of his games next season. She extends him the same invite and he gladly accepts before leaving.

"Okay, so what are you up to? Why'd I have to bring a bathing suit today?" I texted her and told her to bring a bathing suit to today's session, but I didn't answer any of her follow-up questions.

"You'll see. Are you wearing it now or do you need to change?"

"I have it on."

"Great, let's go."

I lead her out to the indoor pool area we have at the center. Water exercises can be a great therapy tool for athletes so we have one on the premises. Normally, there would probably be at least one other client out here with us, but I booked it so that we'd be the only ones today. We haven't used the pool in our sessions yet, but I thought this would be a nice change of pace for her. I also thought it might be a nice way to get her mind off her dad. He's been quiet, not even calling on Christmas, which she doesn't mind, but she's wary about what he might be planning during his silence.

"Hell yes, we're using the pool today? You're getting in with me, right?"

"Of course."

She mumbles something about getting to see me shirtless and wet as

she strips off her shorts and T-shirt to reveal her sinful bathing suit. It's an orange hi-cut one piece that makes the walnut-brown of her skin glow. The straps of the top are thin and her breasts look tantalizing. Her sides can be seen in small cut-outs, and the front of her suit is open so I can see her toned stomach.

"You gonna keep staring or should we get started?" she calls me out.

"I'm gonna stare a little more."

She laughs as she ties her hair up in a bun and then moves to the stairs by the shallow end of the pool. I quickly strip off my shirt and sweats to reveal my swim trunks and then I jump in the water so I can help her down the steps.

"Okay, so let's start with a couple of these." I instruct her to move through some of the stretches we do each session. She does them with ease. "See, water exercises are low impact so you're able to do them with a little less pain than you might outside of the pool. I thought it might be nice to switch it up today."

"You'd be right. The water feels so good."

"I'm glad to hear it. Let's do some walking." We spend the next few minutes walking in waist-deep water to get her muscles moving and then we move on to simple range of motion exercises and light swimming, careful to avoid kicking. She moves through them with ease, only needing to stop a couple of times.

At one point I lift her out of the pool to sit on the edge so she can fix her hair and take a moment to rest. The sunlight peeks through the windows, illuminating her body, and I'm stunned by how goddess-like she looks. She catches me staring and because she can't help but taunt me, she leans back on her palms, pushing her breasts out farther.

"Break's over. Back in the pool, Olivia."

"Yes, sir." A low growl escapes my chest. As I help her settle back into the water, I wrap my arm around her waist and carry her a little deeper until the water comes up to her chest. I place her down against the wall.

"Stand up straight, legs shoulder width apart." She complies immediately which only makes me harder.

I step closer to her until our bodies connect and my dick stands against her stomach. Her breath hitches at the contact. "Now what?"

I step a little to the side so that I'm standing on either side of her unaffected leg, making sure I'm not in the way of her injured leg. "You're going to slowly raise this leg to your waist." I trail my hand up her leg to rest on her waist.

"Fuck," she breathes. "Do you get this close to all your clients?"

"No, just you."

Her face heats. "Good answer."

"Do as I say, Olivia. I want ten of them."

She licks her lips and without taking her eyes off me, she slowly lifts her leg. Her leg brushes against my side on the way up and back down. I watch the heavy rise and fall of her chest and the tremble in her arms through each lift. My fingers rub soft circles into her opposite hip throughout the entire exercise. On her tenth rep, I catch her leg while it's still at her waist. "How did that feel?"

"G-good."

"Good. Pain level?"

"Low."

"Good. And how does this feel?" I press the heel of my hand against her clit and she gasps.

"Better. So much better."

She hooks her leg around my waist, and I reach around to grab her ass while my other hand continues rubbing circles against her clit. When she starts whimpering, I press my lips to hers. I trace my tongue along her bottom lip until she grants me entrance. She sucks my tongue into her mouth and bites my bottom lip once her release hits her. It's not enough. I need more of her, all of her. I lift her to the edge of the pool and pull the bottom of her swimsuit to the side, burying my face between the apex of her thighs.

"Oh fuck, Kai. Right fucking there," she cries. I didn't need her to tell me. I know her body inside and out. I know what strokes of my tongue make her cry out. Which move of my fingers makes her eyes roll to the back of her head. Where to stroke her with my dick to make her toes curl. I've studied

her body and her reactions to me with a fine-tooth comb. I've graduated with a PhD in her pleasure and made it my mission to be her best student.

I bring my mouth back to her clit, enjoying the sting of pain from her fisting my hair. I suck on her sensitive nub while my fingers work her. I take note of the telltale signs of her release coming. The clenching of her walls, the slight tremble in her legs, the drop of her jaw. I suck harder and when she comes I soak it up like a starved man and then pull her into a sloppy kiss so that she can taste herself. I lose myself in the kiss but still manage to pull my trunks down enough to free my throbbing dick and slam her down on it. She lets out a throaty moan in my mouth that reverberates through my body, seeping into my bones.

"Good fucking girl. You take me so well." Her pussy clenches around me and her mouth opens to say something, but the words die on her throat when I angle her so that my strokes hit her deeper. I get her bathing suit top down far enough to expose her peaked nipples and pull one between my teeth. I'm sure to give both breasts equal attention; I wouldn't want them thinking I had a favorite. Her right breast is slightly bigger than the left and the nipple on her right side is a little more sensitive than the left so I tease and bite that one until I can tell by her eyes that it's painfully tender and then I soothe the pain with my tongue. I suckle her left nipple and massage it until her eyes roll.

"Shit, I'm gonna come," she groans.

"Let it go."

And she does, and I follow her moments later. If we weren't pruning from the water, I could stay here forever.

"Best session ever," she sighs.

As we close up and head out for the night I send a quick text to Faith.

Me: No one has a session booked in the pool tomorrow right?

Faith: No, why?

Me: Good. We should probably drain it.

Faith: *throw up emoji* if I weren't so happy for you I'd be disgusted

Me: That's why you're my favorite

Faith: Right. You know there's cameras in the pool area right?

Me: I got that handled

I had honestly forgotten about the cameras in there. No matter, I'll just delete them after I find them.

Right after I get myself a copy.

CHAPTER
Twenty-Five

Olivia

Ciara: Y'all please tell this man that my doctor said I could still fly so I can go to Deep Creek?

Ciara has been complaining that she wants to go to Deep Creek, Maryland, to be surrounded by snow because she's tired of being hot while extremely pregnant. I'm guessing Lincoln isn't going for it since she's now created a group chat with everyone, even her friends from back in Baltimore.

Lincoln: This felt necessary? Who tf wants to be in a group chat with thirteen people?

Ciara: It felt very necessary because you're trying to stop me from living my best life

Lincoln: You're eight months pregnant!

Sasha: I mean she said her doctor said she could still travel

Lincoln: No one asked you sis

Sasha: Pretty sure that was the point of this whole group chat

Isaiah: Ugh no one wants to be present for y'all's weird foreplay a.k.a. fighting

Isaiah: *inserts gif of Schmidt from New Girl gagging*

Nina: Your form of foreplay ain't much better

Isaiah: *inserts gif of Deadpool gasping*

Isaiah: There's too many kids for foreplay

Shane: There's always time for foreplay

Dom: I don't wanna be here

Unknown number: Lincoln bring my woman back to me! Stop holding her hostage—Simone

Ciara: Tell him sis!

Lincoln: Jesus

Kai hands me my morning tea in bed. "It just feels so early for all this mess."

"I mean she really wants her Deep Creek trip."

"And I don't know why Linc is acting like he won't move mountains to make it happen for her." My mind drifts to a possible solution for them. I exit out of the group chat conversation and call Tyson. He was nice enough to loan me his plane once; he just might do it again.

Once I've squared the details away with him, I go back to the group chat where I see the messages have fallen into complete chaos. Poor Brittany, who I haven't met in person but seems very sweet, tried to referee for a moment but gave up quickly. I look over at Kai who's sitting watching the messages come up with a smile on his face but isn't responding.

Me: What if she could fly private? Would that make a difference?

Nina: Bitchhhh, you got private plane money?

Me: No but I know someone who does

Simone: Is this the Liv I keep hearing about?

Ciara: Yep that's her

Simone: Livvvv, nice to meet you boo. Question, this person with the private plane. Man or woman?

Me: Lol you too. Man

Simone: Single?

Me: Definitely

Simone: Saving your number, we'll talk

Simone: *inserts gif of Mr. Krabs with dollar signs in his eyes*

Lincoln: My wife has informed me that if I make her miss her chance to fly private then she'll divorce me so I guess we're going to Deep Creek

Nina: *inserts gif of Cardi B dancing with the word yassss*

Sasha: *inserts gif of Regina George from Mean Girls saying 'get in loser, we're going shopping*

Shane: *inserts gif of Arnold Schwarzenegger yelling 'get to the choppa'*

Isaiah: *inserts gif of French Montana on a private plane dancing*

Brittany: *inserts gif of Oprah yelling 'yay'*

Dom: Still don't wanna be here

Sasha: Oh stop it, you grump

One week later, we're stepping off the plane in Maryland where we meet up with Ciara's friends Brittany, Simone, and Sarah.

Sarah's family owns a house in Deep Creek Lake where we'll be staying. It's got enough bedrooms for everyone to pair up, and Shane complains that he's being forced to room with Dom.

"Who the fuck else would you room with?" Isaiah asks.

"I was thinking maybe Simone."

Everyone laughs, including Simone. Simone is rooming with Sasha since Carter opted to stay home with Nevaeh instead of coming along. "No thanks, boo. I don't share my space with men, but if you're good I might take you for a ride this weekend." Shane falls to his knees in front of her while Isaiah and Kai clown him.

Once everyone has a chance to settle into their rooms and change, we head out to the resort. Since the trip was planned last minute, we only have a long weekend to be here before everyone has to get back to work.

Once we get to Wisp resort, Ciara and I sit in the lounge to grab hot chocolate and people watch. It makes me laugh how hard she fought to come here just to sit in a lounge since she can't ski, snowboard, or snowtube with her being so far along. She looks so happy just being here though.

Kai and Lincoln offer to sit in the lounge with us, but we send them off with everyone, so they join Shane and Dom to try snowboarding. Isaiah and Nina head off to try skiing while Brittany, Sarah, Sasha, and Simone go the snowtubing route.

From where Ciara and I sit, we can see each of the slopes so we're treated to the view of Nina and Isaiah busting their asses repeatedly on their slope. I worry that Ciara is going to go into early labor when she laughs so hard after Simone's tube stops in the middle of the hill and Brittany's crashes into her, sending them both flying into a pile of snow. The guys are boring to watch because they're actually pretty decent. They're not experts by any means but they don't seem to fall as much as everyone else. I will say, Kai looks sexy as hell on that board though.

"So, how are things going?" Ciara pulls me out of my dirty thoughts.

"They're good. How's the writing going?"

"I just finished the latest right before we left, so once edits are done I should be good to publish before the baby comes and then I can take a break."

"That's amazing, Ci."

"Thank you. But let's not skip over the fact that all you gave me was a 'they're good.' That's all you got?"

I laugh. "Was I supposed to have something else?"

"You don't have to. Just saying you can if you want to."

I think her therapy sessions have been going too well because she's starting to sound like one. "I, um, called that therapist. I did end up getting referred to a different one, but I started sessions with her this week."

"Really? Aww, that's wonderful!"

"Yeah, I think it's time I shed this extra weight I've been carrying in the form of my dad. I'm finally realizing I can't do it alone."

"It's not that you can't do it alone, it's that you don't have to. That was a tough lesson for me to learn, but so important."

"I'm not fully there yet."

"That's okay. Have you had any problems with your dad lately?"

"Not lately. Quiet from that man is never good." Quiet when there's nothing going on is one thing because we really never talk unless there's an issue. But quiet when I know I'm doing something that upsets him? That's when my anxiety sets in.

"And maybe that's what he wants is for you to be so stressed about what he's gonna do that you're not enjoying your time with Kai."

"Probably. But that doesn't mean he's not also up to something."

"So prepare for the worst. But let yourself live. Because that is the ultimate fuck you to him."

Those words stay with me even when the crew comes back and joins us for a round of hot chocolate before we head back to the cabin.

Once we get back, we make a big family dinner and hang out for a little while, but it's clear everyone is exhausted from their show of athleticism, or lack thereof for some, and the group scatters to their respective bedrooms. I know it's real when Shane doesn't even make a joke about helping Simone to sleep.

When Kai and I get to our room, I help him strip out of his clothes then join him in the shower where he makes me come twice before we finally wash our bodies and get out.

I expect him to fall asleep the minute his head hits the pillow but instead he pulls me into his arms and kisses my neck.

"Damn, don't you get tired?"

"Are you tired?"

"No, but I also didn't spend my day snowboarding and then licking my pussy in the shower."

"Nothing exhausting about that. That was my midnight snack. But I'm hungry for a meal now."

My mouth waters at that. Fuck, the effect this man has on me is ridiculous. He moves so quickly, I'm startled, but then he gets whatever he was looking for out of his bag and brings them back to the bed.

"You brought all this on the plane?" I look from him down to the sex toys he's laid out on the bed. My rose, a butt plug, a blindfold, and lube. We've used the rose and butt plugs in bed before but never at the same time. He would decide to explore this while we're in a house full of people.

"Do you want to play, love?"

"Yes, sir."

"What's your safe word?"

"Honey." I picked it because that's what he said I taste like. I had plenty of sex in my absence from Kai, and I had plenty of great sex too, but I'd never had sex where I needed a safe word until Kai two point oh.

He instructs me to lie on the bed where he promptly ties the blindfold around my eyes, plunging me into darkness. Not knowing what he's going to do or when only heightens my pleasure. Goose bumps erupt all over my skin, and I shudder at the slightest movement. I feel the faint touch of his fingertips over my ribs, and my body bucks.

He tsks. "So eager."

"Kai, please." I don't even know what I'm begging for, I just know I need him to give it to me.

"Please what?"

"I need…I need…"

"Closed mouths don't get fed, Olivia. What do you need?"

"Your dick."

"Where do you want it?"

"My mouth."

"What's your safe signal?"

"Three taps to your side."

He falls quiet. I strain to see if I can hear anything, the rustling of the sheets, his briefs hitting the floor, anything. But there's nothing. I kick my legs out in frustration. Where is he?

And then I feel it. The fleshy tip of his dick dusting my lips. The distinct salty bead of pre-cum hitting my upper lip. The heat of my mouth welcomes him immediately, but he pulls away and then I feel my head lift and a pillow finds its way under my neck. The bed dips under his weight and I open my mouth, waiting for him to come back to me. He slaps his dick against my waiting tongue, making me squirm. He slides past my waiting lips to the back of my throat. "Suck."

With that, I suction my lips around him and do as he says. I can't see him but I can hear his grunts of approval, letting them lead my movements. When I let my spit run down his dick and my chin, I hear his harsh breath. "Fuck," he groans. I smile around his dick. This feels good. Not his dick in my mouth, although that feels good too, but the knowledge that even in this position, with him straddling my face and me not having the benefit of my sight, I have the control here. I'm the one driving him crazy.

He plunges his hands into my hair, releasing it from the ponytail I had it in, and pumps into my mouth, moaning when I gag. I reach up to massage his balls while I continue sucking and running my tongue over him. I suck until I feel his cum pour down my throat and I keep sucking even after it stops. I suck until he growls and rips himself free of me.

"Come here," I plead. I want him to taste himself on me the way he always does to me. He grants my wish and presses his lips against me. I bite his bottom lip and lave it with my tongue. His kiss is carnal. It's punishing in a way that sends heat straight to my core.

He trails his lips down my neck to my breasts, sucking and teasing me there. Then as he nips and sucks, he brings the rose up to tease the other. "Oh my God." I squirm beneath his hold. He has my wrists above my head in one of his hands while he tortures me. When I cry out, he plants kisses on the spot between my breasts then works his way down my stomach to my pussy.

"Your pretty pussy looks so empty. We should fill her up, don't you think?"

Oh my God, yes. I wiggle under his hold again, and this time he lets me go but only so he can grab my hips and pull me to the edge of the bed. A deep, heady moan falls from my lips when his tongue licks up my folds. He works me to a state of oblivion where I can't even remember my own name and then he folds my legs toward my ears. "You okay?" he asks.

"Yes, sir."

He laughs. "Tell me again. What's your safe word?"

"Honey."

He kisses the back of my thigh as something wet hits my ass. I recognize it as the lube, but my legs already begin shaking when he coats my asshole with it and primes me with his fingers. My heart is racing. His scent surrounds me, but I still can't tell exactly where his face is or what he's going to do next.

There it is. The slightly chilly intrusion against my hole. I take a deep breath and relax myself so my body will accept it, and he praises me as I do. When it's firmly planted, my senses feel even more heightened. Everything feels so intense. I reach up to massage my breasts, trying to find the rose so I can use that too but instead I hear his voice in my ear. "Take a deep breath for me." When I do, he suctions the rose to my clit.

"Fuck!" I cry. My body is convulsing with need. Every move I make only serves to heighten the stimulation. I can't run from it and I don't want to. His hand runs across my throat, applying a gentle pressure that sets every nerve ending in my body off. He rips the blindfold off of me and the light in the room is an adjustment, but my focus is firmly planted on him. This is real ecstasy. Or I thought it was, until his dick pushes into me and sends me to the brink. He starts with slow strokes and then plunges deeper into me.

The pressure on my throat increases a little more as does the intensity of our skin slapping together. I fist the sheets as my toes curl so tight I'm not sure they'll ever unfurl. He offers me a little relief by removing the rose, and the moment he pulls out of me, my pussy resembles a waterfall, making him

let out an appeased hum. He wastes no time plunging back inside of me and putting the rose back in its place.

Shit. I feel myself climbing higher and higher up the scales of pleasure. Past the point of ecstasy and euphoria and reaching pure bliss. Heaven. Intoxication.

And then the waves pull me under. The fall is steep but the ride is incredible and when I crash I crash into him. I feel his release when he lets go, filling me up, and then I let the waves take me. I vaguely hear his words of praise as he pulls out of me and then slowly removes the butt plug. I vaguely feel his lips on my throat, my wrists, and my thighs. I'm present enough to know when he leaves the room and then when he comes back to scoop me into his arms and place me in the warm bath he ran for me. I'm present enough to feel him get in the bath across from me and pull my legs into his lap so he can massage them, but I start fading into the joyous peace of sleep not too long after.

The next morning, when we pull ourselves out of bed, we make our way downstairs where everyone is already eating.

"Hey sleepyheads. We made pancakes, eggs, and bacon," Sasha points out.

"Thank you," we say in unison. Kai kisses my forehead and then grabs plates for both of us while I grab two glasses of orange juice. I feel eyes on me, but when I look up I don't find any.

Shane asks if we're going back to the resort today but Simone cuts him off. "I'm sorry, are we going to act like we didn't all hear them putting in work last night? Had me missing my toy and had Sasha ready to call her man."

The kitchen falls silent and then we all burst out laughing. "Oops, sorry guys," I offer.

"You can be sorry that I didn't think to bring my toy because that shit was hot."

Kai shakes his head in mock embarrassment, but I see the grin he hides behind his hand.

Everyone decides that we should head back to the resort today, so we all disperse to change and get ready, but I'm drawn to Kai's voice in the living room. He doesn't sound angry but he sounds annoyed. I only catch the tail end of his conversation before he hangs up and heads in my direction.

"What was that about?"

He sighs. "That was Faith. Another client canceled their therapy with me."

"Wait, what? Another? This isn't the first one?"

"No, one canceled the other day too."

"Did they say why?"

"They opted to use another service." Fuck. I knew the quiet couldn't be trusted. "It might not be him. I've had this happen before."

"No, nothing's coincidence with him." I stomp off to our room in search of my phone and when I find it, I dial the monster in question.

"Jason Harding's phone." My lip snarls at the voice on the other line. Myra. Answering my dad's phone on a Saturday. I guess they've given up all pretense of a professional-only relationship.

"Hello, Myra. Can you please put my father on the phone?"

"Oh, hello Olivia." I roll my eyes. I called his cell phone so she damn well knew it was me. Bitch. "Sorry, he's not available at the moment. Can I take a message?"

"As a matter of fact, you can. You can tell him to back the fuck down."

"Excuse me?"

"You heard me. Tell him to back the fuck down and stay out of my business, and yes, that business does include Kai."

"You never did learn any respect, did you?"

"Respect is earned. And Myra?"

"Yes?"

"You can stay the fuck out of my business too." I hang up before she can reply.

It's been a couple of hours since I left my message for my dad. He hasn't

called me back, but I didn't really expect that. I'm not sure what I am expecting though. Kai sent our friends off to the resort without us, but all we've done is sit here since they left.

An idea is swirling around in my mind but I think it's a little crazy. It's a lot crazy, actually, but something in my heart is telling me it's the right thing to do.

"You gotta talk to me, love. What's going on in that pretty head of yours?"

He always knows. Part of me wants to revert to my old ways of trying to handle everything myself, but I know that's not the right way to handle things anymore. I need Kai by my side if I'm going to do this, and that's okay to admit. "I think I need to go see my mom."

I can tell my answer shocks him, but he nods as if he's already on board. "You know where she is?"

"I looked her up a long time ago; I just never went to see her. She took her maiden name back but she legally changed her name from Beverly to Jennifer. Jennifer Watkins. She's not dancing or singing anymore, but she still works on Broadway as a choreographer."

"Okay."

"Okay? That's it?"

"You say this is what you need so this is what we'll do. Let's go." He makes it seem so easy and for him maybe it is. For me, I don't think I'll breathe until this is over.

We pack our bags and call the crew to let them know our plan. They offer to come with us but I insist that they stay. They'll take Tyson's plane back home while Kai and I take a rental car and drive up to New York. We'll fly back from there.

The five-hour drive up to New York gives me too much time to think of what I'll say to my mom when I see her. Will she even recognize me? She hasn't seen me since I was twelve. I don't even know what I want from her, but I just feel if I'm going to take my father head-on that she might have some insight she can offer me. His obsession with me started with his obsession

of getting her back, so maybe I can even get her to talk to him or something. I don't know. I have no idea what I'm doing.

We make it to our hotel in New York with enough time to shower and change for the show. The show is beautiful. It's called *Lost in Transformation*. It centers around a girl named Amaryllis who wakes up from an accident and has no idea who she is so she starts over, and as she remembers glimpses from her past life she realizes she's much better off this time around. The dance style screams my mother. She was always so graceful. When I watched her dance around the house, her moves were always languid and flowy. She knew how to capture an entire emotion in one movement.

I'm so engrossed in the show I almost forget why we're here. "What do you think you're going to say to her?" Kai asks during intermission.

"I honestly have no idea." I search the crowd to see if I see her, but I know chances are she's backstage with the dancers. When intermission is over, I immerse myself back into the show. I know my mom didn't write the show but I can't help but to compare Amaryllis to her. The life she builds for herself after her accident is beautiful. She falls in love, she finds a job she loves, friends she cares about. She creates a home. The glimpses she gets from her old life are full of nothing but pain, abuse, and loneliness. Is that how she felt with us? I never saw my father raise a hand to her, but who knows what he was doing when I wasn't around. At this point, I would put nothing past that man. If he was abusing her, why did she leave me with him? Was that the only way she could get away? I've spent so much of my life hating her for leaving me behind, but now I just have so many questions. I intend to get those answers tonight.

When the show ends, the crowd heads for the exits while Kai and I make our way toward the stage. A man with two teenage kids lingers by the stage as well. The man and his son don't capture my attention but I'm struck when the daughter turns in my direction. She looks…like me. Same eyes, same nose, same lips, same head shape. The same facial features that I get from my mom. The woman in question walks from behind the stage and into the arms of the unrecognizable man. He plants a quick but sweet

kiss on her lips before stepping aside so the teens can wrap her up in a hug, and the boy presents her with flowers that make her face light up in delight.

She has a new family. They both look somewhere between sixteen and eighteen so that means she started over not too long after leaving me behind. I have a brother and a sister. And a stepdad. My heart is pounding. I wonder if they know I exist. If I were to walk up to them right now would I be blowing their lives up? I've never seen my mom look this happy before. She's never looked at me the way she looks at those kids, and she's definitely never looked at my dad the way she looks at the man on her arm.

I look over at the young replica of myself and wonder what kind of relationship she has with my…with our…mom. Does she feel supported and loved or stifled and hated? Does *she* dance? Is she following the former Beverly Harding's legacy or was she allowed to forge a different path?

I can't do this. I can't force my way into her life when the woman who gave birth to me clearly doesn't want me there. For twenty years, my dad has been chasing a ghost that isn't even haunting him. I refuse to do the same.

"Let's go home, Kai."

He gives me a sad smile and grabs my wrist. "Are you sure?"

I look back at Jennifer Watkins and her family. "I'm sure."

CHAPTER
Twenty-Six

Kai

J ASON HARDING IS A FUCKING PEST. IN THE MONTH SINCE WE'VE BEEN back home from New York, I've lost a few more clients. Not enough to really affect my business but enough that I'm irritated. When I try to ask them what's driving their decision, they're cagey about it, all but confirming for me that this is in fact the work of that fucker.

I call my friend that is looking into Jason's dealings, and he lets me know that he has a lead he's following but he's not clueing me in until he has something concrete, so I leave him to do what he does best.

In the meantime, I think it's time I face my own ghosts since Olivia is facing hers. After deciding not to approach her mom, I thought she'd be upset but she wasn't. She was just resigned to the fact that she'd never have parents she could count on. She didn't hide away her emotions; she leaned in to them. She's been keeping up with her therapist who is encouraging her to let go of her parents completely because not having parents doesn't mean she doesn't have family. She's been making time for Ciara, Nina, and Sasha and

calling Angie and Justine more often to check in. She filled them in on what's going on with her dad, and though they were upset that she hadn't given them the full story before, they understood where she was coming from.

With Olivia spending the afternoon at Neon Nights with Nina, I decide to head to my condo. I let Lily know she can head out early, grateful that her report is that Po Po is having a good day, and then I head back to Po Po's bedroom.

"Little Wolf, how are you?" she asks as she sits up.

"You don't have to sit up on my behalf, Po Po."

"Nonsense. I want to sit up while I talk to my grandson. Help me, will you?"

I help her sit up and then I sit beside her but keep a little distance between us. "What's on your mind, Wolf?"

I scrub my hand down my face. There's no easy way to have this conversation. I just have to rip the Band-Aid off. I tell her all the things I overheard and her face pales.

"Little Wolf," she says as she puts her hand on top of mine, but I move it, ignoring the hurt I see on her face. "I'm ashamed that you heard those things."

"So, you said it then?"

"I was opposed to Lisa marrying Xavier, yes. But you misunderstood my reasoning, just as your dad did back then. I explained it to him and Patrice, but if I had known you knew I would've extended the same courtesy to you."

So Auntie did know. I'm even more confused now. "Well, here's your chance. How could you stand in my face all my life and claim to love me, love Kylie, while simultaneously hating half of what makes us...*us*?"

"I have never h-h-hated any part of you, Kai." She shakes her head and takes a moment to clear her mind. "Please understand. When I said I didn't want Lisa to marry Xavier, it had nothing to do with him being Black and everything to do with him being American."

That sets me back. "What?"

"When Lisa and I came to America, she was a teenager but she just adapted so quickly. I didn't. I wanted to hold on to Guangzhou. Our traditions, our religion, our everything. It was all I knew. And Lisa didn't do

anything w-w-wrong, she was just more ready than me. She had already learned English before we came over so I had to depend on her to translate for me at first, which I hated. And then she found new interests. She wanted to practice Christianity instead of Buddhism. She didn't want to come to church with me anymore. She wanted to go out with her friends instead of going to the market with me. I felt like I was losing my daughter to this country. Then Xavier came along, and I felt like I was losing even more of her because she wanted to move away from me to be with him, and she was my lifeline. Without her, I didn't know how to function in this country. That wasn't fair to her. And it wasn't fair to Xavier for me to try to keep them apart for my own selfish reasons."

Shit. I wasn't expecting that. I can understand her motives now and now see that I didn't hear the full story when I overheard my parents talking. Po Po was just scared and tried to cling to the only person who also understood what she was going through. She proceeds to tell me how she made a point to find a network of friends that understood her but how she also made sure to connect with people that she didn't understand either, so that she could learn new things. She connected with both my dad and aunt. She did what she needed to do to feel whole on her own here. She made this her home.

"Thank you. I wish I had talked to you sooner. I was just so shocked and hurt by what I thought I knew."

"Understandable. I'm sorry I gave you the impression that I would ever think that way. I,"—she takes a deep breath—"I hope you know that when you were born, it was one of the happiest days of my life. You were so beautiful, with a head full of hair. I named you, you know?"

"You did?"

"Yes. Lisa wanted my input for your name and I wanted to pick something that broadened past the horizons of our culture. When I was searching, I came across the name Kai and it had so many different meanings. In Mandarin it meant victory, in Hawaiian it meant ocean, in Finnish it meant rejoice, in Navajo it meant Willow Tree, in Scottish it meant the keeper of keys, and in Scandinavian it meant Earth. I had never seen one name have so many meanings to so many different people. I knew that was the name for

you because I wanted you to have a name that meant you could be whoever you wanted to be. And I called you my little wolf because you were always quiet, more likely to observe first before making a decision, but when you or your family were threatened you were quick to put a stop to it."

I grab her hand and squeeze. She puts her other hand on top of our joined ones and smiles up at me. I don't know if I can immediately drop everything I thought I knew, but I'm now confident that we'll get back to the way we were.

"Did you name Kylie too?"

She shakes her head, smiling. "No, that's all your mom. She got really into that Kylie Minogue when she was pregnant with her."

For the first time in a long time, the laugh that escapes my lips toward Po Po is genuine.

"Can I take this off now?"

"Not yet," I answer.

"Gotta say, wearing a blindfold in broad daylight for hours feels weird." I laugh at that. I have a surprise for Olivia but I couldn't let her see where we were headed or she'd know immediately, so I blindfolded her. I was concerned about being pulled over with a blindfolded woman in my car but thank God, we avoided that.

Once I park in the garage, I tell Olivia she can take the blindfold off and wait for recognition to hit her.

"Hold up, are we at Rice?"

"Yep."

"Holy shit! Is Coach Naughton still here?"

"She sure is. I actually organized our visit with her. She's letting us do our physical therapy at their facility, and she wants to see you."

She launches herself at me, kissing me all over my face before kissing me so deeply that I'm about to take her in this car.

"Thank you," she says when she pulls away.

"One of these days you've gotta stop thanking me for doing what I'm supposed to do."

"Bringing me to see my old coach is what you're supposed to do?"

"Making you happy is what I'm supposed to do."

When we make it to Coach Naughton's office, her assistant coach lets us know that she's meeting with a student so she gives us free rein to tour the gym where Coach will find us.

We check out the field and Olivia spends a moment remembering how much she loved it. I know she wishes she had stayed in school, playing under Coach Naughton and working with her teammates. I know she wishes she had done a lot of things differently back then, but all we can do is move forward. I hope seeing the field today and Coach will help her do that.

We make our way back into the locker room from the field when Olivia pushes me against the lockers. "What are you doing?"

"You know what I always wanted to do when we went here?" she purrs in my ear.

"What's that?"

"I wanted to sneak you in here and have my way with you. Some of the other girls did it but I never tried."

"Oh really?"

"Yeah, and since making me happy is your job and all."

"Say no more." I drop to my knees and pull her shorts and panties down, inhaling the scent of her perfect pussy before I pick her up by her legs and back her up against the closest wall. Her scent intoxicates me and the sounds she makes when I drag my tongue through her folds nearly break me. With her back against the wall and her legs wrapped firmly around my shoulders, I take one hand out from under her ass so that I can stretch her with my fingers.

Her walls clench my fingers while I suck on her clit, and I look up from my position to find her bottom lip trapped behind her teeth. She locks eyes with me and immediately knows what I want, so she releases her lip and lets her whimpers fall freely.

In the distance, I hear voices. They're not right on top of us but they're definitely making their way toward us.

I look back to Olivia and chuckle when I see the horrified expression on her face.

"Kai, you gotta stop."

I stop eating my entrée for long enough to say one word. "No."

Her answering cry sounds like a mixture of lust and worry. "Oh my God, Kai. Please."

"Do you want people to see me eating your pretty pussy, Olivia?"

Her mouth parts but no words come out. Truthfully, I would have no problem with someone finding us this way. It seems that she has the same thought. I know the thought of getting caught turns her on, but I know she's worried that Coach might be one of those people and she doesn't want that. "No," she sighs.

"Then I guess you better hurry and give me what I want then, huh?"

"Fuck."

"What was that?"

Her hooded eyes come back to me. "Yes, sir."

I increase the pressure of my fingers and suck her clit harder. The voices get a little louder but I keep up the pressure.

Her hands grip my scalp and pull me farther into her, fucking my face. When I feel her orgasm coming, I pull my fingers out and bring them around to her ass, pushing in ever so slightly. She grinds harder, chasing that high until the evidence of her arousal is all over my beard.

I get her on the ground and back into her bottoms before I duck into the bathrooms because there's no way I can hide my throbbing erection from anyone.

I hear the voices enter the locker room and then I hear Olivia's voice greeting Coach Naughton and whoever else is with her. I hear her make up some story about me running into someone I know but catching up with them later before their voices trail off as they leave.

I'll give them some time to catch up by themselves before I find them for our workout. Right now, I'm too focused on what other dreams I can make come true for Olivia.

CHAPTER
Twenty-Seven

Olivia

CANNOT BELIEVE I HAD KAI EAT ME OUT IN MY COLLEGE LOCKER ROOM. I can't believe I almost got caught letting Kai eat me out in my college locker room, and I can't believe that the thought of getting caught turned me on as much as it did.

I know we had full-on sex in a public bathroom at the karaoke bar and that turned me on too but this was different. This was a place I know with the possibility of getting caught by someone I know. The added risk of that shouldn't have had that kind of effect on me, but it really did and I almost didn't let Kai stop. Get it together, Liv.

I turn to focus on whatever Coach is saying but she's just eyeing me with a knowing smirk. Oh fuck, she knows.

She leads me back to her office and I happily accept the water she offers me.

"Liv, it's so good to see you again. I just want to say I'm so proud of you. I've been following your career, and you've made quite a name for yourself."

"Thank you, Coach. Really, that means a lot to me. And I just want to say I'm sorry."

Her eyebrows peak. "Sorry? For what?"

"For leaving you and the team behind."

"To go pro? Never heard anyone apologize for that."

I tip my head to the side. "Coach, you know I should've stayed all four years. That's the norm."

"You had the opportunity to go, and I assumed you had your reasons for taking it."

I let out a frustrated sigh. "Do you remember what you told me years ago when I told you about my dad?"

She considers me for a moment. "Yes, I believe I told you I knew men like your dad and to not let anyone take the power you have inside of you. Something along those lines, right?"

"Exactly. I wish I had listened to you back then but I didn't. I let my dad take my power, and I'm just now taking, or trying to take, it back."

Understanding lines her features and then gives way to anger. "Good for you for taking it back. Doesn't matter when you do it as long as you do."

"Thank you."

"And now that you're really a grown-ass woman, I can be frank. Your dad's a prick."

I snort with laughter. "Honestly, prick is too gentle a word for him."

We spend some time catching up on our personal lives and professional lives before we make our way to the weight room to meet up with Kai, who I really hope has found a breath mint or something.

The letter in my pocket feels like hot lead against my skin. It's been staring me in the face for weeks and still I've done nothing with it. It's time.

Is it strange that I'm a little more on edge about confessing to Kylie than I was to confess to Kai? The look she gave me when she first saw me in Kai's condo, full of disdain and hurt, was a kick in the chest, but I deserved it.

I called myself doing the right thing, the heroic thing even, by leaving and taking my father's watchful eye with me all those years ago, but all I did was leave a trail of pain behind. I broke the heart of the boy I loved. I cut off contact with my friends. I abandoned my coach and my team. I cut off the two people that treated me more like a daughter than the two people who gave birth to me. I kept in contact with Patrice but I put her in a position where she couldn't share a huge portion of her life with me, and I forced her to lie to them. I cut off the girl who looked up to me and who I loved like a sister. She was fifteen when I left. An age where having a big sister could be so meaningful, so crucial, and I let her down. I did to her what my mother did to me—I left her when she needed me most. I should've been there to give her advice about boys and interests, and help her shop for her homecoming dress, and soothe her first broken heart. Instead, I allowed fear to rule me and turn me into a version of myself I never wanted to know.

Take back your power.

The elevator ride up to Kai's floor is normally short, but today each number the elevator bank illuminates feels like it's taunting me, as if asking if I'm really sure about this.

Finally, I stop on his level and force my feet to move to his door where I slip the letter with Kylie's name scribbled across the front underneath.

I'm halfway back to the elevators when I hear a door swing open.

"What's this, some kind of Dear John letter?"

Fuck. So much for her probably being at work at this time.

I steel my nerves and then turn back to face the girl who is no longer a girl but a beautiful woman with so much disappointment in her eyes.

"Umm, not really. My, uh, my therapist told me if I didn't feel like I could say the words out loud that I should write them down. Get them out that way."

"Sooo, this is what? An apology tour? Is everyone getting a letter?" She flings the letter in the air.

"No. Just you."

Her eyes soften for a moment but then as if she's preparing for me to cut her down, she masks her face back into indifference. "And your plan was to just leave it here for me to find and then...nothing?"

"I was going to give you time to read it and digest it, then I was going to call you and hope like hell you were willing to talk to me."

Her stance transitions from one of confident defiance to one of uncertainty. "Right. Well, just so you know I already know about your psycho dad. Mom told me."

Figures. I expected that; it's why my letter glosses over my dad's actions instead of poring over every detail. That wasn't the point of the letter anyway. I didn't want to focus on his wrongdoings, I wanted to focus on mine. And more importantly on how I was going to do better going forward.

"That's okay."

She stares at the letter for a moment, like it'll read itself out loud if she stares long enough. The silence permeates the air, stifling it. "Okay. Well...I guess I'll read it then and maybe call you."

"I'd like that. But if you don't, I'll call you."

She laughs and then claps her hand over her mouth. "Sounds like you." She hesitates. "Hey, Liv?"

"Yeah?"

"I didn't actually burn your bracelet."

I smile and wait for her to get back inside the condo before I head back down to my car. My moment of peace only lasts for a moment because my phone chimes with a news alert, and the headline sends my mind into overdrive.

Kai Morris, Pro Athlete Physical Therapist, Accused of Swindling Clients Out of Money and Sexual Harassment

That motherfucker. I knew he was just biding his time, but I was hoping we would have something to neutralize him before he could act on his plan.

I race home and am relieved to find Kai's car in the driveway.

"Kai!"

"In here," he calls from the bedroom. He's sitting on the bed, head in his hands. I drop to my knees in front of him and rub my hands up his thighs. "You shouldn't be in that position for a long time; it's not good for your knee."

Of course he would be thinking about my knee at a time like this. "Fuck the knee, Kai. I'm so sorry."

He pushes himself back on the bed and pats his legs, so I quickly get up and straddle his lap with my legs behind him on the bed. "I'm not."

"What? Kai, this is bad. This could ruin you."

"No, it won't. We're going to take him down, I'm confident in that. And even if these bogus-ass accusations don't go away when all is said and done, fuck it. I don't regret a single moment of being with you. You with me?"

"I'm with you."

A FaceTime call from Angie comes through so I answer. "How's Kai doing? And how are you? Tell him we know it's all bullshit. What do you need us to do?"

"Slow down, Angie. We're okay. We're figuring things out." Justine commandeers Angie's phone and demands to talk to Kai, so I leave them to it in favor of answering the door which someone is trying their hardest to knock down.

I peek through the curtain to make sure it's not cops trying to force their way in here, but it's not cops at all. It's Ciara, Nina, Shane, Sasha, Lincoln, Isaiah, Dom, and a woman that looks familiar but I'm not sure why.

"Hey," Ciara greets when I open the door.

"What are you all doing here?"

"We saw the news post and we knew that could only be the work of your trash-ass daddy so we're here to help," Sasha adds.

"And we brought backup. Liv, this is my sister, Reggie. She's a family lawyer but she's scary as fuck and can practice criminal law too." At Lincoln's introduction, Reggie steps up and shakes my hand, assuring me that she can take care of Kai.

"You guys dropped everything to be here right now?"

"Of course. It's Kai." Nina shrugs.

"I'm gonna try my best not to go into labor while we're working but no promises."

Stepping back inside where Justine and Angie are still plotting with Kai and looking at the makeshift family Kai's built, I've never been more grateful, but it's time to bring in more reinforcements.

I pull out my phone and call my full arsenal.

CHAPTER
Twenty-Eight

Kai

I**T'S BEEN THREE WEEKS SINCE THE NEWS STORY ABOUT MY SUPPOSED** misconduct broke. I've been losing clients left and right all while trying to keep my staff calm and continue working with the clients who want to stick by me.

Ciara has given birth to a healthy baby girl but is still adamant about helping me in whatever way she can, despite my protests. Reggie has been working on cease and desist letters left and right.

I'm still waiting to hear from my private investigator resource, but he assures me he's on the cusp of something that will solve all of our problems. Hopefully, I'll still have a practice to save by the time he gets back to me.

Currently, I'm working with Olivia on some progression testing now that she's at the six-month mark. Typically, I like to do this step toward the latter end of the spectrum; however, most professional athletes want to get back to the game before the one-year mark so it's better for me to start test-ing at the six-month mark so I can gauge how far off we are from that goal.

"Okay, love, you're going to stand on this with your big toe on the line." She moves her right foot up so that her big toe aligns with exactly the spot I've pointed out on the y-balance test kit. "Then you're going to use your toe on your left foot to try to push this peg out as far as you can, then back to standing position."

I have her do a trial of the movement on each side before I begin the actual measurements, starting with her right anterior, then moving to her left anterior, her right and left posteromedial, and her right and left posterolateral.

Once I have her numbers I'll be able to compare them to healthy athletes within her same age, gender, and sport. Based on what I'm seeing though, I'm feeling confident that she should actually be ready to return before the one-year mark. That worries me for more reasons than one, but I'll be damned if I try to hold her back in any way. As long as she can do so safely, I'll make sure she gets back on that field.

"That's good. Meet me by the treadmills. I just gotta get my camera so we can do your running gait assessment."

As I make my way over to where Olivia is waiting, I take a minute just to observe her. Her long, dark tresses are pulled into a bun that frames her heart-shaped face. Her lime-green tank top pops against the rich brown of her skin while her gray athletic shorts call attention to her toned legs. It's almost distracting, the way her beauty radiates off her.

I've been spending so much time trying to figure out how I can get her to stay that I didn't consider what I could do to prepare to go with her. If Olivia wants to be in North Carolina then that's where I'll be. No more half measures.

I make my way over to her and am undone by the smile she sends my way. "Hey, you ready? Wait, hold on. Let me reapply some lotion. I don't wanna look ashy on your video."

A deep laugh rumbles in my chest as I grab her by the waist for a heart-stopping kiss. When I release her, she shockingly looks around, as if expecting there to be a crowd watching our PDA. Everyone who's still here knows the two of us are together and they've got more important things to

worry about than me showing my girlfriend some affection. "Your legs look perfectly moisturized. Let's do this."

I get the treadmill started for Olivia and then let her run for a few minutes so she can find her stride before I start recording. I take a fifteen-second video from the side and then I move to the back so I can record her hips, knees, and ankles before zooming in on her feet.

I film for long enough that when I review the footage I'll be able to pinpoint any deviations that might hinder her recovery. Usually, I would review this myself and then with her during our next session, but since my schedule is a lot clearer now I'm able to review it with her now.

I play back the video of her running at a slower speed so I can see where her feet land, how far in front of her they are, and a few other things so I can measure her progression. "Hey, if this business goes to shit, what do you think about being my model on Feet Finder?"

Her eyes grow wide and then slam shut. "Oh my God, there could be a whole market dedicated to physical therapy. Let's get that y-balance thingy in here too." She leans her head against my chest. "Is it terrible to make jokes about this?"

"Eh, if we're going to hell at least we'll go together."

Her chuckle vibrates against my body before she looks up at me with sincere eyes. "Kai, I really am—"

I shake my head, cutting her off before she can continue. "I don't want to hear sorry from you, Olivia. No more sorries. Not ones that don't belong to you anyway."

"I don't think you're gonna get a sorry from Jason."

"I don't need one. His downfall will be all the apology I need, but it is not your job to apologize on his behalf. Got it?"

She stands at attention and salutes me. "Yes, sir."

"Keep playing, Olivia. Think I won't strip you down in front of my entire staff and show them what a good girl you are for me?"

The subtle clench of her thighs tells me that it's time to get her out of here and back home.

Olivia has been acting strange for the last few days. She claims that she needs to fly back to North Carolina to meet with her coach, which makes sense, but she was adamant that I not go with her. I don't mind her going alone, of course, it's just that she's acting cagey about the whole thing which has me on edge. Is Jason doing something I need to know about?

I find her in the bathroom packing up her skin care products into a toiletry bag. "So, we should probably talk about what we're gonna do once you move back to North Carolina."

Distractedly, she misses her target and drops a bottle of face cleanser on the floor. "Huh?"

My eyebrows furrow in concern. "Is everything okay?"

"Oh, yeah. Just nervous about my flight. You know I'm a boujee bitch, used to flying private."

"We flew commercial home from New York."

"And it was terrible." She giggles, but it doesn't reach her eyes and I'm not buying it.

"Mm-hmm, so back to my question then." I repeat the question and notice that she meets my eyes in the mirror but doesn't turn to look at me.

"I don't know. I'm not worried about it though. We'll figure it out."

I cross my arms in front of my chest. "I could always move."

"No!" She schools her initial look of terror. "I mean, that's not necessary. Look, let's talk about all of this when I get back, okay?"

I silently agree but my mind is reeling. I don't know what's gotten into her, but if she thinks I'm letting her go without a fight this time, she hasn't been paying attention for the last six months.

CHAPTER
Twenty-Nine

Olivia

I'VE GOTTA SAY, LIV. THIS IS THE FASTEST DEAL I'VE EVER GOTTEN squared away. Houston was very eager," my agent, Belinda, claims as she tucks my freshly signed papers away.

"They're lucky to have you," Ivy Haven, my head coach in North Carolina, agrees. Coach Haven and I have been close from the moment I joined the team, so I knew when I called her with my decision she would support me rather than tear me down.

"Thanks, Coach. You know y'all will always have my heart though."

"Mm-hmm, we'll see about that when we're on that field."

"Oh no, on the field I'm dusting everyone's ass but after that though."

She cackles and pats me on the shoulder. "There's that confidence. Working with Kai really did work wonders for you. You might even come back to the game better than before."

Working with Kai is the best decision I've made in thirteen years. "That's the goal, Coach."

After all my meetings are tied up, I head over to Angie and Justine's place for a surprise visit.

I expect to have to track them down when I get inside, but they're waiting for me in the kitchen and Justine hands me a margarita. "How'd you know I was coming?"

Angie rolls her eyes. "How did we know she was coming? Claro que si, she was coming. I wish she would come back and not come see us. Idiota," she mumbles, more to herself and Justine, then pulls me into a hug.

Justine lets out a small laugh behind the rim of her glass. "I think she meant how did we know she was coming at this exact time, babe."

Angie looks at me for confirmation, which the rise of my eyebrow provides, and then shrugs with no apology. Dramatic ass.

Justine whispers to me behind Angie's back that she's already had a few margaritas so to ignore her. I'm shocked she's allowing herself to indulge with the U.S. Women's National Team season in full swing and the National Women's Soccer League season about to start, and she must realize this because she offers me an explanation without me asking. "This is your going away party!"

I chortle. "Awww, you do love me."

She strains her thumb and forefinger together. "Un poco. Now drink, bitch."

Four margaritas later, the three of us are lying on the couch reminiscing on the fun times we've had in this city. Justine's family is scattered all over the US, but her parents live in LA in a house Tyson bought for them. Angie's family is split between Honduras and Florida. Up until this year, the only other family I had was Patrice in Atlanta. With our demanding work schedules, it's hard for us to see our families so we relied on each other to fill those gaps. I was fine with being away from them for this past year because I thought I'd be coming back. It feels weird to know that I won't now. We've lived in different cities before, so I know our friendship will stand the test of time but still. It feels like the end of an era, but the beginning of a new one.

"Who am I gonna make rosquillas with now? Her noncooking ass?" Angie whines. Justine throws a pillow at her.

"I know where my skills lie and I stick to that." By skills she means she makes the drinks while we make the food.

"Mm-hmmmm, you've got a skillful mouth too, babe," Angie hums.

"Told you, four drinks in and the freak comes out to play."

I hand her a ten-dollar bill to satisfy our bet and then shake my head at Angie. "You couldn't hold out two more drinks before you started getting nasty?"

Angie starts singing "Nasty" by Ariana Grande but falls back into her chair when she tries to get up and give Justine a lap dance.

"You're so cute when you're sloppy." Justine boops Angie on the nose. I laugh then excuse myself to their guest bedroom to leave them to do whatever drunk married couples do.

"Te amo, Livvy!" Angie singsongs after me.

"Te amo, chica borracha," I singsong back, Justine's laughter and Angie's growling following me until I close the bedroom door.

The next morning, Angie is up early praying for death and begging the blender to be quieter as she makes her protein shake in preparation for practice while I'm waiting for the Uber that's going to take me to the airport and home to my man.

I feel like shit for the way I left things with him. I was acting shady as all hell when I promised no more secrets, but he caught me off guard with his questions, and I'm hoping he'll realize that it's a good secret this time.

When I get back to the house, Kai is still sleeping. I didn't tell him I was flying home so early because I wanted to surprise him, but now that I'm here watching him lying on his back in nothing but black boxer briefs, I have a different surprise in mind.

I saunter over to his side of the bed and pull the blanket completely off his legs and straddle him. His dick instantly comes to life for me, straining to be freed from his briefs, and who am I to deny him. Kai stirs as I lower myself onto his shins so that I can pull the band of his briefs down.

"This is one hell of a wake-up call," he says as he yawns.

"I aim to please."

He bucks his hips up, forcing me to lift myself, so that he can fully

remove his briefs. His dick flops right onto his stomach. The barbell looks especially shiny, begging for attention. My mouth waters with the thought of getting my mouth around him so I spring into action. I lean forward, hiking my ass into the air, and trace my tongue down his length, reveling in the beautiful contradiction of his silky smooth skin against the hard ridges of him.

"Jesus, you're so fucking incredible." I laugh while his dick sits against the back of my throat which only makes his groan louder.

I close my mouth tighter and reach up to massage and grip his balls, humming with pleasure at his sharp inhale. I suck him hard and sloppily, breathing through my nose so I don't have to let up.

He tries to grab me to pull me up the bed, but I place my hands on his chest and push back, releasing him with a pop. "Lie back, and let me take care of you."

"Fuck," he groans.

His hands fly to my hair, pumping up into my mouth, and I welcome his harsh strokes with my tongue. His grip on my hair teases the edges of cruelty but never dances over. I slide my hand down to my swollen clit to relieve some of the pressure, moaning around him as I instantly feel my orgasm on the horizon.

I can feel Kai's coming too, so I double down my efforts, bobbing my head with intense velocity, swirling my tongue faster, and sucking harder.

"Ah shit," he grumbles moments before his release coats my throat. I flash my tongue, covered in his cum, at him for a second before swallowing it down and laughing when his head flies back onto his pillow.

"Welcome home, love." His voice is a contented sigh as he pulls me against his chest.

CHAPTER
Thirty

Olivia

I'VE IMAGINED HOW THIS DAY WOULD GO IN MY HEAD A MILLION TIMES. The day when I'd be able to put my father in his place for good.

The file that Kai's connection was able to produce for us along with the dealings Reggie made are about to grant my wish. My father was smart. We never lived above our means, never brought unnecessary attention to ourselves, but what's done in the dark always comes to light.

My head is held high and my shoulders are back as I strut into my father's office, coming face to face with Myra.

"Liv, your father is not available for a meeting at this time. I'm happy to set an appointment for you, though."

"That won't be necessary, Myra. He'll see me now." I stalk past her, ignoring her cries for my attention as my backup, Sasha, Nina, Ciara, and two-month-old Naomi strapped to Ciara's chest, block her path. I glance back to find her eyes bloodshot red with fury. "You know what, Myra? Since I'm all

about women empowerment, let me give you a piece of advice. You might want to dust off that résumé."

With that, I march into my father's office, surprising him and his guest who I recognize to be Momentum's CFO, Cory Hanson.

"Olivia, what do you think you're doing?"

"Freeing myself from you. I don't mind doing so in front of company, but I'm not sure if you want that."

Cory looks back and forth between us, his lips tightening in confusion.

My father commences yet another silent battle of wills with me, but I've got all the will in the world now. He seems to come to his senses and shake out of it. "Cory, excuse us for a moment. You know how daughters are."

"Sure, we'll touch base later." He nods at me on his way out but I don't acknowledge it. Fuck him and every other misogynistic asshole at this company.

"What do you want, Liv? I thought you would've come to me begging for Kai's livelihood back by now, but you must not really care about him."

"Why would I beg you for something he didn't lose?"

He smiles. "It's only a matter of time. He's losing clients left and right. The accusations will only keep coming."

"No, they won't."

"Excuse me?"

"You're excused. I actually came here to offer you the chance to beg me for your livelihood."

At this, he bends over in a full belly laugh. Good, I look forward to the moment I shove that laughter back down his throat and make him choke on it.

"And what would I possibly beg you for? Please enlighten me."

I hand him the file and let him read for himself.

There it is. The draining of color from his face. The fall of that sadistic grin from his face. The angry scowl meant to hide the utter fear traveling through his blood.

I grab the file back from him and open to the first page. "Let's see, there's all the proof of the threats and bribes you made to countless women

to force them to make false sexual assault allegations against Dante Moore and Kai Morris and a few others. There's also the proof of the threats and bribes thrown at numerous athletes to get them to accuse Kai of scamming. Being as they're all athletes endorsed by Momentum, I'm sure the public is going to eat that up. Now, sadly, I know all of that means nothing at the end of the day. You'll settle out of court in the civil cases, cough up a ridiculous amount of cash, and beat all criminal charges. It's disgusting but I'm not naive enough to think that's not how this world works. What you can't beat, though? The proof of your embezzlement from Momentum over the last fifteen years. Now one thing big corporations don't like is when you steal their money. They'll happily throw your ass to the wolves after that, and you'll trade in your beautiful home for a six by six cell. Now ask me what you can do to stop me from releasing this?"

"You honestly think that—"

I raise my hand to silence him. "I said ask me what you can do to stop me?"

His jaw tightens and I can see his mind working overtime. "What can I do?"

"You can come clean about the allegations. All of them. You'll have to pay a shit ton of money, yes, but it's a good thing you've got all that stolen money to pull from, huh? Momentum is absolutely going to make you resign, and no one in this industry will hire you again, but would you rather forcibly retire on a boat somewhere tropical or would you rather spend the rest of your life behind bars?"

"I have more money than you and more power than you. I can easily make all of this disappear."

"I don't know if you know this but when you embezzle money, they don't let you keep it." I tip my head to the side, studying this man I was once afraid of. "You have power because you stole it from me and countless others. I'm taking it back. You should be grateful for the grace I'm extending you."

"Your grace? You are a waste of space. You're the reason your mother

left us and yet I still poured all my time and resources into making you a star and this is how you repay me."

Once upon a time, those words would've cut me. Now they barely break the skin.

"I don't care why she left. The two of you didn't deserve me, so consider this your severance package. You make it right with Kai, Dante, and the others and you get to keep your freedom. You step one toe out of line, I will ruin you. You ever try to contact me again, I will ruin you. Those are the terms. There are no other options."

I fling the file at him, letting the papers float to the floor around him. "Here, you can keep those. I've got plenty more copies."

Former COO of Momentum, Jason Harding, Confesses To Witness Intimidation. Steps Down From Position.

Have I mentioned that I love flying private? Kai and I are making the most of all this space, barely able to keep our hands off of each other after today's headline.

We had a commercial flight booked, but Tyson called and insisted I take his plane in celebration so here we are, joining the Mile High Club in style.

I love Portland in April. It rains a lot and the temperatures can be a mixed bag, but the delicate bloom of flowers visible this time of year is always a wonder to behold. I have so much to show Kai for his first time here, but first I grab us an Uber to get to our most important reason for this visit.

"How did I know I would see your face after today's news story?" Dante wraps me up in a hug that lifts me off the ground the moment he opens the door. He looks amazing. Construction has kept his hard body in top shape. His penny-brown skin is rich and smooth. Time has been kind to him. It owed him that at least.

"Nowhere else I'd rather be. I had to put eyes on you after that came out. Make sure you're good."

"I'm better than good, Livvy." He looks over to Kai, who's patiently standing behind me. "Is this him?"

"Dante, meet Kai. Kai, meet Dante."

The two shake hands and then pull each other into an embrace.

"Good to meet you, man. I'm glad this one finally got her shit together," Dante says as he points his thumb over to me.

Kai chuckles and pulls me under his arm. "Me too."

"Okay, enough bonding."

Dante leads us inside to his beautiful home that looks professionally decorated. I know why but I point it out anyway.

Dante's face heats. "That's all Tati. She's got that gift, you know?" Tatiana is his gorgeous interior designer girlfriend that he met on a job and mother of his child.

Right then, what sounds like a stampede but is actually just two feet attached to a very excited little girl rolls through the foyer.

"Daddy, daddy! Do we have compwany?"

He scoops her into his arms and nuzzles her cheek. "We do, baby girl. This is Daddy's friend Liv and her friend Kai. Can you say hi?"

"Hi!" She waves excitedly. Willow Moore is one hundred percent her dad. I don't see a lick of Tatiana in her which Dante tells me is a running joke between the two of them that she carried her for all those months and she had the audacity to have his face.

Willow takes us on a tour around her bedroom and her homemade playground in the backyard before Tatiana comes home and Willow loses interest in us. Tatiana gives me a long hug and introduces herself to Kai, then grabs Willow's hand and offers to show Kai to the kitchen for a drink, leaving Dante and me alone to talk.

We get comfortable in the eggshell chairs he has hanging on his back patio. "So, how do you feel now that it's over?" he asks.

"Me? I should be asking you that. You're finally free from the stain he left on you."

Dante waves me off. "I told you; I was free a long time ago. I made peace with my lost basketball career. I found a life that works better for me. Makes me happier. I wouldn't have Tati and Willow if I hadn't lost everything first."

"True."

"So I ask again, how do *you* feel?"

"Hmm. I don't know. I thought that once I was rid of my dad's influence I'd feel so much different—like a whole new person."

"You don't?"

"I do but I don't, you know? I think I thought it would be a cure-all. That I'd stop feeling so much regret and guilt for my part in everything but it didn't wash that away, just made the tide not so high. I'm working on it though. Therapy is helping a lot."

"Good. Healing is a continuous process."

"Where'd you learn that?"

"My mentor."

"I love that."

"Thanks. Can't let you be the only evolved person around here, can I?"

I snicker. "Can't have that."

"So now that you've finally come to your senses, I guess now is a good time to confess something to you."

"Oh God, what is it?"

Dante proceeds to blow my mind by telling me that the money I've been sending him every month for the last ten years has never seen the light of day. He's put it all into a trust with the intention of turning it over to me the moment I "got my shit together."

"I told you I didn't need it, Livvy."

"I know, but holy shit."

"Well, we can go together to get it signed over to you tomorrow. What are you gonna do with it? If you don't mind me asking."

An idea promptly springs to my mind. "Actually, let me run something by you."

After giving Kai the full tourist experience, we take a long shower and settle into bed.

"I'm proud of you, you know?"

Keeping my hand on his chest, I pull my head up to look at him. "Oh yeah?"

"Yeah. You fought tooth and nail to get the reins of your life back. That's incredible. All that's left is the game. So, what's next?"

I smirk and lean up to kiss his nose. "You'll see."

CHAPTER
Thirty-One

Kai
One week later

I'M CROWDED BETWEEN JOURNALIST AFTER JOURNALIST FIGHTING FOR a spot at the front of Austin's City Hall where a press conference is being held. I'm pretty sure the conference is supposed to be focused on the NWSL, but the questions seem to be centered around Jason Harding's disappearance. His civil suits have begun rolling in as well as his criminal charges, but we already know how those will go down.

According to news outlets, he's been meeting with his lawyers privately but has otherwise not been seen. My name as well as Dante's and three other athletes he's attacked have been cleared, but people are speculating if any others will come forward.

There's demand from Momentum to investigate more of the higher-ups of their company and demand for more diversity in their leadership positions.

A lot of questions are being thrown at Olivia as well, as expected since

she's his daughter. They want to know if she knew anything about her father's actions, but she's handling the questions like a pro, courtesy of the press coach Angie put her in touch with.

"Olivia, what are your plans for next season?" a reporter asks.

"I'm so glad you asked that. I've learned a lot these last few months, about myself and life as well. I won't address Jason Harding's effect on that because quite frankly, he doesn't deserve that spotlight from me, but I will address where I go from here. All my life, my focus has been on soccer and nothing else, and that worked until it didn't. I lost myself and frankly I lost my passion for this sport. I've wanted to walk away from it all so many times. But, in the time I've been in Austin, I've rediscovered not only my passion for my career but also my passion for myself. My physical, mental, and spiritual health. I have my family to thank for that. Not the family I was born to but the family that has found me and wrapped me up in their warmth. And I especially have the love of my life to thank for that. So thank you, Kai." A resounding gasp rumbles among the crowd and then a hush falls over them as they wait for her to continue. "I've found myself again, and now that I have I feel reborn and ready to make all of you proud. With that being said, I'm honored that the USWNT will have me again for this upcoming season." The crowd, who has been hanging on to her every word, claps fiercely for that statement. "But as far as the NWSL, I'm proud to say that as of next season, I am now a member of the Houston Vibe." She unzips her hoodie to reveal her new uniform, and the crowd goes wild.

Question after question rolls in but I'm stunned still. Houston. She got herself transferred to Houston. For me.

The crowd's chant become nothing more than roaring thunder in my ears as I push my way to the front of the City Hall steps. A reporter notices me and tries to ask me a question, but I only have eyes for one person and she excuses herself the moment she sees me headed her way.

She wraps her arms around my neck and I wrap mine around her waist. "So, what do you think? Houston to Austin isn't so bad."

"Not bad at all. And what do you think about making that distance even shorter?"

"I'd say that would make me very happy."

"And making you happy is my job after all."

Crowd be damned, our tongues meet in a kiss that'll have me apologizing to my mom later.

Five months later

"Mr. Morris, come with me, please." A security guard leads me away from everyone. We're in Kansas City at Children's Mercy Park for the USWNT's game against Nigeria and Olivia's first game back.

The family refused to miss Olivia's first game back so everyone is here— Kylie, Auntie, my parents, Lincoln, Ciara, Isaiah, Nina, Sasha, Carter, Nevaeh, Shane, Dom, Reggie, and Michael. Lincoln and Ciara's daughter is home with Ciara's mom while Isaiah and Nina's three kids are with his parents and Reggie and Michael's kids are being trusted to stay home alone. Brittany, Simone, and Sarah wanted to join but they sent us a video of them watching together on TV. We're sitting with Justine as well, who's excited that she has more people to shout with her.

Olivia has worked her ass off to get to this point, between transitioning back to practice with her new team and entering the beginning stages of planning her foundation with Dante. They will focus on being a resource for children who have experienced trauma, helping them to better strengthen their mental health, as well as teaching them financial literacy and other key life skills.

The security guard leads me down a long hallway where the roar of the crowd gets lighter and lighter. He opens a door for me and shuts the door behind me. I look around but don't see anyone at first but then her scent surrounds me. Olivia steps out donned in her USWNT uniform and cleats with her hair in a long ponytail and a headband wrapped around her edges.

"What are you up to, Olivia Harding?" The smile in my voice can't be contained.

"Well, first I wanted to say thank you for being here."

"Where else would I be?"

She hums contentedly and reaches for my hand. When I grab it she leads me to a bench and pushes me down. "Second, since you are here, I figured I should take advantage. A girl's gotta have her traditions, you know?"

I lick my lips, not knowing where this is going. "So what do you need from me?"

"I can always count on you to ask the right questions, Kai. I need you to sit back and enjoy the show."

She presses something on her phone and the sound of "The Boy is Mine" fills the room.

The End

Epilogue

Kai
Seven months later

"Love, I'm home," I call out when I step into our new home in Houston. We're still in the process of unpacking, but the fact that we own a house together in the city where everything fell apart before is beautifully poetic.

Olivia doesn't answer my calls, so I go in search of her. Not finding her in the kitchen or living room, I head upstairs.

I find her sitting on the floor against our bed with her knees up to her chest and a piece of paper in her hands.

"Olivia? You okay?"

She's frozen to the spot; I'm not even sure if she heard me. I take a knee beside her and gently rub her shoulder, alerting her to my presence. She sniffles and looks up at me, her eyes glossy with unshed tears.

"What's wrong? How can I help?"

A small giggle escapes her lips, and a strand of hair falls from her

ponytail right over her eye, so I grasp it between my fingers, twirling it slightly.

"Nothing, I'm fine. I'm just remembering that I was writing letters well before my therapist suggested it."

She looks down at the paper she's holding again. I follow her gaze, and one thing stands out; my name is at the top of the page.

"You wrote me a letter?"

"Several. I just found them when I was unpacking."

"When?"

"Throughout the years we were apart. I wanted to send them to you, but I just—I couldn't." She shakes her head. "I wouldn't. I'm sorry."

"What have I told you about the sorrys?"

A tear glides down her cheek; I lean to kiss it away.

"Do you—do you want to read them now?"

My words catch in my throat. We've talked in detail about our time apart but a chance to read her thoughts in those moments? I don't think I can pass it up.

"I…" I cut myself off, nodding instead.

She picks up a pile of letters by her side and hands them all to me before grabbing my face and pulling me in for a deep kiss.

"I never stopped loving you," she says as she stands and heads for the door.

"You're not gonna stay while I read?"

"Oh no, my heart can't take that. But come find me when you're done."

She closes the door behind her, and as if pulled by a magnetic force, my eyes immediately turn back to the first letter. I take in the delicate script of her handwriting, tracing it with my fingertips.

Without another thought, I begin reading.

June 10, 2010

Dear Kai,

I'm not sure if you saw it on the news or not, but I did it. I made it to the pros. I'm officially in Orlando now. Orlando. That's...so far from you.

I fucking hate it.

God, I miss you. I hate that you looked at me with such pain the last time I saw you. I never wanted that. I only wanted to save you.

I wish I could tell you how sorry I am. Better yet, I wish I could tell you the truth. You deserve that. But I know you, Kai. I know you'll sacrifice everything for me. I can't allow you to do that. Of course, you'll say you'll never resent me for it, but you should. I'd resent myself enough for the both of us.

Being here in Orlando is nothing like I imagined. It doesn't feel right without you here, but I'm going to do everything in my power to make you proud.

Love, Olivia

May 15, 2011

Dear Kai,

This year has been insane. Orlando is... complicated. I kind of hate it, but I can't tell if that's because I actually hate it or I'm just miserable. Angie thinks it's a little bit of both.

I just realized you don't know Angie. How crazy is it that you don't know someone I call my best friend? Do you have new friends I haven't met? A new love? I never thought we'd go a day without speaking, let alone two years. It feels like a giant piece of me is missing.

Anyway, I wanted to say happy graduation day. I wish I could be there with you. I wish I had the strength to sit in the audience for you. But please know that I am thinking about you: today and every other day.

Love, Olivia

January 1, 2012

Dear Kai,

I had a dream that we had a daughter.

Not when we were nineteen, though. We were older. I know because you had the slightest wrinkle lines around your eyes, but it didn't make you look old. You looked distinguished. Like you'd spent your whole life laughing freely.

In my dream, she was about five, and she was perfect. She had my cheeks and my nose with your eyes and your lips.

She had a Barbie truck but wanted to drag race with it. Doesn't that sound like something our kid would do?

We were happy. So happy. It felt so real.

I cried in my shower until the water went cold when I woke up.

Do you think dreams show our potential futures? Or just the ones we gave up?

Love, Olivia

October 13, 2012

Dear Kai,

It's hard to believe that Kylie is eighteen now. I saw her birthday post on Instagram and was in awe of how gorgeous she is. I wanted to call her but...I don't have her number. I thought about reaching out on Instagram, but well, I'll just say it, I'm scared.

I'm not proud to admit that I spent way too much time zooming in on the photo she posted because you were in the background. You look good, Kai. Is that weird to say? You've always looked good; it was just crazy seeing you in a recent photo. Your IG being private makes it really hard to cyber-stalk you. Sorry, that was too much. And besides, I don't deserve to see how you're doing. Hopefully, you've moved on and have found someone who can give you what you need.

I love you. That will never change. Be well.

Love, Olivia

December 25, 2012

Merry Christmas, Kai.

I got you a gift this year. Silly, I know, but I couldn't resist.

You've told me that Po Po has called you Wolf for as long as you can remember. I've always wondered how she knew so early on how perfect that name would be for you.

Everyone loves you. Your demeanor naturally calms people down, yet you're a bit of a loner, clinging only to those you deem special. I was always honored to be one of those people. Someone you'd protect with everything you had and love so deeply it was impossible not to feel.

When I saw that picture of you a few months ago, I noticed you were wearing my mother's cross. I remember the day I gave it to you like it was yesterday. You took my pain and wore it around your neck so I wouldn't have to. You were always doing that, but it wasn't fair to you.

You shouldn't have to wear my pain. You should wear something that represents you; the intelligent, kind, playful, devoted man you are. When I saw this, I knew I had to get it for you. I hope one day you'll see it.

P.S. I found the picture in the same store. Po Po always called me Tulip. I don't know why and I don't think I want to know. Keeps the magic alive, you know? But I wonder if maybe this picture was made for us.

Love, Olivia

I drop the letters on my lap and look down beside me. Tucked slightly under the bed lies a nondescript brown box. When I pop it open, I find a gold chain. At the end of it, there is a small amber pendant with a 3D howling wolf in it. It's perfectly polished as if it's brand new.

Taped to the inside of the box is a beautiful drawing of a gray wolf standing amongst a field of pink and purple tulips. The photo is laminated, so it hasn't lost an ounce of its vibrancy.

The fingers on my right hand trace a delicate path across the face of the

pendant, taking in the fine details, while my left hand caresses the cross I still wear around my neck.

I reach up and unclasp the cross, laying it on the bed. I should've said goodbye to it long ago, but it was how I held on to Olivia through the years. Now, we can both let go of the past. I slip the chain around my neck and clutch the pendant against my chest.

My body aches to find Olivia, but I know she wants me to read all the letters before I do, so I press on.

February 20, 2013

Dear Kai,

You want to know a secret?

When I found out the WPS was shutting down, I was happy.

It's hard to still be passionate about something when your heart only beats at half the speed.

Now, I'm in Portland. Another new city without you, and I'm even more lost this time.

I met someone else.

He's not you. No one is, but he's sweet and makes me laugh. He wants me to give him a chance.

And here's the kicker; he knows about you.

I told him, thinking it would scare him away. It didn't. He's still here and still trying.

Every day I tell myself I'm gonna let you go, and then every day, I prove myself to be a liar.

Maybe I like being a liar.

Maybe it's who I am.

I don't know if I'll ever get over you, but I think I have to try.

Right?

Love, Olivia

August 17, 2013

Dear Kai,

"Absence and death are the same, only that in death there is no suffering."

Have you ever heard that before? It's from Theodore Roosevelt. I heard it the other day and thought how fucking accurate.

All this suffering and for what?

Because of me, a man lost his career and reputation. The very thing I tried to save you from, I let happen to someone else. What's wrong with me?

I wish I could take it all back. I wish I could go back in time and fix everything. But where would I go? Back to when I decided to stay with him even though I was warned? Back to the moment I left you behind? Or maybe even further? Back to the day we met and make it so I never darken your doorstep? Or back to the very beginning of my story and just...make it stop?

I just want it all to stop.

-Olivia

June 19, 2014

Dear Kai,

I almost made it an entire year without writing to you.

But today, as I was settling in my new place in North Carolina, you were heavy on my mind, and I just needed to say something.

I needed to say thank you.

Thank you, Kai.

Thank you for the time we had. I wouldn't trade it for the world.

I think I'm ready to let you go. I think I'll lose myself in grief and regret if I don't.

Sometimes the pain is so bad I'm afraid it'll swallow me whole. I'm afraid I'll want it to.

I'm sorry we didn't get the future we planned. I'm sorry for the hurt I caused. I've followed your career, so I know you're a hot-shot PT. I am so

incredibly proud of you. I knew you would do it, and I know you'll continue flourishing on your own.

I don't expect your forgiveness, but I do hope you forget me.

Best, Olivia

July 5, 2015

Dear Kai,

It's hilarious how you think you're past something, and then one moment brings everything crumbling down around you.

I let you go. I swear I did.

But today, my team won the World Cup.

The World Cup. Can you believe that?

And do you know how I felt when we won?

Numb.

This was everything I'd been working towards my whole life, but when it happened, I felt nothing because all I wanted to do was run into your arms and celebrate.

I wanted to share it with you.

Ain't that a bitch?

Maybe I'm not meant to let you go. Maybe my fate is to push you to the far back of my mind where I can't reach you every day but where you can still pop up to remind me of my shortcomings when I start to forget.

Honestly? I'll take it.

Love, Olivia

From there, the letters aren't actual letters but more random notes where she shares things that made her think of me or musings about my life and what she wishes for me.

They continue until the year before her accident. The message is clear: I was never too far from her mind. She loved me even when she told herself she didn't.

It's enough for me.

It's always been enough.

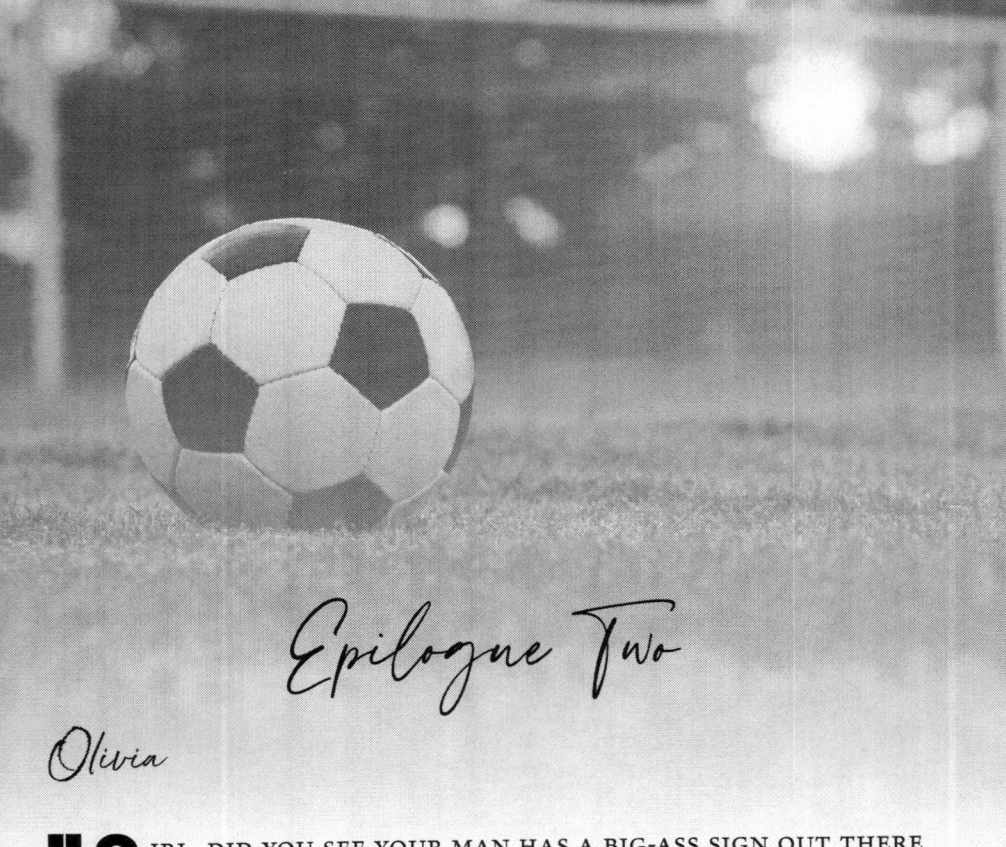

Epilogue Two

Olivia

"**G**IRL, DID YOU SEE YOUR MAN HAS A BIG-ASS SIGN OUT THERE that says, 'Harding Goes Hard AF'? It's so corny but cute."

Of course he does. When he was back here for my pregame ritual he made no mention of a sign, but he did seem overly enthusiastic. I think he might be more excited for this game than I am.

With his busy schedule, he's not able to make it to every game and I wouldn't expect him to. We bought a home in Houston together, and he has been busy getting his new practice up and running here. He still has his practice in Austin as well, and he bounces back and forth between the two locations, but primary management for that location falls under Faith now. I've honestly been shocked and impressed that he's been able to make it to as many domestic games as he has, but this is the game I knew he wouldn't miss. This is my first official game with the Houston Vibe. And who are we playing? Of course, my old team, the North Carolina Meadow.

Angie and I were on the phone for an hour last night taunting each other over who was going to win. I love playing with her on the USWNT but I'm going to love wiping the field with her ass this season just as much.

I slip my phone out of my locker one last time and find messages from everyone wishing me luck before the game and then there's one from Dante.

Dante: Willow said to bring her a trophy after you win today. I told her that's not how it works but she said how will you know you won if you don't get a trophy and I had nothing for that sooo you might wanna pick one up before you get here

If you would've told me that I'd feel anything but regret toward Dante after what happened or that I'd become Auntie Wivvy to his daughter or that we'd become business partners who started a foundation together using my guilt money, I would've called you crazy.

I've never been happier being wrong.

I type out a quick response to him letting him know she'll get her trophy. Houston is playing Portland later this week, so I will see the cutie pie soon enough. Maybe I'll make one out of Angie's tears.

I tune back in to Coach Lopez hyping us up. Then it's time to step onto the field.

The ringing in my ears from the crowd's eagerness never gets old.

The feel of the Bermuda grass beneath my cleats is a high I never want to come down from.

Hearing Houston's fans cheering us on is electrifying. I look out to where I know Kai and Justine are sitting and blow them a kiss. I'm so glad Justine is able to be here for this even though she'll fly out right after because her season just started as well and she has a game tomorrow.

My eyes troll North Carolina's side looking for Angie, and when I find her she's already staring me down with an evil smirk. She makes the "you're dead" gesture at me and I stick my tongue out at her and flip her off. The hammering of the crowd reaches deafening heights.

Two to one, Houston. After the game, Coach Haven daps me up and whispers in my ear that she won't let the team go easy on me next time,

making us both laugh. Angie wraps her arms around my neck, pulling me in close and saying, "The way I see it, esto es un empate."

I pull away from her and point to the scoreboard. "A tie? Oh, so that big-ass two and that big-ass one means nothing, huh?"

She puts her finger over my lips. "Silencio. Fuck that score. I scored a goal and so did you so you and I are one to one."

She and I make plans to settle the supposed true winner of today's game before I make my way over to the stands.

I sign a few autographs and then I hear a soothing voice cut in.

"Excuse me, ma'am, I'm a huge fan. Could you sign my jersey?" I turn expecting to see Kai, and I do, but standing behind him is practically the whole damn family. Justine, Shane, Mr. and Mrs. Morris, Auntie, Po Po, Kylie, Ciara, Nina, and Sasha. The other guys I'm sure are working or on kid duty.

"I can't believe you all came! Thank you."

"We wouldn't miss this," Sasha squeals.

"Miss what?"

"You signing my jersey." Kai pushes the jersey to me but it looks different; I just can't figure out why. When my gaze finds its way to the top of the jersey, I realize the difference. It says Morris instead of Harding.

"Aww, you had a jersey customized?"

"I was hoping it might be the name on your jersey soon."

I beam at him but then his words register. Wait, what?

"Told you she wouldn't get it," Kylie laughs.

"Are you...?"

He pulls out a box and opens it to reveal a gorgeous pear-shaped engagement ring with a chocolate diamond that matches my eyes. "I am. What do you say, Olivia? You wanna make my life complete and marry me?"

The family waits with bated breath for my answer, as if there was a chance I'd say no. My story with Kai may have taken a long detour, but the ending was written in the stars a long time ago.

"Yes, sir."

Shane

I don't get the significance of Olivia's custom-made jersey saying "the boy is mine" on the front, but she let out a full belly laugh when she saw it so I guess she's happy.

I'm happy for her and Kai. They deserve this and each other. I give Liv a sweaty hug and pull Kai in for a bro hug and congratulate them on the pending nuptials. I know Liv will be happy to shed that Harding name. Maybe it will stop people from harassing her about her father's whereabouts. None of us give a damn where he is, so long as he keeps his ass out of Texas.

I'm in the middle of telling Kai that I expect to be named best man since I feel I played a crucial role in them reuniting when my phone pings with an email.

Of course it's from the bane of my existence, Lauren Brentwood. I can't even get away from this woman on a Saturday afternoon.

We started as marketing consultants at Thrive Marketing at the same time years ago, and it's been hell ever since. My lip snarls as I read her email with a progress report on each consultant's projects. Does she want a cookie for working on a weekend?

I remove everyone from the email except my buddy Larry, and send him a reply making fun of Lauren for her lack of social life. The email may also imply that if she got some dick maybe she'd loosen up a bit and have something better to do on a Saturday. Petty and unprofessional, I know. But the woman drives me insane.

When my phone chimes again, I open the email app expecting a funny reply from Larry, but instead my face pales at the response I receive from Lauren herself.

From: LBrentwood@thrivemarketing.com
To: SEvans@thrivemarketing.com
Subject: RE: Thrive Project Status Report
Hi Shane,
I hope you're having a wonderful weekend although whatever you have

going on can't be that exciting since you took the time to read my email on a Saturday afternoon instead of waiting until Monday morning like most people. Perhaps it's your social life that should have Larry concerned.

I appreciate your heartfelt advice, but maybe if you spent less time worrying about whose face I'm sitting on, this email would've ended up in the correct inbox. But then again, your attention to detail, or lack thereof, is probably part of the reason Mr. Spencer handed your last project to me, so no surprise there.

Enjoy the rest of your weekend. I hope you're able to stop fantasizing about my pussy long enough to enjoy it.

Best,

Lauren Brentwood

Fuck me. I scan the email again, noticing that I did in fact send my reply to Lauren Brentwood instead of Larry Brenner. Their close email addresses have tripped me up a few times in the past, but this is by far the worst one to fuck up.

Monday morning is going to be a shit show.

The end

Want to see Shane and Lauren's story? Stay tuned for Book 4 of the Lost & Found series!

Want more of Kai and Olivia? Click here for a special bonus epilogue: dl.bookfunnel.com/awl2f6i4zd

ABOUT
the Author

Natasha is an indie contemporary romance author living in Baltimore, MD with her family and fur baby.

She likes to write about everyday heroes who are a bit haunted and heroines who are sweet but also badass.

When she's not writing, she's usually reading, playing with her adorable dog, or hunting down delicious gluten free snacks.

Stay Connected!

Newsletter Sign Up (https://geni.us/NBNewsletterSignUp)
Goodreads (https://geni.us/GoodreadsNatashaBishop)
Instagram (Natasha Bishop (@natashabishopwrites))
Tik Tok (https://geni.us/NBTikTok)
Facebook Reader Group (https://geni.us/BishBrigade)
Facebook Author Page (https://geni.us/NBAuthorPage)
Amazon (https://geni.us/NBAmazonAuthorPage)
Linktr.ee (https://linktr.ee/NatashaBishop)
Website (Authornatashabishop.com)

Made in the USA
Middletown, DE
23 February 2024

50226679R00179

To all the GEBs and custom earmuffs out there, this is for you.

Thanks Torri!

WHERE WE FOUND OUR

Passion

NATASHA BISHOP